Allegations of Love

also by
Kevin Brophy

Novels
Almost Heaven (1997)

Autobiography
Walking the Line: Scenes from an Army Childhood (1994)
In the Company of Wolves (1999)

Allegations
of Love

Kevin Brophy

**Wynkin
deWorde**

2003

Published in 2003
by

**Wynkin
deWorde**

Wynkin deWorde Ltd.,

PO Box 257, Tuam Road, Galway, Ireland.
e-mail: info@deworde.com

A CIP catalogue record for this book is available from the British Library

ISBN: 0-9542607-4-0

Typeset by Patricia Hope, Skerries, Co. Dublin, Ireland
Cover illustration by Roger Derham.
Jacket Design by Design Direct, Galway, Ireland
Printed by Betaprint, Dublin, Ireland

Dedication

For
Galway,
the lost town that I loved.

Chapter 1

Towards the end of her visit, when I told Bee that I was going to set down a record of these events, she gave me a long look, which was at once, both searching and pitying. '*Sunt lacrimae rerum,*' she quoted. Bee is sixteen years-old and Latin is one of her A-level subjects.

'Kind of,' I said, remembering the Virgilian phrase from my own schooldays: *these are the tears of things.* 'But it's not all tears, show-off.'

But I was smiling as I teased her; I'm proud of the way she is not afraid, at sixteen, to gird her conversation and arguments with the classical tags and literary allusions of her learning. Bee is the one truly good thing about my whole life, her existence almost a justification for my own. We were sitting at this very table, where I'm now writing, just a couple of months ago, when she leaned her head of cropped, dark hair across the table and rested it on my shoulder. I saw then, for just a moment, myself in the long-ago, stooped over the same table, in the same kitchen.

'You should have called me, Dad. You shouldn't have been alone at that time.'

'It's not your job to be worrying about your old man,' I said with mock-sternness. 'Your job is to get straight As in your exams and then become the leading classical scholar of your generation at that Disneyland University you're so determined to get into.'

'Cambridge, Dad!' she protested. 'King's College, Cambridge . . . and don't change the subject.'

'King's, Queen's, what's the difference? Your old man's *alma mater* might have been beyond you, but I could have dropped a word in the right ears to give you a leg-in.'

'Oh, yes! I would love that. The Bogtrotter's Academy for leprechauns and other little people!'

We laughed easily together, joshing each other a lot, whenever we managed to get together. I dote on my beautiful, brilliant, teenage daughter, and I see no reason to conceal my besottedness from her or from anybody else. Beatrice Best, only daughter of her scribbler father, Daniel, will leave her mark upon the world.

Her beauty is her mother's: nobody could ever accuse the Best's of being beautiful; strong-featured, yes, tall and big-boned too, but never beautiful. I could see Elizabeth in Bee's high cheekbones and honeyed skin; when I touched, for a moment, my daughter's crop of dark, rich hair I could almost remember the first time I had laid my trembling hand on her mother's cheek.

'C'mon, my beautiful, English daughter,' I said, rising from the table. 'It's time I was driving you to the station.'

Bee takes her height from me: when she stood up in her platform shoes, she was more than my six feet.

'Can we walk, Dad? I like your quaint little West-of-Ireland town.'

'Watch it,' I said. I looked at the clock on the mantelpiece, checking that we had time before Bee's bus left for Shannon. She had expressly forbidden me to drive her to the airport and I knew better than to argue with her.

'Damn!' She looked at the clock as well and uttered one of her milder expletives. 'I'm sorry, Dad, it's too far for you to walk . . . Why don't we just take the car? Or better still, I'll head off by myself, there's no need for you to come with –'

'No need at all,' I interrupted her. 'Except the pleasure of walking beside my beautiful daughter.'

'You're sure you can manage?'

'Get your coat,' I said. 'And stop fussing like an old grandmother.'

Her platform-shoes clop-clopped along the hall and up the stairs. I could hear the door of her room open upstairs as she collected her bag. Although I'd had the little room completely re-decorated and had put in a new bed and dressing-table to stand on top of the fresh blue carpet, I had been unable to remove my past entirely; on my way to bed, in the larger room across the small landing, I sometimes pushed in the door of this small bedroom and in the unlighted silence I'd feel I could hear my own boyish breathing, from decades ago, so sure and confident that morning would come and my mother would call me and I would hurry downstairs to help my father with the dogs.

This behavioral pattern had been an occasional habit before Jeff had given me the news; now it seemed to me that I was forever staring through that opened door at the small boy who lay asleep under the grey blankets with his father's old overcoat on top during the winter nights.

'Dad?'

I saw the look of concern on her face when I turned to her.

'Are you okay? I can stay for the weekend, if you like.'

'Your mother is expecting you,' I said. 'And you have to be in school on Monday morning. Straight As, remember?'

There was no need to show Bee the shades that haunted my days now. Afterwards, she could read about them in my words – or at least as much as I chose to reveal. That's why I prefer words on paper; the reader, unlike a listener, has neither body language nor sad smiles nor swallowing noises to embellish your carefully-doled-out thoughts. The full stops between your sentences cannot expose your pain like the silences between your spoken words.

My daughter could not hear the early-morning barking of the hounds in the small backyard. She could not smell the fuzzy animal warmth of them when you unlatched the green kennel-doors and she could not feel their muzzles nosing against you, their tongues wet and pink and welcoming at the start of another day.

So I closed the door on those distant mornings and stepped out with my daughter onto the pavement of Paternoster Lane. I felt her big, dark eyes upon me as I double-locked the door and pocketed the keys. In that other time, when the dogs yelped in the backyard and my grandparents still lived in the house at the other end of the street, you could leave your front door open all day.

Bee's rucksack dangled with studied nonchalance from her left shoulder. 'Wouldn't it be easier to carry it?' I said. 'If you put it on both shoulders?'

'Dad!'

We both knew it was a game I played; I was not such an old fogey as I sometimes pretended. I could tell, as we made our way along the narrow streets, that Bee was deliberately slowing herself to my pace. Jeff had suggested, tentatively, that perhaps I should think about using a stick, but I had dismissed the idea angrily. I was only 48 years-old after all, not 98 and wasn't yet ready to throw in the towel.

When I felt Bee link her arm into mine, I kept my eyes resolutely ahead. I couldn't trust myself to look at her. Paternoster Lane was wrapped in its usual mid-afternoon somnolence; there are no children here anymore, just middle-aged relics like myself and childless yuppie couples who had been drawn to the street by its nearness to the city centre. Today, however, the street seemed loud with whispers, half-heard echoes from days that were gone.

'All right, Dad?'

'Of course,' I said, and the words came out grumpily. 'Mind yourself now, crossing the road.'

She laughed but said nothing. I knew what she was thinking: I survive on the streets of London, and here's my old man warning me about the traffic on a side street in a small town in the West of Ireland.

There was something in the afternoon – the stillness of the October air, the hint of winter in the grey, cloudy skies – and somehow my daughter had never seemed so precious as now,

4

walking slowly past the closed doors of the little houses, the blind windows where not even a curtain twitched to acknowledge our passing.

Bee was all I had. I kept coming back to that. Jeff's news, delivered with gruff gentleness, had made me look back, do a kind of stocktaking. The liabilities made a lengthy list: I could check them off in my sleep. The assets hardly registered: a magazine by-line that would soon be forgotten, a single book that had somehow conned the reading public into believing it was "a minor masterpiece". Bee was the only asset that counted.

We walked in silence along Dominick Street and crossed over O'Brien's Bridge, in the shadow of the Protestant church. On our right stood the new hotel, all grey stone and maintenance-free PVC windows to see in the millennium. At the top of the incline, opposite yet another fast-food joint, the street was flanked by scaffolding; the iron framework was draped in builder's sheets of green, plastic netting that had come to seem like the town's natural habitation

'They're always building here,' Bee said, wonderingly. 'Every time I come, that green stuff is hanging down somewhere.'

'It's progress, Bee.' I tried to keep the sourness out of my voice.

'It's greed, Dad,' Bee said. 'Nothing more than simple greed.'

I loved it when she expounded about the tyrannies of government and the evils of multinationals. Who knew what lay beyond a degree from King's College, Cambridge? Busy Bee might find other ways to save the whales and re-house the denizens of cardboard cities.

'It's a lovely old town,' she said. 'But the way they're pulling things down and changing things . . . it makes you think they don't even have a plan.'

In her voice I could hear the crusading impatience that infuriated her mother; Elizabeth's concerns were always closer to home. "Why don't you *do* something about it, Daniel Best? You could write about it, you know?", she once demanded. "I have to live here!", I remember replying, avoiding the challenge.

'I have to live here,' I said to my daughter.

'Listen to me!' Bee laughed. 'You'd think I knew everything.'

You will know more than I ever knew, I wanted to tell her; you will achieve more than I ever did, because you have in you a capacity to give far more than I ever could. And in your giving, you will be happy, happier than I ever could be. I don't pray anymore but, if I did pray, if I *could* pray, that would be my prayer for you.

Of course, I told Bee no such thing. I had no wish to burden her with my fears, my unsatisfied dreams. Only reluctantly had I given her a highly edited version of what, according to Jeff, lay in store for me. I felt I owed her that. I could remember – how could I ever forget? – the desolation of the house in Paternoster Lane, all those years ago, empty without my father's winking, long-suffering presence.

Bee's bus was waiting at the station when we rounded the corner of the Square. In a way, I was glad that my slow progress meant we had arrived barely in time. I had no heart for a long-drawn-out farewell in the lee of a departing bus while the already-seated passengers looked down on us from the windows and the driver eyed us through the open doorway. We embraced and I held the tears back as I kissed her on the forehead.

'I'll be back for the New Year, Dad.' She gave me another hurried squeeze. 'I'll have to stay with Mum for Christmas, but I'll come over for the New Year. I promise.'

There ought to be a law against it; a beautiful teenager trying to make bits of herself to bring a little happiness into the fractured, fucked-up lives of her parents.

'I promise,' Bee said again.

The driver revved the engine noisily, startling us apart.

'Look after yourself, Bee.' It was getting harder to hold back the tears.

'You too, Dad. That's your only job now, looking after yourself.'

'Are ye comin' or goin'?' the driver called down to us. 'Or will ye wait for the next one?' He was trying to scowl, but his ruddy face broke into a grin when Bee smiled at him.

I watched her, achingly young and beautiful, climb aboard the bus. The driver gave a cursory look at her return ticket before he bent towards the gear stick. Bee looked back down at me, tall and slim in jeans and a black biker's jacket. The door of the bus swung shut and she was gone, still waving at me through a window as the driver pulled the huge vehicle away from the pavement.

I stood awhile, after the bus had rounded the corner and disappeared from view, as much to get my breath back as to blink back the tears that filled my eyes. I thought of taking a taxi home but decided against it: there was still power in my legs. But I knew I needed a drink. A large whiskey in the pub on the corner would dull the pain of Bee's going. It would also give me heart for the walk, the slow walk, back to Paternoster Lane. Beyond that lay the rest of the task I had set myself. I crossed the road gingerly towards Garvey's pub trying to ignore the creeping tiredness in my legs and the dull ache in my heart.

Chapter 2

I'm not sure I'd have bothered at all to write down this account of events, if it hadn't been for Jeff's news, that day in his surgery, a couple of months before Bee came over to spend her half-term with me. After all, I have nothing extravagant to set down in these pages. My yarn is nothing more than the usual sad recitation of most of our lives: love and betrayal, greed and guilt; some of it my own. Nothing you wouldn't find in any ordinary, contemporary life, hidden in the folds of its own mortgaged respectability.

Your perspective tends to alter a bit when you are finally told what you knew all along anyway – that the lumps in your armpit are malignant. It was the result you'd been expecting, all through the 48-hour wait since they'd dug out their samples from the biopsy in the university hospital, but the weird bit, the hope-springs-eternal bit, is that the news still shocks you. You wonder why Jeff's rugby-player's face, all squashed nose and cauliflower ears, is fading and blurring into a meaty mash from a butcher's block. His lips, swollen beyond recognition, are still moving but you can hear no sound from between their fleshy pinkness. You realise that it's difficult to breathe. Jeff, huge and bulky in his dark-brown suit, has hauled himself upright out of his chair on the other side of the desk and is starting to make his lumbering way around the desk towards you, but you wave him away.

The moment of terror has passed.

You hear yourself say that it's okay, you're okay.

You're not okay, you know you're not, but the glib phrases issue from your conditioned mouth. You've just been sentenced to a premature grave but some part of you instinctively observes the proprieties and insists to Jeff that you're okay.

'I'm sorry, Dan. Really sorry.'

Jeff's misshapen features have by now re-arranged themselves into their usual grotesqueness, the nose that was twice broken on the rugby field, the pair of ears that were squashed and chewed in countless scrums because protective headgear was for wimps and Nancy-boys. At school I used to wonder why Jeff was so determined to get into medical school: the level of points required for entry seemed beyond the reach of his lumbering brain, yet he had successfully plodded his way through enough math's, history, science, and the literature of three languages to win his place. As soon as he made it into the medical faculty, Jeff promptly forgot the entire history of civilisation, its literature included, and concentrated on improving his rugby and learning to be a doctor. His choice of profession still puzzled me. Until now, I'd had little reason to visit Jeff's, or any other doctor's, surgery and what I'd seen of Jeff on my rare visits had not shaken my view that nature had intended him to dig trenches and build houses. He rattled on about prognosis and treatment but I wasn't taking it in.

'I'll call you,' I said. 'Tomorrow, at the latest. Tell me then, not now.'

'It is important,' Jeff said. 'To begin treatment as soon as possible, even a day could count.'

I shook my head. 'I wanted to digest the news,' I told him. 'Anyway, what difference could a day make now,' I added.

'Where there's life, there's . . .' Jeff said.

I snorted.

'It's true,' Jeff said earnestly. 'There's always hope.'

10

While I'd been waiting for the results of the biopsy, I'd been hiding my hope from myself, but it had been real, coiled within me, waiting to leap up and clap its hands in exultation for a good result. The game was lost now. The referee had blown the whistle and your name wouldn't feature in the next round of life's fabulous championship. 'Life's a bitch,' I quoted from some otherwise forgotten cartoon. 'And then you die!'

'We have to be positive, Dan,' Jeff said. 'It's the only way.'

'They're not *our* lumps,' I said slowly. 'They're mine.'

His squashed face gave nothing away. 'You shouldn't be alone tonight, Dan,' he said. 'Are you still seeing Dolly Hynes?'

My puzzlement, fury even, must have shown in my expression.

'It's a small town, Dan,' Jeff said, shrugging apologetically. 'Seriously, you're better off being with people right now . . . and I want you to phone me tomorrow, without fail. Otherwise, I'm coming round to Paternoster-fucking-Lane to get you. Understand?'

I suppose I should have seen and heard the true doctor's concern in his attitude; perhaps I should have realised, finally, that Jeff had been born to be a GP. I didn't, of course. When I looked at him, overweight and prosperous, all I could see was a fellow of my own age who didn't have malignant lumps in his armpits. This was my new perspective on the world.

Anyway, my sour instinct was not incorrect. It wouldn't be too long before I learned that Jeff's world was not confined to house calls and writing prescriptions and it was what happened next that really got me started on writing this account of the life and varied times of Daniel Best, scribe. A pen has always seemed to me to be what nature intended you to hold in your hand; I've always been driven to explain the world to itself in my personal words. It's not improbable that, sentenced to death, as I saw myself, I would have felt impelled to record, in some way, the events leading up to my departure. Writers, even magazine columnists like myself, are inclined to a generous view of their own importance in the scheme of things.

But the unexpected, almost trivial, incident that occurred in

11

Jeff's reception area began a small chain of events that forced the pen into my hand and these words on paper.

Jeff's practice occupies the ground floor of a house in the Crescent. Polished brass plates on the gate piers and on the wall beside the front door tell you that the upper floors of the property are used by medical specialists; a pediatrician, a cardiologist, an oncologist. It's one of the four houses on the Crescent still used in its entirety by medics. When I was growing up, medical families occupied almost all of the houses, in the bow-shaped terrace. Once, on an occasion that I could recall only dimly, when my mother had marched me from Paternoster Lane, past the Jesuit Church and around the corner on to this street of high houses with tall windows and waiting in an unheated room with faded carpets and high ceilings to be called into the doctor's room, I had sensed her discomfiture. I remember being surprised that the doctor was a woman: she was tall and bony and her hands were cold as she examined the ears that had been paining me for over a week. An orange-coloured ten-shilling note changed hands before we left, my mother mumbling her thanks, clutching the prescription that the doctor had scribbled on the green-and-gold leather top of the dark desk. And I can still remember the awe in mother's voice that night, at home in our own kitchen – after she had trickled the precious, expensive drops into my screaming ears – as she tried to describe for my father the splendours of the doctor's establishment. If one of the big lads who played hurling on the street in the evenings took a good swing with his hurley, he could nearly drive the ball up and over the roofs from the Lane into the doctor's garden but, listening to my mother's voice, you'd think the Crescent was at the end of the world's most fabulous rainbow. Listening to her, keeping my head tilted so that the hard-bought drops from the chemist's shop in Dominick Street could work their wonders inside my wretched ears, remembering the gold tooling that had edged the dark top of the desk, I was inclined to agree with her.

'She took your money, didn't she?' My father's voice was as mild as if he were talking to the dogs when he was unhappy with them. 'She put her hand out and she took the ten-bob note from you, didn't she?'

I remember my father as a tall man, with a deep voice that came from a barrel-chest, but his words then, as always, were delivered without intensity or malice. When he was gone, it was his gentleness I missed: even when, under my mother's orders, he set himself to scold me for some domestic misdemeanour, the softness of his voice and the barely-suppressed grin on his face let you know that he thought the whole thing was a cod and that the pair of us would be better off out walking the dogs. Most of the time I have been able to hide from myself how much I miss him.

My neck was getting stiff, still standing with my head tilted sideways beside my mother's chair. I caught, from my tilted angle, the look he shot at her, warm and private, from beneath his dark brows.

'Sure you have this place looking like a palace, love . . .'

'No thanks to you and your mouldy dogs!' The moulting presence of the greyhounds was like a running sore with my mother.

'And I wouldn't want to live anywhere else,' my father finished, smiling across the kitchen at both of us.

Nowadays most doctors didn't wish to live on the Crescent. They have moved out to the town's burgeoning suburbs or to more spacious homes on the outskirts of the town and have taken their practices with them. Only some consultants and a handful of GPs from old family practices, like barnacled survivors, are now to be numbered among the solicitors and accountants who have taken over the Crescent.

Not that I was thinking any such thoughts when I stepped out of Jeff's office that day and pulled the door shut behind me. I'm not sure that I was capable of any kind of thought right then. An image of my father, stroking the fine-haired flesh of the dogs, flashed through my mind, but you couldn't call it a thought. It was a fleeting image, no more than that, but it blotted out the spacious corridor, the cream-coloured walls, and the heavy-duty, beige carpet. I leaned against Jeff's door, measuring the distance past the ladies' and gents' toilets and the facing doors of Jeff's two partners. It must have been all of a dozen paces to the reception desk and I wanted to be sure I could make it. I wanted to hand over my £20 note to pay for my visit. I am my mother's son too.

The corridor bellies out into a wider reception area, which is dominated by a chest-high, semi-circular counter. This area is presided over by Kay Cummins, a spinster of indeterminate years, over-weight, round-faced, bossily efficient and unfailingly kind. I know her as a nodding acquaintance in the evening walks on the promenade, her blubbery body poured into her tracksuit, her round face red with the useless exertions of trying to walk her way towards a more acceptable figure. We always smile and wave at each other as we pass in our separate universes.

I was standing with my twenty-pound note in my hand, when I realised that Kay was not in her accustomed place behind the counter. I thought I heard someone crying and for a moment I wondered if it was myself.

'Mr Best? Please, would you mind helping . . .'

Kay was bent over a straight-backed chair outside the counter. The sobbing noise seemed to come from within her. I had to look closely to see a crying girl, buried in the encircling centre of Kay's massive arms. Somehow Kay's words penetrated my dazed mind. She'd called a taxi for the girl; she'd phoned a second time, but still the car hadn't arrived. The poor girl was obviously distressed; would I mind giving her a lift home?

Still in a daze, I heard myself saying yes, the car was outside. I started on a rambling explanation of how I usually walked but Kay wasn't listening to me. She was too busy making shushing noises, consoling the sobbing creature inside her embrace. The girl who emerged from that embrace had about her a doll-like beauty, with cropped, yellow hair and huge eyes in a finely sculpted face. She was tiny but perfectly shaped; her hips flared against a short, tight skirt while above a slender waist, a white, cotton sweater was stretched by high, firm breasts.

I don't know if I observed all of that then, or later. I did notice the way her mascara was smudged across her crying eyes, the way her full lips were down-turned with sorrow and anger.

Kay and I were shepherding the weeping girl between us towards the front door, past the waiting-room on the left, when I heard Jeff's voice behind us.

'Kay! What's going on?'

'It's all right, doctor,' Kay said. 'Kelly is just a little upset, but Mr Best is going to give her a lift home.'

'But Dan can't . . . He's not up to it right now.'

I waved him away, pulling open the front door.

'I'm okay, Jeff,' I said. 'Don't worry.'

Kay let the girl go then, and she seemed to sag, lifeless, against me.

'I'm okay,' I said to Kay. 'I'll get her home.' Kay had given me the name of a block of flats just off Eyre Square.

'But you can't –'

The door swinging shut cut off whatever Jeff was going to tell me I couldn't do. I steered the girl along the garden path, conscious now of her body leaning on mine. She could have been nineteen or 29, these days I find it hard to tell. And why was she crying? Had one of the other partners in the practice been talking to her also, about the difference a day could make? I could smell the womanliness of her as I eased her through the narrow gateway out on to the footpath. Despite everything, I was curious about her. And somewhere at the back of my mind I was wondering about the odd, frightened expression on Jeff's face as the front door of the surgery swung shut.

Chapter 3

By the time we pulled up outside the block of apartments in College Court, she'd managed to get the crying under control. She mumbled a thank-you, her doll-like face streaked with dried tears. She left the door of the car hanging open as she turned to climb the steps to her flat. There was nothing doll-like about her legs, about the firm thighs encased in their tiny sheath of black skirt. Even as I watched her haul herself abjectly up the stone steps, I could not ignore the sexuality that seemed to scream at me from her diminutive frame.

I hadn't been unaware of it in the car either, as she slumped beside me in the front seat while I negotiated the town centre in my old Mercedes. There were moments in that brief journey around the docks and the Square when I forgot about the lumps in my armpit and the weight in my heart.

At the top of the flight of steps she began to search through her handbag. She was leaning against the heavy door, varnished darkly and, embroidered with the fake medieval hinges so beloved of our town's developers. I could see the frustration in her face, the pouting lips puckered impatiently. She straightened, holding in her hand a bunch of keys. I watched her search, select, try to push the key home. It didn't fit. Her frown deepened. She tried another, unsuccessfully. The ring of keys seemed to slip from her grasp and there was a harsh, jangling noise as it bounced off the stone. For a second she looked at the ground. I saw her face crumple once more into tears and then she let her handbag go and it too hit the ground and its contents spewed across the wide, stone step. Kelly slumped against the door, her face a mask of anguish and dejection.

She hardly seemed aware of me, standing beside her, trying to console her, telling her everything would be okay, we'll just get you inside and get you a nice cup of tea, all the platitudinous, clucking noises that we learn over a lifetime. I stooped to retrieve her bag, stuffing the scattered cosmetics and packets of cigarettes back inside, and began the process of selecting the right key. The key ring was attached to a brass disc inscribed: Manchester United Players Loo. It was the sort of thing Bee might have. Kelly Carpenter made no objection when I finally pushed open the door and put my arm around her to help her inside.

Through open doors off the narrow hallway I had a glimpse of unmade beds and scattered women's underwear. Bras and knickers hung from the white, plastic-coated clotheshorse that was tented above the sides of the cream-coloured bath. A large TV and accompanying video-machine stood in the corner of the spacious living-room area that opened off the end of the hall; a matt-black, hi-fi rack system rested on top of an oak sideboard, flanked by piled-up heaps of CDs. Even as I was lowering the girl onto the four-seater couch, I was wondering who shared this apartment with her; the paperbacks and ring-binders stacked in the tall bookcase were the stuff of college life, but no student could afford the shiny gear and expensive furniture that were housed in this apartment.

She nodded, as if she understood, when I said that I was going to make some tea. The kitchen was straight out of the pages of the Sunday supplements with its gleaming gadgetry, dark tiled walls and split-level cooker. On either side of the double-sized sink stood a white washing machine and its matching dishwasher.

The tea, coffee and sugar were stored in a row of labeled pots with pneumatic caps. When I pulled open the drawer, searching for spoons, I was struck by an array of silver cutlery that would grace the gift list of any blushing bride. Kelly Carpenter, I had observed, wore no wedding ring but perhaps she was just married and had been on the receiving end of a very profitable wedding shower.

She seemed more composed when I went back into the living-room. She was perched on the edge of the couch, her hands curled and still in her lap, her legs drawn tightly together. Her lips moved in a kind of thank-you smile as I handed her the beaker. I watched her blow at the hot tea, like a child, before she sipped at it. I felt her eyes on me over the rim of the beaker. You could see worlds in those almond-shaped and cornflower blue eyes. They were measuring me; I knew that, wondering about me.

'I'm pregnant,' she said at last.

The way she said it, I knew she wanted no congratulations.

'You'll be fine,' I said at last. 'You're young and healthy –'

'Don't! Just fucking don't!' The blue eyes were dull and lifeless now. 'I can't have it . . . My father will fucking kill me.'

I didn't want to hear this. I wanted to be gone. I had my own wounds to lick, my own ghosts to greet.

'Len is no better.' I might as well not have been there; her half-sobbed words spilled out into some personal desert. 'He only wants me for the one thing.'

'Is Len your boy-friend?' I was thinking I could call him before escaping to my own lair.

'He's some fucking boy-friend.' Her laugh was bitter. 'He'll be just as pleased as my oul' fella will, with the news but for once in his life Len can lump it. He's going to have to pay to get rid of it. He's been happy enough to pay for everything else . . . now he can pay for my fucking abortion. Can you see me going back up to Ballinrobe with my tail between my legs and a baby in my arms? The whole town laughing at me, and then my oul' fella reading the riot act from morning 'til night? Not likely . . . not *fucking* likely!'

19

Her words mapped a sad, ugly terrain that I had no wish to travel. 'You're upset,' I said, as gently as I could. 'And tomorrow you'll wish you hadn't said these things to me . . . you don't know me.'

She lifted her hand then and looked at me as if for the first time. 'You sound just like Len. Cautious. Keep it quiet. Take me to bed but don't let us be seen together, not even for a coffee.' The bitterness was draining out of her; defiance had briefly taken its place. 'Well, he can't sweep this under his fitted fucking carpets. The whole fucking town is going to know about this baby 'cos I'm going to make sure they know about it.'

I thought of telling her that unmarried motherhood was without stigma in modern Ireland, that the streets were full of single mothers with little Jason's and Natasha's in their lightweight pushchairs, but only for a moment. Kelly Carpenter, I figured, was having an affair with some married sugar-daddy and she didn't know if she wanted a baby or an abortion.

And, it was none of my business. 'I'm sorry,' I said. 'But I have to go. You should discuss this with . . . with Len.'

'You're all fucking talk, Mr Daniel Best, you know that?'

I was unprepared for her vehemence.

'You think I don't know who you are? You think I haven't heard you on the radio spouting out remedies for everything from here to eternity? You think I haven't read your *Morning-fucking-Prince* and cried for that little fellow?' She stood up suddenly and for a moment I had the feeling she was about to strike me. 'You're all talk, just like the rest of them . . . Now get the fuck out of my house.'

Even tears and anger could not conceal the porcelain beauty of the face that was turned up to me. I murmured my apologies and began to make my way towards the hall.

'And take that *fucker* with you!'

Something smashed against the wall in front of me. I turned to face her, hardly believing she had thrown something at me. Her face was streaked with tears, her arm still raised in a throwing posture.

'I only missed,' she said. 'Because I wanted to.'

I stooped to pick up the picture she had thrown at me. I turned the frame over in my hands; its glass was badly splintered by the impact. The frame held a colour snapshot, the kind of memento you'd click after a sunny day in the country or at the beach. Kelly's face was open-mouthed in laughter; the man in the photograph was half-turned away from the camera, as if he had tried too late to escape the moment. Even behind the cracked web of the glass, there was no mistaking that face: especially behind glass. I had seen the face first on one of those early, empty days after my father was gone and the world was changed; through the window of the big house on Taylor's Hill; later, when we were both young men, at the end of the period of my life that had begun with my father's going, I had seen that face once more through cobwebbed, frosted glass. On that occasion it had been the cracked glass of a car windscreen; his face then had looked even more frightened than it was in the photograph I was holding in my hand.

I walked back across the deep carpet and handed the picture to Kelly Carpenter. I swallowed, trying to keep my voice steady. 'Tell me about you and Leonard Crotty!'

Had the face in the photograph been anybody else but Leonard Crotty, I'd have kept on going. I'd probably have picked up the picture and placed it back on the oak sideboard beside the black hi-fi: it would have been a fairly serious venial sin to be untidy in the old house on Paternoster Lane. I might have turned, briefly, to say good-bye before opening the hall door and stepping out in the newly-minted world of College Court. I'd have driven through the orderly complex of redbrick apartments, hurrying towards the sanctuary of my own foetal lair, and I'd have thought no more of Kelly Carpenter and her unwanted pregnancy.

I perhaps should have done all that but the sight of Leonard Crotty's smug, irksome face brought me back to Kelly Carpenter's side and drew me into her life. Or at least it drew her into mine.

F/1021509

Time was when Leonard and I saw each other every day. Later, when he went away to boarding school and we met only during the school holidays, my mother would delight in saying, as she busied herself tidying and cleaning while I waited for her in Crotty's kitchen on Taylor's Hill, that "Wasn't it great that he and I were still thick as thieves?". By then, in my teens, my childhood reservations about Leonard had come to the surface again; in any case, I felt that my mother was trying too hard to engineer an intimacy between me and her employer's son. I was embarrassed by these efforts. Her scheming, it seemed to me, was transparently obvious to the entire Crotty household, and worst of all, to Leonard. One time, back in our own house she had broached the subject of my getting work with Crotty's, when I was finished my schooling, and this could come about if I "played my cards right".

The prospect of being Leonard's creature horrified me and I had left our kitchen in tears. I had not argued with my mother. Deep inside me, I knew that she and I could not risk a major quarrel: by then we had nobody except each other.

In one sense, I became his creature anyway. When he came between Jean and me, I was driven to the edge of madness by grief and jealousy and fury. I still live, every day of my life, with the consequences of my moment of insanity. And every day I blame Leonard for his part in my fall. In the years since I came back to town, we have sometimes passed each other on the street – in a place this size you will eventually get to pass everybody on the street – and we have nodded and perhaps muttered "Hello". We have nothing to say to each other because there is too much to be said.

Perhaps it was the scent of revenge that drew me back into the living-room in College Court. Revenge is, after all, a dish best eaten cold. How cold can you get? Over a quarter of a century had passed since I had skulked in the darkened garden of the house on Taylor's Hill, waiting to destroy Leonard Crotty, not realising as I crouched there, drunk but cold-blooded, that I would succeed only in destroying my own dreams. Now there was another girl crying and, once more, I could see Leonard's frightened features behind splintered glass.

It was more than the prospect of retribution that set me writing this account. The motives of the human heart, I have learned are never pure metal. Aalways they are impure compounds, alloys. In my long career of scribbling, I think I always wanted to write another book, one that would show not just the glory of morning but also the knavery of the night. I wasn't surprised when Kelly protested, accusingly, that she knew who I was, that she had read my book; it is, after all, prescribed reading for teenagers in English schools and, perhaps as a result of this, has become a staple of non-prescribed reading for many Irish teenagers. The truth is, as always, more complex. The *Prince of Morning* was a truthful but spectacularly incomplete portrait of working-class life in Ireland. The "authentic voice of the boy-story-teller" is a concoction of loneliness and imagination. When I wrote the book, twenty years ago, I did so as an exercise in forgetting, not remembering. It was as if, in trying to re-create those first years of life in Paternoster Lane, I could wipe out the memory of the events that followed.

Try explaining that to an earnest, mature student from Wisconsin or Sunderland who has fetched up on your doorstep on a wet Saturday afternoon with wonder in her voice and a well-thumbed copy of your book in her trembling hands. They glance nervously into the hall as if they expect the old greyhounds to come charging past them or as if they might hear Granda Flanagan's raspy voice from the kitchen, wheezing out its recitation of the power and the glory of the British Army. I haven't the heart to tell them of the dull years that followed; I give them tea and biscuits, sign their copies of The Prince of Morning and send them off to Alberta or Welwyn Garden City with their dreams of someone else's childhood splendidly, glowingly intact.

Just this once, I want to tell it like it was. It's my last shot. That's why this record is a memoir: fact, non-fiction. Whatever you call that which is not made up, contrived, squeezed into unnatural shapes and pastures. It did cross my mind to turn this into a novel. Change Kelly's name, conceal Leonard's identify and Jeff's and all the other identities within a litany of pseudonyms. And locate all these improbable names in some made-up town that would be unrecognizable, some plausible conurbation in a non-existent Ireland.

The notion was short-lived. Anybody who bothers to read this story, deserves the truth. *Especially you Bee!* I have done things I'm not proud of, my Honey Bee, but I'd prefer you to hear about them from me rather than from some stranger. When I learned the truth of my father's going, I wept, for me, for him. But I think I was angry too, my pity notwithstanding: I should have heard it from him, not from the frightened lips of an ageing corner-boy

I owe the truth to myself also. Words have been both my tools and my stock-in-trade for my entire working life. Somehow, in all my columns, in all my words, I have contrived to hide myself from my readers. Even from myself. I venture opinions on the madnesses of the world, yet the mouthpiece of these opinions is a fiction. The author I project in my pieces; wise, whimsical, acerbic, does not exist. He is not real. Not like the lumps in my armpit, the lumps I refuse to have treated.

Anyway, I am no novelist. I am a recorder of events, an interpreter of the daftness of my fellow man. When I was asked by Gabriel, all those years ago, to take on a column on a three-months trial, I was flattered; in those first months after *The Prince of Morning* was published, I was flattered and astonished by just about everything. I used to prowl the bookshops of London just to look at my book. Sometimes, when I'd see my name in yet another review, I wouldn't be able to breathe. I'm going to be found out now, I'd think; somebody is going to tumble to it at last: my book and myself are a pair of frauds. Miraculously, it didn't happen. Gabriel's offer seemed to confirm my escape. My publisher was screaming for a sequel, even pleading for it, but I knew there were no more books in me and although the columns for Gabriel's US magazine flowed easily and drew a satisfactory readers' mailbag, the fear of discovery was still strong. Every once in a while, even after years of commenting on the comings-and-goings of the high-

and-the-mighty and the weird-and-the-wacky in Britain and Ireland, I'd figure that my exposure was imminent. Some little, old lady in Sacramento or Abilene, would unmask NewsTruth's Western European correspondent for the sham that he was. It hasn't happened. So here's me, doing it myself now, when the consequences are inconsequential.

No novel then, but just a record of what I have done and left undone. I don't have the skills to clothe these facts in novelistic costumes, to fashion these figures from my personal landscape into characters that are at once fictional but dimly recognizable as their originals. That twilight territory where a nod is as good as a wink and the hurler clings to the ditch.

My record is of Galway, the town that I both love and loathe, sprawling between ocean and lake on the westernmost edge of Europe. I have defaced no signposts, altered no maps. The streets and the lanes of this, my hometown, bear their own names in these pages. So do the men and women and the boys and girls who walk these streets. Even old Mutt and Corrib Prince, their cool noses and wet tongues invading my childish palms in the dark mornings behind our kitchen. This once, the dead and the living deserve the truth: and the nearly dead.

When I left the apartment in College Court about an hour later, Kelly was, if not relaxed, at least dry-eyed. Perhaps my presence had been a comfort to her; I hoped so, or perhaps she was simply all cried-out. Mostly I just listened to her; the words tumbled out of her after a while, as if she had been too long without a listener. Leonard would be away overnight in Dublin.

'A business trip', she said, trying to twist her kissing mouth into a grimace. 'But he'd be sure to call to the apartment on his return . . . He always comes looking for me after he's been away, like he . . . like he . . .' She couldn't find the words to finish; looking at her, I felt, guiltily, a sudden rush of sexual desire. This evaporated to anger as I imagined Leonard Crotty, powerful, middle-aged and arrogant, arriving, enveloping and devouring such loveliness.

It seemed obvious to me that Kelly didn't know her own mind; I urged her not to make a hasty decision. 'Leonard was sure to be supportive,' I said, gritting my teeth. 'Whatever her decision. And you can count on me,' I told her.

I reminded her of that again, when I stood up to leave. I pressed into her hands one of the cards I so rarely use, reciting aloud my phone number as you might for a child. She was turning the card over in her fingers when I was leaving, her shoulders slumped as she perched on the edge of the couch. I turned in the doorway to look back at her and saw her staring vacantly at the card, as if she were wondering what it was. She did not look up as I closed the door behind me.

Chapter 4

It's strange, the way that last year of the old life at Number 1, Paternoster Lane shines in my memory. I mean our life when my father was still with us, and the dogs were in the yard whining or yelping and my mother in the kitchen, smiling. I can remember that year better than I can recall the day before yesterday. Not just the vague remembered view of a long vista, either, but well-defined details, like chiseled, golden images that are highlighted against a background of rich brocade. Sometimes I'll be standing at the sink in the kitchen – not the old kitchen of that time but the newer, larger model, pushed back into the yard – and from outside, I'll hear my father's voice, talking in that gentle tone that he used for everybody. I look out through the double-glazed window and I can see myself, in short, corduroy trousers and green-and-gold striped braces, stooping beside the kennels, stroking old Mutt, telling Prince to behave himself and to keep his paws off the good shirt I wear to school.

I couldn't imagine a life without our greyhounds. You had to feed them. Water them. Brush them. Keep them dry and warm. When the kennels leaked and Dad was patching the roof with fresh tarpaulin you had to listen to Granda Flanagan's croaked criticisms. My father never raised his voice in response to the old man's barbs; he'd just wink at me, across the sloped wooden roof of the kennel and go on nailing down the sheet of tarpaulin. Sometimes he'd shoot me the same wink when Mam was ranting on about the cost of meat for the dogs, but he'd do it in a more leisurely way and, sometimes, he'd repeat the wink, just to make sure my mother would catch him doing it; you'd see the indignation on her face, sharper and leaner than Dad's, and she'd set about him with a rolled-up copy of the *Connacht Tribune* and he'd mock-plead for mercy, crouching for shelter behind me, trying unsuccessfully to stifle his own laughter, until my mother herself could no longer resist the laughter.

Sometimes my father would die slowly on the kitchen floor, groaning and writhing like a fellow on the screen in the Estoria, clutching his stomach, where the bullet was lodged, and he'd beg me, on his death-bed, to protect his helpless dogs when he was no longer there to look after them. Mammy would give him a last clout of the newspaper before she threw its torn pages on top of him. "I don't know what kind of loodramauns you are at all", she'd say, or something like: "You have more respect for the dogs than for the woman of the house!". She'd turn away then, but she'd let me see the glimmer of a smile, so I'd know she was only joking.

Did I dream that golden time? Are these golden-glow images no more than the wishful products of a sentimental imagination? It might be easier if it were so. Once you recognise illusions for what they are, you can begin the process of dumping them out of your life. You can dump reality too, excavate it from your heartland and unload it on the slagheap, but what then will you store in its place? Sometimes the only way to know yourself is to love your pain.

That last year was real, and it remains so in my heart. Especially the walking; the dogs were walked twice a day, once before Dad ate his breakfast and again, in the evening, after he'd eaten his dinner. I was always a permanent fixture on the evening procession; it was the morning walk that was the problem.

'No. Definitely not!' My mother was adamant. 'You're too young and you're too small to be gettin' up at cockcrow to walk those so-'n-so dogs. You need your sleep and I'm goin' to make sure you get it.'

'But –'

'No buts.' There was no glimmer of a smile on her face now. 'D'you think I want the Brother sendin' for me to ask me why you're fallin' asleep in the class every mornin' before it's even ten o'clock? D'you think I want the whole street to be laughin' at me, lettin' my son out walkin' a pair of stupid dogs at some ungodly hour of the mornin' when it's still as black as night?'

My mother could continue for a long time like that. She never even seemed to pause to draw breath.

Behind her back, my father's wink was forlorn. We both knew that no amount of winking codology could solve this dilemma.

'And you can forget about tryin' to get around me with your oul' nonsense, Tom Best,' my mother declared, as if she could read both our minds. 'The lad is too young and that's that!'

'I was only going to say, Breda,' my father said. 'That you're dead right . . . The lad is too young and he needs his sleep.'

My mother eyed him suspiciously, as if she were anticipating an ambush.

'He needs to build up his strength first,' my father went on smoothly, 'before he can come out with me and the dogs in the mornings –'

'But when I'm older –'

'Daniel!' My mother's voice was sharp. 'Don't be interruptin' your father!'

'Sure Danny meant no harm.' I felt his fingers ruffle my hair and I wished again that I had a helmet of dark curls like his. 'D'you think it might be okay, love,' he said sweetly, avoiding my mother's eyes. 'To let him out with me when he's reached the age of reason?'

'The age of reason?'

'The very thing, love; the age of reason.' I watched him sneak a glance at my mother then, gauging the temperature. 'Reaching the age of reason would mean the lad could help me with the dogs and not just be walking along behind them like an ornament . . . like some other ornaments I could mention, if I wasn't a gentleman and married to a lady.'

My mother chose to ignore the barely-veiled reference to Granda Flanagan. 'And when d'you imagine my son might reach this age of reason, Tom Best?' she asked, sarcastically.

'Sure you're the scholar here, love,' my father said. 'You're the one that knows better than me what our holy Mother Church says about that.'

'Our holy Mother Church?' Mammy sounded incredulous.

'Correct me if I'm wrong,' Dad said. 'But aren't we told that we make our First Holy Communion when we reach the age of reason?'

I didn't dare breathe: my First Communion was only a few months away.

'You're a rogue, Tom Best,' my mother said at last. 'But sure I knew that when I married you.'

My father said nothing. When he looked at me, I knew that he was trying not to smile.

'The age of reason.' My mother shook her head, as if wondering at herself. 'I must be losin' my own.'

'After his First Communion then,' Dad said. 'What d'you think, love?'

'We'll see.' Her eyes moved from my father to me, and back again. 'We'll see.'

My father winked at me. This time he made certain my mother couldn't see him. I looked over at the calendar from Taylors' Bar and Grocery on the kitchen wall, beside the Sacred Heart lamp. As soon as I got the chance, I began to count the days until I reached the age of reason. There were 73 days left and I can still recall the anguish I felt, counting the black figures on the clutch of white, flimsy pages gummed to the yellow cardboard below the picture of Taylors' Bar and Grocery, as the number of days mounted under my moving finger. When you're seven years-old, ten weeks and three days seems further than forever. I know differently now, conscious of days slipping through my fingers like fine sand.

Being alone with my father and the dogs on his morning walk, before he went to work at Crotty's, was the end of my rainbow in that year of 1957. At school we chanted our prayers in unison – *Our Father, Hail Mary, The Morning Offering* – while Brother Edmond beat time with the cane on his desk, like some latter-day galley-master who longed to deliver us from the evil of our own ignorance; there were twice-daily inquisitions to test your grasp of the tenets of the faith of our fathers, and the same hooked cane flashed fearfully on the palms of those found wanting. Stinging fingers and screaming palms marked our road to holiness. Nobody plotted rebellion. You shook your wounded paw and got on with it. It was the way the world was.

And anyway, every day brought the rainbow's end and a little closer. You could forgive Brother Edmond his obsession with mortal sins and venial sins and the difference between them: the Brother didn't know about dogs and having your Dad all to yourself on the morning circuit around the sleeping roads, past the unopened curtains and the still-locked doors. The Brothers didn't know everything.

My mother was not so ignorant. 'You have that child moidhered,' she said to my father at the table one morning. 'He's gettin' ready to receive his First Holy Communion and his prayers are the last thing on his mind. All he can think about is walkin' them bloody dogs, God forgive me for swearin', first thing in the mornin' . . .' She gave up, to glare at my father.

He looked sternly at me. 'Your mother is worried about you, Danny.' I looked in vain for a hint of a smile in his dark eyes. 'Say the *I Confess* for her.'

I recited the Confiteor at a gallop.

'Now the *Act of Contrition*.'

'*Oh, my God, I am heartily sorry for having offended Thee, and I detest my sins above every other evil . . .*' I didn't draw breath until I had stumbled across the finishing line.

'D'you see that?' My father turned to my mother. 'He's word

perfect, so there's nothing to worry about. Sure isn't he a credit to you, love?'

'Ye're a right pair,' my mother said.

I suffered myself to be fitted out in a new, navy-blue serge suit with white shirt and dark blue tie. When the morning arrived and I was led, fully dressed and groomed, into my parents' room, I hardly recognised the fellow who stared back at me from the tall mirror on the door of the wardrobe. The black, patent-leather shoes felt heavy on my feet and the unaccustomed tie was threatening to choke me. Beside me I heard my father stifle laughter when I said that I'd better go and show my First Communion outfit to Mutt and Prince.

'We'll give it a skip this morning, Danny boy,' my father said.

My mother was muttering to herself that he had me ruined entirely, as we made our way across Helen Street and along New Road to St Joseph's Church. The day's sacramental passage remains largely unremembered. Everything; the tasteless white disc on my tongue, the blessing of prayer books and rosary beads, even the collecting of shillings and tanners and one half-crown in neighbours' houses that afternoon was no more than a postponement of the following morning. Only then would I be alone on the quiet roads with Dad and the dogs. Only then, truly, would I have reached the age of reason.

Man proposes, as my mother used to intone, and God disposes. Robbie Burns made poetry out of the notion: *The best-laid plans of mice and men Gang aft agley*. I didn't know about Robbie Burns back then but I knew how he felt.

On the morning after I reached the age of reason, I overslept. I just knew, the moment I woke, that something was wrong. The new, navy-blue trousers were folded neatly on the chair beside my bed, the jacket draped carefully over the rail-back of the chair. The patent-leather shoes gleamed from under the chair, the balled, white ankle-socks exactly as I had left them, stuffed into the open mouths of the shoes. My room was its usual self, the plain brown linoleum shiny with its once-weekly coat of polish, my pile of comics stacked neatly on top of the small chest of drawers. The sun was too bright, the silence too loud, on this first morning of my reason-blessed life.

I couldn't hear the dogs.

I didn't know, pelting down the stairs in my nightshirt, that in a year or so I would hear a deeper silence. That morning when my mother turned from the range and smiled across the kitchen at me, I didn't want hear the concern – even the pleading – in her voice.

'You were sound asleep, *a ghra*,' she said. 'I couldn't bear to waken you.'

'You promised! You *promised* to call me!'

'I did, Danny. I called you once and there wasn't a gug out of you.' I shook off her hand. 'You were exhausted after all the excitement yesterday.'

Couldn't she tell that my excitement was for the morning to come? That all that holy stuff in the church couldn't hold a candle to the glory of my first morning walk with Dad and Prince and Mutt? 'I'll catch up on them,' I said, turning back towards the stairs. 'Dad told me the way he goes in the morning.'

She pulled me back. 'They'll be home in a minute, Danny,' she said. 'It's nearly 7.30. You know your father has to be at work by 8.00.'

I brooded over my loss all day. When I look at myself in the group photograph taken that morning; we had to wear our Communion outfits to school to pose for Mr Farrell's camera in the school yard, I can see no trace of the anger and resentment I felt.

Even at seven years-old you put on your public face; or perhaps at seven you learn to put it on. When I came back to this house, I put away in the attic most of the pictures my mother had hung on the walls, but this group shot I left in its place, above the sideboard in the small sitting-room that looks out on to the street. I'm not sure why. Perhaps to remind myself of a time when I knew better than now who I was and where I belonged: I can still put a name to every grinning face in our tiered ranks, although it is years since I have met anybody from that class. Or perhaps I keep it on the wall of the front room to remind myself of the day when I began to learn that life has its own mulish way of screwing-up the schemes and hopes of mice and men.

By 6.00 that evening, none of it mattered. The bells of the churches had barely finished ringing the Angelus, when my father came swinging around the corner of the Lane. He was carrying his jacket in his left hand; sweat was beaded on his brow as if he had run all the way home from Crotty's Builders Providers.

'You're early, Tom.' My mother was already running the tap into the basin for my father to wash.

He grinned at me, lathering his hands and arms. 'Sure I thought I'd get home quick . . . We have to make up to Danny boy for this morning.' When he bent under the tap to rinse his face and neck, you could see the muscles in his back rippling under his white sleeveless vest.

'You're not thinkin' of goin' off without Granda, or anythin' like that?' There was an edge of sharpness to my mother's voice.

'We wouldn't even think about doing such a thing, would we, Danny?'

I made no comment. My father's patience with Granda Flanagan was a continuing wonder to me. Once, when I tried in my childish way to remonstrate with the old man for saying something "awful" to Dad, my father cut me off, gently but firmly. Not until years later did I begin to understand something of my father's guilt at having taken from Granda Flanagan the daughter he expected to care for him all his life. When Breda Flanagan left her father's house at the other end of Paternoster Lane in 1948 to marry my father in St Joseph's church, she was 31 years-old; a spinster by the standards of the time, whose designated purpose in life was to attend to the needs of her father's ailing flesh. My mother herself seemed unable to forget what she had betrayed and abandoned at the other end of the street; my grandfather's ready and frequent reminders made sure of that.

We knew he was outside when we heard the *rat-tat-tat* of his stick on the front door. It was open, as usual. A second later, we heard his rasping voice.

'Is it tonight you're takin' them animals out to walk, or tomorrow?'

'We'll be right there, General.' This title was the only joke my father allowed himself at Granda Flanagan's expense. It was a joke that seemed to please my grandfather.

Dad pushed back his chair from the table, remembering to bless himself after dinner as per my mother's insistence. I did the same and he grinned at me. It was time to walk the dogs.

Paudge Lydon, an unemployed fellow from across the road who financed his drinking by snatching salmon from above the Wolfe Tone Bridge, had christened our evening walk the "apostolic procession". There was neither rhyme nor reason to the tag but, in the way of these things, the nickname stuck. It made even less sense when you considered that Paudge had somehow picked up on my father's title for Granda Flanagan: Paudge would interrupt his conversation with the other fellows at the corner of our street and draw his skinny frame up to his full five-feet, four-inches and salute elaborately. "General Flanagan, *sir*", you'd hear him bark, as we passed by. "At ease, Paudge", my father always answered, laughing.

Granda didn't laugh. He scowled at Paudge and his cronies with such balefulness that you knew he'd send them over the top if he could at Mons or the Somme or one of those places he never stopped talking about, into the killing-zone of the Germans' machine-guns. My grandfather had survived all of those battles. When I was older, reading history books in the library at the top of the courthouse, I could only shake my head in wonder at Granada Flanagan's war-stories: he had, it seemed, served on every major front in World War I, from Gallipoli to Flanders and had, of course, survived them all through his native intelligence and inventiveness.

His wounds, at least, were not invented.

Because of his wheelchair, we walked on the roadway. The footpaths were too narrow and it was too difficult for me to manoeuvre the chair up and down to cross the road. Paudge and his mates were not the only ones to mark our evening progress. On summer evenings, especially, when front doors were flung open, greetings were hurled at us from every house: "How're you, Tom?" or "Left-right, left-right" or "Is that oul' dog ever goin' to win anythin', Tom?".

I can still hear the wireless pips through open windows on the street, and the newsreader's voice starting on the half-six news. You could set your clock, Paudge used to say, by the commencement of the "apostolic procession".

And I can hear the shushing noise of the rubber tyres on the road; my grandfather's wheezy breathing; my father's voice, returning greetings and cooing to the dogs; they straining against the leash, panting tight against Dad's side until we have negotiated the narrow streets of the town.

Sometimes, on an upward incline, the wheelchair is too much for me and my father leans over and places his hand, hard and scarred from Crotty's yard, alongside mine on the push-bar and the wheels spin easily round. He goes on pushing until we crest the slope and his fingers idle through my hair when he lets go of the chair. Back then, there was little traffic in the town and our procession was, in any case, known to most of the drivers who used the same roads; their car-horns honk cheerfully, they wave through open windows.

'You'd be better off puttin' the oul' fella in the traps at the Sportsground, Tom.'

'Them hounds look like they could use a good feed, Tom.'

'You should put the oul' dogs in the wheelchair, Tom, and the lead on the oul' fella.'

The horn blowing was not always cheerful. 'Keep your shirt on,' Dad would advise some impatient stranger, pulling the dogs and myself in beside the kerb. 'There's room for everybody.'

'Bloody cheek,' my grandfather roars in my memory. 'Did I fight a world war to be shoved aside on the streets of my own town?' He brandishes the knobby blackthorn stick that never leaves his side. 'Did I get the best of Johnny Turk to be walked on top of, back here?

'Keep your shirt on,' my father says.

'If I had my legs back, I'd show these jumped-up gurriers the way a real soldier handles himself.'

Dad grins. I wonder again why he never reacts when Granda Flanagan takes the mickey like this. My father served as a soldier in the barracks on the edge of town for five years, until he married my mother. Not for the first time, I toy with the notion of letting the chair freewheel down some hill.

'Dad was in our own . . . *Irish* army!' I said proudly.

In that moment there is a sudden, hanging silence. On Grattan Road, beside the swamp, we skid to an abrupt halt. My grandfather's hands have gripped the rubber tyres into immobility. His white, grizzled head starts to turn; I am hauled by a bony hand to the side of the chair and I find myself staring into pale, rheumy eyes, not sure if I see anger or hurt in their watery blueness. When I look up at my father for help, I am shocked by the dismay in his face.

'Oh, Danny!' he groans.

And his reproach is no more than that. I still hear it, whenever I drive along that road, between the gentrified coastguards' houses and the playing pitches of the reclaimed swamp. Even if he had known everything I did or did not do afterwards, his voice would have been raised no higher.

The dogs yelp in their muzzles. They can smell the sea and the open road and the promise of a longer leash. My father's command to them is sharply spoken, as if they, and not I, had breached some personal code. And I sense, standing there on the black road beside the swamp, that I have disappointed him with my unchecked words. In his refusal to reprimand me, I become dimly aware of his immense kindness and his immense strength. I have always know it, but I see it now as I have never seen it before, while the dogs wait and my father waits and this helpless cranky old man in a wheelchair waits.

37

'Sorry,' I say. 'I didn't mean it.'

'Shake hands with your granddad.'

I look from my father to the old man. His pale face seems to have grown whiter with rage. I fancy I see sparks of anger in the pale, blue eyes. I meet his gaze and hold out my hand.

'Take the boy's hand when he offers it to you.' My father's anger is diverted towards Granda Flanagan.

My grandfather transfers his stick to his left hand. My hand is enclosed in his bony fingers. I wonder if it is the summer wind that is making the pale eyes more teary than usual. 'I'm sorry, Granda,' I mumble, pulling my hand away.

The distance between us rattles.

'Can we walk the dogs now?' There is irony in my father's words. 'C'mon, Prince, c'mon, Mutt . . . all's quiet on the western front.'

I bend again to the chair. The lines are deep on Granda Flanagan's neck, like trenches cut in dying soil. I hear Dad's voice, rousing the dogs, and we push on, harder now, into the wind.

I have, almost without knowing it, reached the age of reason.

Chapter 5

It was Kelly Carpenter's predicament, rather than my own, which got in the way of sleep that night in Paternoster Lane. The irony of the situation was too obvious to miss: it was the kind of irony that often suffused my column in NewsTruth. There was a kind of classic symmetry about the scenario that appealed to me: while I try to find resources within or without to cope with my own approaching end, I am, by the contrivance of some grinning providence, made the confidant of a young woman who has doubts about how to handle the gift of life. Lying on my back, half-listening to the footsteps of late-night clubbers taking the short-cut home along our road, I wrote and re-wrote the column on the white ceiling of my bedroom. I teased out the situation with macabre humour. I laughed at myself. I wondered about the life the child would lead if he or she were permitted to live and about the life it might have led if the verdict went against it. Kelly's Barbie-doll blankness stared down at me from the ceiling of my dreams. Leonard Crotty tried to hide behind her shoulder.

Gabriel would love it, but I knew that this particular column would get written on nothing more accessible than my night-time ceiling. Leonard was doing nothing illegal by "dipping his wick" in the extra-marital pond; neither was it illegal for him to father what used to be called a bastard. Mrs Crotty might not approve of such activities but no doubt she lived in affluent ignorance.

In my words on the ceiling I could read my own rage, my own hurt; my regrets too. The sky was lightening when I feel asleep.

The phone woke me. It was Jeff. 'You were supposed to call me, Dan.'

I blinked against the light. 'What time is it?'

'It's almost 1.00. I still have a half-full waiting room but broke away to contact you.' I could imagine the frown on the squashed features as he paused to draw breath. 'Now will you get your ass around here so I can make arrangements for you to begin your treatment?'

'I'll call you, Jeff.'

'It's past calling time, Dan. I have a bed booked for you for tomorrow morning in the hospital, 9 am.'

'I'll phone you,' I said.

'9.00, Dan. Tomorrow.'

I put the phone down but then took it off the hook. The ceiling was wiped clean of all the sleepless words I had scribbled there during the night. Now it held only one word: chemotherapy. It was a word I wished neither to see nor to hear nor, more importantly, to speak. Jeff could go fuck himself. I had too often seen the balding, toothless victims of the wonder "treatment" withering their way towards their inevitable end and I had no desire to join their poisoned ranks. Quality meant more than quantity. I'd settle for fewer days, so long as they were normal. Whatever normal might mean in my life.

I showered slowly in the bathroom I'd had built on above the extended kitchen. The backyard had all but disappeared. The bumps under my arm hadn't. They didn't seem any bigger either. Maybe they were growing inwards.

For breakfast I spooned the green, seedy flesh out of a couple of kiwi-fruits and toasted slices of Griffin's bread. Jeff had warned me to avoid coffee, but I figured it didn't matter anymore. Buddy Holly was right, all those years ago.

The coffee-pot sustained me through the afternoon, as I worked on my column. By 5.30 pm the piece was finished, keyed and transmitted to NewsTruth's offices in Manhattan. I switched off the computer with regret. My column had become a way of losing myself, rather than pointing out any truth for any of the readers.

When I first returned here from London, I used to while away the evenings by going for long walks. Back then; I was wondering what to do with myself. The future had stretched no further ahead than the formalities of the funeral. Or so I liked to pretend; a future without Bee was too empty to contemplate.

My promise to cut down on my drinking had won from the court the concession of a weekly two-hour visit with my daughter, but it had turned out to be a pyrrhic victory. Elizabeth sniffed around me like a demented sommelier and Bee fretted lest her wayward father should somehow land himself in troubled waters. I could hear her small, sad voice in my ear on those long marches I made in and around my sprawling town. After a while I realised that I was tracking the different routes of our long-ago apostolic processions. Sometimes Bee was there, straying through time, and I was at once child and father on our evening rambles.

I no longer trusted my legs or lungs enough to carry me on such excursions. I sat into my old Mercedes still enjoying the feeling of having finished my column. The deadline and the writing itself had become important features in my landscape. I nosed the car along the Lane between the rows of parked vehicles. It was a designated disc-parking area by that time and residents like myself had to display our manila-coloured permits inside the windscreen. For all I knew, they could have permits too for bicycle-tyred wheelchairs and apostolic processions.

At the Small Crane pub I swung right, out past the Jesuit church. Although we could almost touch the church from our backyard, my father never went to mass there. "The friars are the men for the likes of us", he'd always say, heading in his Sunday suit for the 10.00 mass at the Dominicans. I remembered his words, driving slowly along Grattan Road, past the swamp and in front of the Dominican church on the old docks. After more than 40 years I could still hear his reason. Something to do with love, I suppose.

The Square had unclogged itself of evening commuter traffic. I drifted slowly past the sober facades of banks and building societies, noting the September residue of back-packers on the Square, thumbing guidebooks and guzzling bottled water and take-away sandwiches. Kelly Carpenter should be among them, loitering her way with youthful intent through strange, promising streets, rather than nursing a pregnant belly in a fancy apartment that was probably paid for by Leonard Crotty. Cruising past her College Court block I noticed that Jeff's car was parked on the road outside. The big Volvo station wagon was easy to recognise, with his "Doctor on Call" sticker on the front windscreen. I pulled in at the far end of the street, sheltering behind a Toyota Land Cruiser. The last thing I wanted was a kerbside lecture from Jeff and an instruction to go to the hospital first thing in the morning.

I wondered if Kelly was Jeff's patient on this visit.

College Court is four storeys high; all the apartments have individual front doors that open directly on to verandahs that run around three sides of the building. I waited and watched the building through my passenger side-door mirror. When the door of Kelly Carpenter's apartment opened a few minutes later, it was Jeff that came out. He stood there a moment, blocking the doorway, blinking in the evening light. I watched him pull the door shut behind him and stride purposefully down the main staircase that linked the verandahs and I went on watching him as he got into his car and drove off around the corner of the block.

I began to wonder what kind of house-calls doctors made without their black bag of tricks. Perhaps Jeff had taken to carrying his around in his pockets.

Driving through the town I'd had a vague notion, half-formed, of calling in to see Kelly. Seeing Jeff's car and then Jeff threw me. Kelly, I remembered, had been seen the day before by one of Jeff's partners, but maybe, I reasoned, house calls were shared out among all the members of the practice. Or perhaps they worked a rota system and today was Jeff's turn. Whatever. There was nothing sinister going on here, just a doctor visiting a patient. Without his bag, I reminded myself, his arms were free to swing confidently as he marched down the steps to his shiny-new, estate car.

I was still mulling these thoughts over as I switched on the ignition. Seamus Fox, who serviced the car and attended to its running repairs, was always telling me that the old Merc was a petrol-guzzler and that the best thing I could do was get rid of it. I should get rid of this interest in Kelly Carpenter too, I knew. I also knew that I couldn't, wouldn't, and that I would hang on to it, just as I hung onto my old car, lovingly ferried back from London years previously.

The unannounced and perhaps by now, unwelcome visit to Kelly could wait for another day. Anyway, I reasoned, maybe she would phone me soon. Then again she might have no need to. Perchance Leonard Crotty, after a lifetime of wheeling and dealing in people's emotions, would suddenly shape up like Sir Galahad.

At the junction with the main road I had to wait for a gap in the traffic. I swung left behind an elderly, rust-spattered Datsun and found myself staring into the dark eyes of a fawn-coloured greyhound. Through the rear window of the old car the dog stared back at me, his eyes unblinking above the cage of his muzzle. We climbed the Magdalene hill slowly, but neither the dog nor I noticed the small houses on the right or the low-slung bunker of City Hall on the left. We went on staring at each other, the dog and myself, as we crested the hill, heading past the grey decay of the old Grammar School and the mortgaged splendour of the big B&Bs on College Road.

I wasn't surprised when the driver in front indicated left and swung into the main entrance of the Sportsground. The two fellows on duty at the gate waved to the driver in recognition. The dog in the back seat of the car turned away from me, as if he could smell the track and the races that would shortly begin. As

I drove past, I had a glimpse of the track rails, white under the floodlights, and beyond, the dark bulk of the stand. It didn't seem to have changed.

I was the one who had changed. What I did remember most from my one-and-only visit to the track, after prolonged pleading with my mother to allow me to go with my father, was my own sense of wonder on that long-ago Friday night. The magic of the Sportsground was somehow richer than any I had imagined. The bright lights were brighter, the sense of mystery darker. Here men in caps and hats and long tweed coats conducted their business with the aplomb of Masonic elders.

'Evening, Tom.'

The clasp of hands before eyes dropped to me.

'Is this the young lad? You're startin' him young.'

My own hand pressed between calloused palms, my hair ruffled, my chin uptilted for better inspection.

'He's the spit of you,' another said, his eyes straying away from me towards Prince. We'd walked him through the streets of the darkening town, dinnerless on a night of racing. Canny eyes all around measured Prince like merchandise.

And found him wanting!

I knew they did. Knew it in the sideways glance, the half-smile that flickered on thin lips. In the yard beyond the stand, where you kitted out the dogs in their colours for each race, you could sense the amused indifference in the other fellows. Prince was drawn in the outside trap of the six runners. The black-and-white horizontal stripes of the Number 6 jacket, looked like a part of his natural colouring.

'Ye have the best draw anyway, Tom,' a young fellow said, fastening the red jacket around his own dog. His companion grinned. I knelt down beside Prince and hugged him. I felt my father's fingers in my hair.

Where we stepped out of the yard and crossed the paved area to the track, we could hear the crowd. They were gathered in the

44

middle of the stand, opposite the finishing line. Below them, on the rails, half-a-dozen bookies were shouting the odds. I understood about odds. Dad had explained them on our morning walks, the ones we did without Granda Flanagan. 'Ten to one, Corrib Prince!' I heard one bookie shout, and I stroked Prince's head as we walked in line towards the row of traps. '20 to one, the Prince!' another voice roared and there was laughter from the huddle of hats and caps around the bookies.

The fellow in charge of the traps wore a white shop-coat that was stretched tight over his belly. I felt his eyes on me as I stooped to kiss Prince and whisper encouragement in his pricked ear. 'Just ignore them, Prince,' I told him. 'You're better than any of them.' He turned to lick me and I felt the leathery hardness of his muzzle bump against my nose. My father cradled the dog in his arms and placed him in the trap. The other dogs were already in; the shop-coated fellow swung the gate shut behind the dogs. My father and I scampered towards the rails with the other handlers.

The lights in the stand were suddenly dimmed. I heard a humming like a distant train on tracks and then the mechanical hare, furry and frozen, swept past us on its knee-high, metal arm. I had a glimpse of the dogs in their cages, snouts poised on paws, and then the traps swung open. The dogs sped by in a coloured blur. I saw Prince's black-and-white combination at the back of the field. Before the first bend two dogs were locked in a heap of flailing limbs and crashed together in the dust. A third animal slammed into them and joined the tumbling, yelping heap. Behind them, untroubled, Prince cruised by on the outside.

Groans from the stand. 'That fucker is always fighting,' someone shouted.

I hardly heard them. *He's going to be third, Dad!* I screamed. 'Look, Prince is third!'

He finished a long way behind the two in front, but I didn't care. I looked back at the bookies to see if they were eating their insulting words but they were bent over their satchels as if they were unaware of Prince's achievement. The lights on the track dimmed and the greyhounds circled, yelping for their lost hare. I rushed towards Prince and pressed myself against his sweating, panting flanks. I glared at the fellow in charge of the red dog, the jacket soiled from tussling on the ground, but he only laughed at me. 'Ye were lucky,' he said. 'Maybe ye can get them all fighting the next night.' I turned my back on him, hugging the dog together.

We had to go home immediately. It was the price of my mother's consent to this first excursion of mine. But first there was business to be done. 'The prize, Dad!' I tugged at his sleeve. 'What's for third?'

He was on his knees in the yard, methodically checking Prince, lifting each leg and feeling with his fingers along its length. '50 bob.' He grinned up at me. 'Your Mam will be pleased.'

Two pounds and ten shillings was a prize to be reckoned with. 'Prince was great,' I said. 'He'll win the next time.'

'Aye,' he said. 'Maybe he will at that.'

We collected the money in the small pebble-dashed shed at the side of the yard. There were bars on the small window; a single, unshaded bulb cast a sickly light on the fellow seated at the desk. His hair was plastered to his skull and his teeth were yellow from cigarettes. They reminded me of Mutt's fading fangs when he tried to smile at us.

'A good night, tonight, Tom. The gossun brought you luck.'

'It comes and goes, Mr Duggan.' I noticed that my father seemed nervous in the presence of this suited fellow. 'It comes and goes.'

'It seems to go a lot in your case, Tom.' The yellow teeth were bared again, laughing at their owner's joke. 'A helluva lot, you might say.'

My father said nothing. He had removed his cap when we'd entered the small office and he was turning it in his hands like a nervous wheel.

The stained teeth flashed again, as if their owner might say more, but he seemed to think better of it. He stooped before the dark green safe in the corner and swung the brass handle downward. I had a glimpse of papers and moneybags as he removed a small cash box, and then the heavy door once more swung shut. The cash box was crammed with money; pound notes, ten-shilling notes, fivers, tenners and some bigger notes I had never seen before. I gasped.

Behind me, Prince farted.

'You should have left him outside.' The plastered skull did not look up.

'Sorry.' My father winked at me. 'Sorry,' he repeated.

I watched him as yellow-toothed Mr Duggan handed over the money; two green, pound notes and an orange, ten-bob note. My father stuffed the notes quickly into his pocket and said thank-you and goodnight in a rush, as if he were about to start coughing.

Outside, with the door safely closed behind us, my father finally burst out laughing. 'Oul' Duggan,' he spluttered. 'He means well but you'd think it was his own money he was handling.' He shook his head in wonder, wiping tears of laughter from his blue eyes. 'The oul' head is always down, counting the money . . . he never looks up . . . Sure he doesn't even know there's stars up there.'

It was dark now; the sky seemed littered with stars. Dogs were still being readied and walked around the yard, and the bookies were still shouting the prices at the foot of the stand, but just for a moment the shouting died and the track-lights dimmed, and there was just Dad and myself and Prince, bound together by our fifty-shilling success under the expanse of stars. For that one moment, they were ours and ours alone.

'You're some boyo, Prince! In oul' Dugg's office!'

I watched him lovingly stroking the dog, loving him. 'Will we go home now, Dad?'

He handed me Prince's lead and we set off together. There were good-humoured whistles and jeers from the fellows in the stand as we passed by; my father waved and shouted back at them. We had to walk around a big, shiny car, which had pulled up just inside the entrance to the Sportsground. The gate attendant was stooped at the driver's side of the car. Through the open window I could see a large, bald, head that was dominated by a greying moustache beneath a bulbous nose.

The driver hailed us in a loud voice that reminded me of a teacher's. 'I hear you did well tonight, Tom.'

'Not so bad, sir, not so bad at all.'

'Just so long as you didn't do too well.' The driver barked a laugh; I felt his eyes turning to me. 'Is this your son and heir?'

'Danny, sir.' My father pushed me slightly forward. 'Say hello to Mr Crotty, Danny.'

'Hello, Mr Crotty.'

The bulbous nose nodded in greeting, the moustache twitched and the small eyes lost interest. 'See you tomorrow, Tom.' The engine revved up as the car moved away.

'Yes, sir,' my father said, but I knew that the driver couldn't hear him.

We were still for a moment, watching the car pull away from us to park under the stand. 'Is that Mr Crotty that owns the yard?' I asked.

'Himself,' my father said. 'In the flesh.'

'He's bald,' I said.

'It happens to the best of us,' my father said as we turned on to College Road.

'It won't happen to you, Dad!'

Under the streetlight I could see the dark curls that had strayed free under the peak his cap. I felt his hand tighten around mine. 'What did Mr Crotty mean, Dad?'

'About what?'

'When he said, "so long as you didn't do too well"? '

We had to walk in single file around a car that had parked on the footpath.

'Sure he was only making oul' talk, Danny, the way rich people do.'

Prince yanked on the lead.

'He's lonesome for Mutt, Dad.' Mutt used to race before I was born, there was a small silver cup with his name on it on the mantelpiece in the front room.

'Everybody's lonesome for something, Danny.'

'I'm not,' I said.

'I'm glad to hear it, Danny boy,' my father said. 'All the same,' he went on, as if to himself, 'you don't miss much, do you?'

I didn't know what he was going on about but I was tired of words now. Ahead lay the familiar face of Paternoster, our own house at the end, and Mutt to welcome us, and my mother too, and the prospect of her excitement when I told her about the race and my father pressed the crisp, paper money into her hand in the warmth of our kitchen. The streetlights glowed that night but it was the stars that lighted our way home.

Attic voices from that long-ago night whispered to me as I drove home; left at the big roundabout below the Sportsground and then the long sweep downhill along Bohermore and into the Square. Back then the sky had been studded with diamonds and all my tomorrows had shone among them. I could not have known then, proudly marching home through the quiet streets with my father and Prince, that within weeks, my diamonds would be swept from the sky and my tomorrows drowned in darkness.

There was, for once, an empty space at the end of the Lane and I pulled in outside the door. I switched off the ignition but I sat a while in the car, listening to the voices in my head. I was in no hurry to go inside. These days, one place felt pretty much like any other.

Chapter 6

Prince ran again a few weeks later. Not even tears could crack my mother's resolve on this occasion.

'It's far too late,' she'd said, her mouth and mind set. 'You'll be in your bed at 9.00 and that's that.'

The look my father gave me over his mug of tea was oddly pleading. 'It's the last race, Danny. Sure it'll be after 10.00 before we get out of the place.'

I snuffled. I had spent the afternoon in the yard with the dogs, stroking them, talking to them. Prince's black and white coat shone from my brushing. I knew that he understood when I told him that he needed to break fast, steer clear of trouble and the race was his. 'It's not fair,' I said.

'You can come the next time . . . I promise.' Dad looked desperately from me to my mother and back again. 'And I'll tell you all about the race in the morning, before I go to work. Honest.'

But I refused to be mollified. 'It's not fair,' I said again.

'That's enough.' My mother's voice was sharp. 'Your bed-time is nine o'clock and that's all about it.'

The pips before the 6.30 news were sounding on the wireless as my father pushed back his chair and stood up from the table.

'I'll be off so,' he said. 'Are you going to help me get him ready, Danny?'

'You're awful early,' my mother said. 'Isn't it the last race he's in?'

'I've a few oul' things to do,' Dad said. 'And anyway, I want to give the dog plenty of time to get settled up there this evening.'

'If you ask me, it's too settled those oul' dogs are, sure they're better fed than ourselves . . .' At my mother's words, Dad grinned across the table at me. We'd heard it all before and my mother knew we had. 'Ye're a right pair of latchigoes,' she finished, but she was laughing.

'Mam –' I started, still hoping, but my father's hand on my arm stayed me.

'Next time, Danny boy,' he said. 'Alright?'

I made a face. 'If I'm awake when you come home, Dad, will you come in and tell me about the race?'

'Course I will.'

'Promise?'

'Cross my heart and hope to die.'

I'd have died for him there and then, the wide smile on his weathered face, the errant curls like a pair of question marks above his blue eyes.

'I'm going to be awake,' I said. 'When you come home.'

Of course I wasn't – awake, I mean. Back then I didn't lie on my back composing versions of what might-have-been on my bedroom ceiling. Sleep comes easily when you're eight years-old, when every night is no more than a necessary interruption between days of discovery.

In the way of these things, I slept later than usual that Saturday morning. I knew, as soon as I opened my eyes, that it was late – the sun was bright in my room, pouring through the yellow, unlined curtains. I wondered, pulling on my shoes and trousers, why I had not been called that morning.

I opened the curtains and lifted the lower half of my window.

Mutt looked up from the pen, barking in response to my call. There was no sign of Prince. I didn't give myself time to think, hurling myself noisily down the stairs and into the kitchen.

My mother was making a cake. She paused in her work, shaping the sticky dough on the kitchen table, and smiled at me.

'The dead arose,' she said.

'Why didn't you call me, Mam? And why isn't Prince out the back? Where's Dad?'

My mother laughed. She sprinkled flour on the dough; her hands moved, effortlessly and expertly, shaping the dough into its usual perfect circle.

'You needed the sleep, Daniel, and your father's at work.' With an ordinary knife she cut a large cross into the face of the cake. 'Prince is out in Bartley's.'

'What's wrong with him?' I asked. Bartley was a grizzled farmer who shared a dark, two-storey house out by the railway line with an equally grizzled, unmarried sister. Twice I'd been there with Dad and an out-of-sorts Mutt. 'Is Prince hurt, Mam?' I remembered the two dogs crashing together on the track, the third animal slamming into their tangled bodies. 'Is he hurt?'

'He's just a bit sore after the race.' She stooped to position the cake in the centre of the baking tray in the oven. 'That's what your Daddy said . . . just a bit sore.' My mother seemed on the verge of laughter; I sensed that she had more to say. It dawned on me at last.

'Did he win, Mam? Did he win?'

She raised her eyebrows and widened her eyes, teasing me.

'He did, didn't he? Didn't he, Mam?'

'He won, Danny,' she said then and she didn't even tell me to stop when I started shouting and dancing in the kitchen.

'I wish that Dad was here, Mam,' I said when I got my breath back.

'Maybe he'll be satisfied now.' My mother seemed to be talking to herself. 'Maybe we'll see a bit more of him at home now if he has the same dogs out of his system.'

I was looking out the window at old Mutt. He was stretched, sleeping as usual, inside the pen. 'I wish Prince was here.'

'You shouldn't be wishing your life away, Daniel.'

'And I wish Dad was here.'

'He'll be home soon,' my mother said. 'For his dinner.'

But he wasn't. The dinner hour came and went without my father's cheery greeting at the door. By 2.30 I was watching the road from the corner of the Lane and my mother was fretting over the range, trying to make sure that "nice bit of mutton" wasn't boiled away to nothing in our usual Saturday stew. 'They must've kept him for a bit of overtime,' my mother said at 2.50, but her tone of voice made me feel she didn't really believe it. Crotty's yard always closed from one to two o'clock; everybody knew that.

'I hope we're going out for Prince tonight,' I said.

'He can have the bit of stew when he comes home tonight,' my mother said. 'I just hope it's not all dried up on him.'

The long afternoon stretched emptily ahead. I sat a while with Mutt but he seemed more interested in sleeping than in my commentary on Prince's triumph. I hauled him to his feet and took him out on to the street. Paudge Lydon, skinny and brylcreemed, was holding up the corner of the Lane as usual. I stopped in front of him, taking in the oiled quiff, the long jaws sucking hungrily on the Woodbine.

'What's up with you, Best?' When Paudge took the butt from his mouth, I could see the yellow strand of tobacco stuck to his lower lip like a piece of loose skin. 'Something on your mind?'

'Prince,' I said. 'He won last night.'

'I heard.' Paudge sucked again on the butt. 'You could've fuckin' told us, Danny boy. I could've had a few bob on him. I'm down to my last fuckin' butt.'

I looked at Paudge with fresh eyes, intrigued by this glimpse of his personal circumstances. 'I'll tell you the next time, Paudge,' I swallowed. 'I promise.'

'You're not the worst, Danny boy,' Paudge said. 'But the trouble is there won't be a fuckin' next time. Lightning like this doesn't strike twice.'

I was afraid to ask Paudge what he meant, he had retreated again to his self-imposed task of watching the world from his wary eyes. I wondered what he saw there, day after day, staring into space. Sometimes Paudge joined the older fellows on the lazy wall at the foot of Dominick Street but mostly he kept his personal sentinel post at the far end of Paternoster.

When I looked out after the Angelus bells, Paudge had gone in for his tea, but there was still no sign of my father. I could sense my mother's uneasiness, pretending not to be watching the alarm clock on the mantelpiece.

The hammering on the door startled us.

'Is he home yet?' It was Granda Flanagan, frowning in his wheelchair.

My mother shook her head. Granda swiveled impatiently in his chair on the footpath. My father had gently but firmly resisted the idea of fashioning our doorway into a sloping ramp that would give my grandfather unaided access.

'He probably met some of them excuses-for-soldiers from up at Renmore.' Granda Flanagan's gob of spit smacked loudly on the pavement. 'They're on the piss by now, that's for sure.'

'If he's gone for a drink, he's welcome to it.' I was no longer surprised by the defiant tone my mother usually adopted towards Granda; it was a fact of life, like Paudge leaning against the corner of the street. 'Tom Best is a hard-workin' man.'

'I'll have a real Tommy any day,' my grandfather said, wheeling away sharply towards his own house. 'Before one of them toy soldiers from the Irish Free State.'

I stood with my mother in our doorway watching him go. I felt her head on my shoulder, drawing me closer to her. 'We'll wait inside,' she said.

Paudge Lydon was back at his post; his eyes watched us as my mother closed the door and we went into the kitchen to wait for my father to come home.

I never saw him again. When my mother called me next morning,

I thought it was still night. She didn't switch on the light in my room; as I struggled with sleep-clumsy fingers to button my shirt and tie my laces, I could hear the noise of the rain falling steadily on the roof. It made the gloom denser, as if the house too were clothing itself with wet darkness. My mother was agitated, rushing me through the ritual of dressing. She seemed not to hear me asking where was Dad.

I was going to stay with Auntie Rita, she told me, just for a few days. She wasn't really my aunt; rather an old school-pal of my mother's who now lived in Athlone. Why, I wanted to know, and why couldn't I wait to go to Mass since it was Sunday?

It was my grandmother who answered me. I hadn't noticed her, bony and skinny, almost invisibly pressed into the kitchen wall. 'Because your Daddy is sick,' she said. 'And your mammy won't be able to look after you. It'll only be for a few days.'

It was all I could get out of them. When they looked at each other, their faces were white and drawn and their eyes were hollow above black smudges. Not even my tears could budge them into answering my litany of questions. They didn't object when I said I didn't want any porridge and pushed the bowl away from me on the rose-tattooed, yellow oilcloth. When I went outside to kiss Mutt goodbye, I clung to his warm neck and told him that Dad and myself wouldn't be able to take him out that day but we'd be back soon for him.

'The two of us would, together. Honest, Mutt,' I cried. The dark pools of his eyes held no explanations for the strangeness of this Sunday morning.

Paternoster Lane was quiet when my mother and Granny Flanagan led me outside. The red van parked at our door had CROTTY'S printed on its sides in big yellow letters. I recognized the driver, a fellow called Bob, who lived in Fairhill; after Mass on Sundays, he and my father often chatted earnestly about the dogs, while the women stood waiting and the white swans cruised in the Claddagh Basin. Bob started to say something to me but then I saw him exchange a glance with my mother and he took my small brown suitcase without a word. My mother kissed me and then so did, unexpectedly, my grandmother; her lips cold and brittle like scorched paper. It was still raining as we drove off; the wipers clattered noisily on the big windscreen of the van.

When we were outside the town, pushing between the green and sodden fields, I asked Bob what was wrong with my dad. His eyes seemed fixated on the wet, grey road. 'He's not good, Danny,' he said. 'He's in hospital.'

I knew that it was pointless, asking any more questions. We drove on in a capsule of sullen silence towards Athlone.

Aunt Rita and her husband were kind to me; the children of the house kept their distance from me. Sometimes I'd catch the boy, a lad about my own age, staring at me and he'd look away guiltily. On the Friday of that week, Aunt Rita called me alone into the front room, overlooking a street not unlike my own. I knew she was going to tell me that my father was dead and gone to heaven. I felt nothing, not even when she put her arms around me and her hot tears rolled onto my face.

Next day, on the journey home, I knew that Bob was trying to hold back tears. The rain fell and the wipers clacked and the load of wooden pallets in the back rumbled as the van crossed the big bridge over the Shannon, but not all the noise in the world could fill the emptiness I felt in my heart. A couple of times since, on the rare occasions when some tale of folly or madness has drawn me and my pen back to Athlone, that awful sense of bleakness has come back to me, like a musty smell in a rarely-opened room. When they built the four-lane by-pass around the town a few years ago, I was glad and that now, on my journeys to Dublin, I had no need even to pass by the door to those days of sorrow.

That, of course, lay ahead in the unknown future. I knew nothing of it as Bob and I drove into Galway. On Paternoster, only our house looked different. The mark of death was pinned to our door, the white card, bordered with black, crowned with a ribbon of darkest crepe. The card was streaked with rain: the ink had run like tears of navy-blue.

At the door, Bob shook hands with me gravely.

'I'm sorry for your troubles, Danny boy,' he said. He nodded to my mother before he drove off in the rain.

My mother said nothing. She stooped in the hallway and I leaned against her but when she kissed me her mouth seemed as cold and dry as Granny Flanagan's. She made no effort to stop me when I brushed past her, dropping my case in the narrow hallway, hurrying through the back door.

The yard was empty. The pen had disappeared. Of the netwire fencing nothing remained. The foot-high concrete base for the fence looked ugly and incomplete in the rain. In the emptiness I called for Mutt and then Prince, but only the rain answered, falling steadily on the empty yard. The rain blinded me, and my tears too. Through the rain I finally saw my mother, standing in the back doorway. Her eyes seemed to look through me, as if I were not there, as if I were not shouting in the rain, demanding to know where Mutt and Prince were.

'They're gone,' she said at last.

'Where, Mammy? Where?'

'They're gone,' she repeated. 'Just gone. Don't ask me again about them!'

Her face was white above the black jumper and black skirt, and her hair was drawn back into a tight bun. Her mouth seemed smaller, creased into a thin line, as if she had nothing more to say to the world. I sensed, with a sad, unwelcome insight, that in a single week our world had changed forever.

I never again asked her about the dogs.

Chapter 7

In the weeks that followed, it was neither the sudden, shattering loss of my father, nor my mother's unfamiliar, stony face that troubled me most. I wept for my father at night, and I was stunned by my mother's withdrawal – it seemed as if I had lost them both together – but it was the threat of going to live in my grandparents' house that made my life almost unbearable.

'Why would you want to be livin' on your own,' my grandmother demanded in our kitchen. 'When you could be with us?'

'It's ridiculous stayin' here by yourself with the lad,' Granda Flanagan rasped. 'There isn't even a feckin' pension out of Crotty's.'

Not like the Connaught Rangers, he might have added, but he didn't need to: I was the one who pushed his chair up to the post office in Eglinton Street every week, to collect his British Army pension.

Nobody asked my opinion but I had learned not to expect that from anyone except Dad. My mother would look from me to her parents, when they assaulted her with their demands, but she said nothing. I interpreted her silence as agreement; within a week of my return from Athlone I was convinced that I would spend the rest of my life in the house where my mother had grown up, a handy target for my grandmother's commands and my grandfather's spittled invective.

I was wrong in my reading of my mother's thin-lipped silence. As I grew older, I came to realize that, in those bleak days after Dad's death, she was trying to devise her own strategy for survival. She had lived for 30 years under her parent's roof, an unpaid workforce-of-one whose particular task was to take charge of my grandfather's wheelchair; she never had a job outside, like the girls of her own age who worked in shops or in hotels or in the laundry; every penny she had, whether to buy the makings of a dress or to go to the pictures, was doled out to her out of the famous pension. When she met my father – where or how, I never did find out – he was still serving in the bloated Irish army of the Emergency; he must have loved her very much, I like to think, to go on calling at Flanagan's door in Paternoster Lane, his army walking-out uniform a sure-fire red flag for Granda Flanagan's impatient contempt. Only when Tom Best had "gone on his ticket" from the Irish Army and found work from Crotty's, was consent given for my mother to leave the Flanagan nest and set up her own home with my father: even then, she wasn't allowed to travel far and "wires were pulled" to ensure that a house at the other end of the Lane – recently made empty by the convenient simultaneous deaths of the old couple who lived there – should be allocated by the Corporation to the newly-weds.

Not so far and yet far enough. My mother had been ceded almost complete control of our household by my father; now, even in grief and in shock, she had no intention of letting her independence go, of returning to the drudgery of life at the other end of the street.

It was my misfortune, and her own, that, in order to retain her freedom of spirit, she had to harden her heart. It can't have been easy: she was 40 years of age, a widow with an eight year-old son in tow. In the years that followed, as she steered her unblinking way on the fiercely independent course she had charted for the two of us, I became accustomed to the thin-lipped hardness, but I never quite forgot the way it used to be, once upon a time, in a house that was the same but was yet changed utterly.

When she called me downstairs that evening – I had taken to lounging on my bed, listlessly turning over pages of comics I had already read – I had no idea that we were about to set off on a journey that would have far-reaching consequences. It was, so far as I could see, just an ordinary weekday evening, but I washed my face and hands when she told me to, and I put on my good white shirt that she had draped across the chair in front of the range. I hated the black tie but I let her fix it under my collar in silence: in the month since my father had died, I had learned not to object and not to ask questions. She checked that my shoes were shining and then handed me my good tweed sports jacket. I shut my eyes against the black diamond of mourning on the left sleeve; it had, briefly, been a talking point on the street but it soon became no more than a reminder of my father's continuing absence.

'Don't you want to know where we're goin'?' she asked, when she was satisfied with my appearance.

I nodded, saying nothing. These days, even to say the time out loud could start me crying.

'Your father has been dead a month now, God rest him,' she said. 'It's time we went to see Mr Crotty.'

'Mr Crotty?' I had a memory of a mountainy head, nodding inside the big car at the entrance to the Sportsground.

'He was your father's boss and he thinks he can fob us off with just the two weeks' holiday pay that was already due to him.' For a moment she pursed her lips so fiercely that her mouth seemed to disappear. 'It's time we went to see him. Up . . . up on Taylor's Hill.'

We took the short cut that September evening, up past the back of the Jesuit church, out onto St Mary's Road. The hill rose up ahead of us, leafy and winding and comfortable. It was only a few minutes' walk from the Lane but you felt, starting up the tree-shadowed slope, you had strayed into a different country.

My mother banged on the heavy door harder than she needed to, as if she might find courage in the clattering of the big, wolf's head doorknocker. I felt dwarfed by the house: it lay behind a high screen of trees, invisible from the road, waiting to ambush any unexpected callers with its huge bulk. My mother lifted her hand again, as if she would strike the door once more with the poll of the iron animal's head, but she seemed to think better of it and she clutched with both hands at her good handbag. It was black, like the clothes she wore; like the scarf on her head. Already, before my eyes, she was ageing into widowhood.

We waited, silently, on the doorstep of the Crotty house, the front door of which was flanked by a pair of bay windows that bellied outwards from the house. Suddenly I realised that I was being watched from the window to my right. The face of the boy looking out at me reminded me of that massive head lit by the dashboard light of the car in the Sportsground, except that this face was freckled, without a moustache, and was topped by a dark-brown thatch. I knew instinctively however, looking at its roundness and its small, inquisitive eyes, that this was the son of my father's boss.

The boy was about my own age; under his frank inspection I drew closer to my mother, but I did not flinch from his gaze. He half-turned away; I saw his lips move as he spoke to someone else in the room, and in a moment was joined at the window by a girl. She was older than him but from their physical similarities was most obviously his sister and as two pairs of round eyes were now examining me, I tugged at my mother's sleeve to point out our observers.

At that moment, the front door of Crotty's house swung open. The woman who confronted us was of medium height, heavy-set and white-haired. Mrs Crotty, as I would learn later, had been a primary schoolteacher before her marriage: there was something of the schoolteacher now in the way she looked at my mother and me, as if she knew more than we did but, if we behaved ourselves, she might admit us to her store of knowledge.

My mother said whom she was, and that she'd like to see Mr

Crotty. Her voice had that same down-at-heel diffidence I had noticed in the doctor's house on the Crescent, just down the hill.

Mrs Crotty led us along a dark hallway to a small sitting-room. Behind us a door opened; when I glanced back I caught a glimpse of the boy behind the window. He made a face at me; the girl beside him, taller and slimmer, laughed.

Mrs Crotty had seen them too. 'Nosey-parkers,' she said lightly. 'Get back to your homework, I'll be in to check it in a few minutes.' She turned to my mother, smiling. 'Children,' she said. 'They're all the same . . .' The smile made her face different, an invitation to a confidence. 'But you know that yourself, Mrs Best,' she added, looking at me.

I blushed, but I had already decided that Mrs Crotty wasn't all that bad.

'I will call my husband,' she said, closing the door behind her.

My mother and I waited, perched in silence on the edge of the armchairs.

When he came into the room, Mr Crotty seemed to entirely fill it with his bulky presence. He shook my mother's hand and nodded in my direction. He knew it was a hard time for us, he said, he hoped we were managing. He remained standing while he addressed us; you got the impression that he wanted to be gone out of that small, cluttered room as quickly as possible. What did we want from him, he asked bluntly.

I heard my mother tell him that a fortnight's wages didn't stretch very far when you had a funeral to pay for and a boy to bring up.

My father, he explained, had been with Crotty's for only a few years; and that my mother had received his full entitlement.

'Eleven years,' she reminded him. 'Eleven years Tom Best was with Crotty's, since before she married him and two weeks pay didn't seem fair. Not fair at all.'

Mr Crotty said his hands were tied by the regulations; he spread his hands to show his helplessness.

'The dogs,' my mother said. 'What about the dogs?'

'What about the dogs?' Mr Crotty wanted to know.

63

'It might just be gossip,' my mother said. 'Only that she'd heard that Mr Crotty and Bartley, had become as thick as thieves over Tom Best's dogs.'

As thick as thieves, I heard her say again, and there was no diffidence in her voice now. I listened, hearing it all, understanding nothing. You don't miss much, my father had told me that night, walking under the stars, but he was wrong.

'What is it that you want?' Mr Crotty asked. 'Don't beat about the bush.'

'Work,' she said. 'I was never afraid of hard work. I do not want nothin' for nothin'.'

'You want to work for Crotty's?'

'Yes, Mr Crotty.'

'What can you do?' he snorted. 'Drive a truck? Load lorries?'

'Anything,' my mother said.

And then again, breaking the silence. 'Anything . . . honest.'

Mr Crotty snorted once more. 'Wait here,' he said, leaving the room.

He left the door ajar. We could hear voices, his and Mrs Crotty's, from deeper inside the house. When he returned, his wife was with him. 'Now,' he said, turning to Mrs Crotty. 'You talk to her.'

Mrs Crotty smiled at my mother. 'Can you cook, Mrs Best?' I heard her ask.

My mother said yes.

Mrs Crotty said she could use a housekeeper. The woman she'd had for years had suddenly decided to marry a widower in County Mayo and she'd be leaving in two weeks. It wasn't all cooking, Mrs Crotty said, there was a heavy load of housework, you had to expect it with a houseful of four daughters and a son, not to mention himself. What did my mother think?

My mother said she thought she'd be well able for it.

'In two weeks then,' Mrs Crotty said.

'On a trial basis first,' Mr Crotty said, as if he suddenly remembered his obligations as one of the town's major employers.

Mrs Crotty smiled. 'Of course,' she said. 'But I've no doubt that Mrs Best would prove to be satisfactory.'

I stood up then, along with my mother. Mrs Crotty shook my mother's hand, and then mine. Mr Crotty followed suit and I felt my small hand would be mangled in his grip. We followed Mrs Crotty along the hall and into the kitchen where my mother would cook meals for the household. It was a big kitchen: tools and utensils hung from hooks around the white-tiled walls. I knew my mother was covertly studying the place, measuring in her mind the days to come.

Mrs Crotty seemed to divine my mother's thought also. 'Don't worry about it, Mrs Best,' she said. 'I'm sure everything will work out.'

She let us out through the back door of the kitchen. She was too kind to labour the point – I would learn that also about Mrs Crotty in the years to come – but we all knew that my mother would not be using the front door again.

Chapter 8

The hammering on the front door was insistent.

Jeff was standing on the pavement, glaring at me. He brushed past me into the hallway. He knew his way: not much had changed since he used to come for help with the math's homework.

'Good morning to you!' I said sarcastically to his back. The orange hazard lights of the Volvo, double-parked in the Lane, were blinking as I closed the front door and followed Jeff into the kitchen.

'What's good about it?' Jeff was making no attempt to conceal his anger. Unlike the previous night, when I had watched him leaving Kelly Carpenter's apartment, he had his old Gladstone bag with him. He hefted it onto the kitchen table now, with an angry, noisy thud. 'What d'you think you're playing at, Dan?' Jeff asked. 'It's two days since you stood in my surgery and I gave you the news . . . and you haven't even started your treatment. So tell me,' he folded his arms, as he leant up against the sink. 'What the *fuck* is going on?'

'I told you,' I said. 'I don't want your so-called treatment.'

'Chemotherapy is different now, Danny. It's not so severe, it's not like the old days, not like –'

'Not like my mother had?' I finished for him. Jeff had not been her doctor, but he had visited her near the end, mindful perhaps of the mugs of tea and slices of cake she had ferried to us in those long-ago schoolboy evenings in the kitchen. He could remember her withering bones as well as I could. I shook my head. 'I'll take my chances, Jeff. No chemotherapy. I prefer to go out with hair on my head and my teeth in my gums.'

'*You could beat this!*' Jeff said. 'You don't have to throw in the towel like this.'

'Don't worry about it,' I said quietly. 'It's my problem.'

I thought he would burst. He clenched his fists and then his mouth. The kitchen seemed filled with an explosive mixture of wrath and indignation. Slowly, visibly, Jeff calmed himself.

'I left a waiting room full of patients to come around here,' he said at last. 'Kay was waving her cards at me but I told her I had to see a patient and that I wouldn't be long. Don't you get it, Dan? You're my patient. Can't you get that into your intellectual, fucking head? I feel responsible for you and . . .' He floundered, casting about for words. 'And you're a friend, for fuck's sake!'

'If you like,' I said. 'I'll put it in writing . . . about not wanting the treatment. Just to cover your ass.'

The silence in the kitchen was dangerous, like something coiled.

'I ought to break your fucking neck for coming out with stuff like that, Dan. D'you really think I'm here because I just want to cover myself? I'm here because . . .' Again the search for words. 'Because you and I go back a long way.' Jeff's eyes scanned the room, as if seeing again the pair of us bent over the geometry cuts and the calculus problems on the kitchen table, while my mother brooded, thin-lipped but attentive. 'What has happened to you, Dan? You were a straight guy back then . . . you were always smart but you were always ordinary too. And look at you now, living here by yourself when there's no need for it. What the fuck are you doing in *Pater-fucking-noster* anyway? You can afford to live anywhere you like . . . Christ, there isn't anybody here from the old days!'

'You're wrong there,' I said. 'Paudge is still here.'

'Paudge!' Jeff snorted. 'Paudge's brain is so pickled with drink by now that he can't even talk to himself. You're telling me you have meaningful discussions with *Paudge-fucking-Lydon* about life, liberty and the pursuit of love?'

'Happiness,' I said. 'It's the pursuit of happiness.'

'Don't patronize me, Dan, you're not giving me a hand with homework now, remember?'

'Sorry. For a moment there I thought you were patronizing me.'

'Aren't they the same thing anyway . . . love and happiness?'

I looked at Jeff, surprised. He'd married a nurse that he'd met during his training; like him, she was large and solid.

'I suppose they can be.'

'*You suppose they can be!*' Jeff laughed. 'You say what you mean, Dan, but maybe what you say doesn't amount to much.' His face grew serious, as if he had remembered something. 'You have told Dolly about this, haven't you?'

Perhaps it was being back in our kitchen that made Jeff so familiar with my private life, I wasn't sure. Perhaps it was our being there together again that took the sting out of the intrusion. I shook my head. 'Not yet, there's time enough.'

'There's time enough for her to hear it from somebody else . . . you know what this town is like. What's she going to feel like then? Pretty small, I'd say, Danny, pretty fucking small. Don't you think she has a right to hear it first from you?'

I thought of Dolly, bubbling amidst her blooms: in the few years since she'd returned from Manchester – or was it Coventry? – she'd made her flower-shop the most popular and successful in the town.

'I guess you're right,' I said. In our years together she had given me her all and asked for little in return.

'It's a comfort to know I'm doing something right,' Jeff said dryly. He started to talk again about the chemotherapy, but I shook my head and he backed off. 'I'm not sure what can I do for somebody who refuses to be treated,' he joked. 'But I'll have a word with my colleagues. Maybe they've come up against awkward bastards like you before, although I confess, I haven't.' He took his bag from the table and we walked out into the hall. 'You don't have to be on your own in this, Dan. No man is an island and all that stuff. I'll help, if you let me. So will Dolly Hynes, I'd say, but you'll have to let her in as well. Okay?'

'Okay,' I said. I was touched, no doubt about it. Perhaps, after all, Jeff had chosen exactly the right profession.

'By the way, thanks for helping out with that lassie the other day,' he said. 'That girl at the surgery.'

'It was nothing,' I said, opening the front door. The orange lights were still blinking in the Volvo; the card inside the windscreen still declared: Doctor on Call. But I was curious about Kelly. 'How is she anyway?' I asked, casually.

'I wouldn't know,' Jeff said. 'I don't even know the kid's name, but I'm sure Trish is looking after her well.' Dr Trish Cunningham was one of Jeff's partners.

He took my hand and shook it. Through the open window of his car, he started telling me again how effective chemotherapy was but I was no longer hearing him. I watched him drive off along the street, puzzled, wondering why Jeff claimed not even to know Kelly Carpenter's name. I might have lumps, malignant ones, in my armpit, but there was, as yet anyway, nothing wrong with my eyesight, and I knew what I had seen in College Court the previous night.

You could smell Dolly's Flowers before you could see the shop. Dolly compensated for the shop's narrow frontage – it was no more than the width of a double doorway – by filling the entrance with blooms and hanging baskets of draping flowers outside the upper windows. The effect, rather like Dolly herself, was brash but cheerful: a scented, in-your-face display that ranged from Impressionist pastel shades in springtime to the broader, Disney-like acrylic colours of summer. Today was a Disney-day and the shoe-shops to either side looked brogue-dull beside the primary splashes of Dolly's roses, gladioli, lupins and ferns.

I stood a while on the opposite side of the street, outside the bank, partly to admire the shop, but also to get my thoughts in order before approaching Dolly. Not that Dolly Hynes could ever be called unapproachable – the success of her business was testament, most of all, to her easy-going nature – but the fact was, that I hadn't spoken to her for a couple of weeks. She'd phoned, and I had put her off with a line about a new series of articles. In her good-humored way, she'd offered to come round and undertake a through examination of my articles but I had taken refuge in silence and put her off.

Through the endless flickering August stream of back-packers and pushchairs, I watched her working in the shop. One customer stood inside, his short, tweedy figure dwarfed by Dolly's ample size. When he came out minutes later, blinking in the bright sunshine, he seemed even smaller; in the milling press of tourists he cradled the large bunch of flowers protectively against his thin chest before he turned away, facing towards home in the suburbs, a birthday perhaps, or an anniversary. At least, I told myself, skirting a braying bunch of Spanish students, I wouldn't have to endure such an old age, remembering dates, ferrying flowers, enduring silences.

Thank God for Dolly. Although she always had the right word of grief of congratulations for her clients, she never allowed sentimentality to cloud her personal vision. Regardless of whether she and I had vigorously pleasured each other the night before – with Dolly it was always vigorous – she rose at 6am each morning to swim for an hour before work, the sole exception being Sundays, when she got up at 7.30 to play 18 holes of competent golf with a couple of her cronies. You could see the regime of exercise in her body: she was wide-shouldered with full breasts and hips that flared above firm buttocks. Dolly Hynes was a big girl, but every inch and ounce of her was aggressively female: when she took you in her arms and drew you in between surprisingly slender thighs, you knew that you were going to have a memorable experience.

I felt the familiar glow of warmth and desire flooding through me as I crossed the street. About this much, at least, Jeff was right; besides, I wanted to pillow my head on those ample breasts and, for a moment anyway, allow myself to be comforted.

She saw me coming. She looked up from the table where she was putting the finishing touches to a large bouquet, tying the crimson nylon tape in a bow around the cellophane-wrapped flowers, and her soft features broke into a characteristic smile. Dolly's smile is a thing of beauty. Her face, soft and round and almost fleshy, is devoid of the fineness and angularity which so often are the marks of beauty, but that face is transformed when she smiles. It's like the sun rising, the way her whole face changes – eyes and skin and lips and teeth seem to merge into a liquid oneness that washes you with tranquility. She put the flowers aside now and leaned back against the table.

'Hello, stranger,' she said, as I kissed her lightly on the lips.

'More fool me,' I said. 'I'm sorry.'

I drew her to the back of the shop, into the tiny cubicle where the boxes were stored, along with the sweeping brush and the bucket and the mop and the vacuum cleaner. Once, not long after we had met, we had made love, quickly and noisily, in this small space, pushing the cleaning things about us in our haste towards consummation.

I went to close the cupboard door but Dolly held it ajar with her foot.

'Not now, Daniel,' she laughed. 'Bad timing.'

I didn't want to talk. I put my arms around her and kissed her again. Her mouth, as always, was full and soft and inviting. I wondered now, my tongue pushing between her lips, why I had stayed away. My hands roamed, caressing her; under the light, grey skirt I could feel the soft roundness of her buttocks. The skirt lifted easily and I pushed my hand between her legs. I felt her stiffen, drawing away from me.

'It's been too long,' I said, reaching for her again.

She stepped back from me. The blue plastic bucket tumbled under her feet and she swore. 'We need to talk, Daniel.'

'There is a time and a place,' I said, smiling, pushing my cupped hand once more between her legs.

'No.' She shimmied, pulling the short skirt back down, to cover her tanned thighs. I felt her hands on my chest, propelling me gently but firmly out of the storage space and back into the shop. 'We need to talk,' she said again, no longer smiling.

'I'll come around tonight,' I said. I was ready to talk now, preferably propped against her breasts. 'We can talk in bed.'

'Leave it a while, Daniel . . . Not tonight.'

'What's the problem, Dolly? Tell me.'

The shop was suddenly darkened. A young man was standing in the narrow doorway, blocking out the sun.

'I have to go,' she said, nodding towards her customer. 'I'll call you.'

'*No!*' I was tired of puzzles. 'Tell me now whatever it is you want to say.'

'You're hurting me, Daniel.'

I let go of her wrist then, murmuring an apology. 'I still want to know what the problem is,' I said.

'The problem is us, Daniel, you and me. I didn't want to have it come out like this, but . . .' Dolly shrugged her shoulders.

'But what?' I demanded.

Dolly hesitated, looking towards the front of the shop. The young fellow had finally decided to enter the shop; you could sense the nervousness in him, surveying the buckets of flowers, even back here at the rear of the long, narrow premises. 'We're going nowhere, Daniel,' she said quietly. 'We've been seeing each other for almost five years now but we're no closer now than the day we started. There's nothing happening between us, can't you see that?'

'What do you want to happen?'

'Don't play games with me, Daniel. I don't deserve that. And I know that you know what I mean.'

And I did. I knew that she wanted the kind of togetherness, the kind of wordless intimacy, which I had been unable to discover with anybody or in anybody since Elizabeth. My marriage had died because of this vacuum I nourished inside myself; now, I realized, another relationship was dying here, in Dolly's Flowers, amid the scented blooms and bouquets and wreaths.

'I'm sorry,' I said.

Dolly shrugged. 'That's exactly what I mean', she said. 'Five years of . . . of I don't-know-what-of something, come to an end and you just say sorry and that's that.'

'It was your idea,' I said. 'Not mine. Remember?'

'Fuck you,' Dolly said. The young fellow was mooching among the plastic buckets inside the door but Dolly seemed not to care about her customer anymore. 'You're supposed to fight for me, Daniel.'

I'm too tired to fight for anything, I wanted to tell her. Of course, I didn't say that, or anything like that. Pride wouldn't allow me to tell her my own news: I couldn't have borne her pity, not now, especially not now, when she wanted out. Perhaps she just wanted more than I could give: or more than I wanted to give. 'I'm sorry,' I said again. Perhaps it was all for the best anyway: in the long run, I'd be sparing her the pain of my going.

She shook her head sadly. I could see the hurt in her eyes. 'I want us to be friends, Daniel.'

'Of course,' I said. I wasn't sure if I meant it.

We walked together towards the front of the shop. The young fellow straightened himself as we approached. He was about twenty; there were still adolescent spots around the corners of his mouth. He hasn't much money, I thought, and he's embarrassed about buying flowers for his first serious girlfriend. There were some things, at least, that I didn't have to worry about.

Dolly smiled at him. 'Take your time,' she said, and he blushed, bending again to his inspection of roses and carnations. She turned back to me. 'So. We will be friends then?'

'Why not?' I answered.

'Good. I'm going to need friends now,' she said quietly.

'Why particularly now?' I asked.

'I'm in the process of buying these premises . . .' She smiled sadly when she noticed the look of surprise on my face. 'I'd have told you Daniel, but I haven't seen you in some time. I'm borrowing the money, of course, but that's not all. I'm buying a new apartment as well, so there's going to be a lot of pressure on me for some time,' Dolly shrugged. 'Maybe it's all this worry about money that started me worrying about us, Daniel . . . I need some certainties in my life, I hope you see that.'

I could have hit her then with the bitter irony of my own circumstances, but Dolly didn't deserve that kind of hurt.

'Where are you buying?' I was doing no more than making polite conversation. I wanted to be gone now, to survey the altered landscape of my life.

'It's a new development,' she hesitated. 'Up at the Spinney.'

'The Spinney?'

'They're very nice,' Dolly hurried on. 'I've only seen plans as yet, of course, but they seem to fit in really well with the area, it's low rise, lots of green space –'

'But they can't be building on the Spinney!' I interrupted her. 'That battle was won long ago.'

'Don't look at me like that, Daniel. I know all about your campaign for the site, but I'm not the builder or the developer . . . I'm just somebody buying a good home that I hope will be a good investment as well.'

'Who's the builder?' I demanded.

I didn't care if the pimpled flower-seeker heard me now; when I had first come back to live again at Paternoster, I had waged a kind of one-man war to save the Spinney from the suburban sprawl of developers and auctioneers. I had won that war, or at least I thought I had won it.

'I can't even remember the name of the builder. Prospector something-or-other . . .' Again she hesitated. 'It was Len put me on to it. He said it was too good a chance to miss, as most of the apartments will be sold from the plans before they're even advertised.'

'Fucking Leonard Crotty!' I understood her hesitancy now. I had never told her of what had happened between Leonard and myself, but she knew that there was no love lost between us. 'I might have known he'd have his finger in this pie as well.'

'Len is only doing his job,' Dolly said. 'Someone has to do it.'

'Yes,' I said. 'Someone has to do it . . . and Leonard's cronies at the golf club get first bite at the cherry. That way the great and the good are kept happy and the kids and the great unwashed who like to mess around in the Spinney can go fuck themselves.'

'Don't fight with me, Daniel.' The pimpled youth, blushing, had retreated to the back of the store. 'Please don't fight with me.'

I looked at her then, more with sadness than with anger. 'No,' I said. 'I haven't the energy to have a fight.'

But I knew I was lying. It would take bigger lumps than mine to stop me getting into this fight. I touched Dolly's face, tentatively, with my hand before I stepped out into the afternoon sunlight of Shop Street.

Chapter 9

'I've never been up here,' Kelly said.

It was on the tip of my tongue to say that I was surprised that her precious Leonard hadn't shown her the place, but thought better of it. I had no quarrel with Kelly. Up here, standing on top of one of the boulders that littered the Spinney, you could see her for what she was, a gorgeous youngster in blue jeans and a fawn sweatshirt who had been too long out of the sun. She shaded her eyes with her neat little hand, looking south against the sun at the city that lay sprawled beneath us.

'The whole place looks fantastic from up here!'

The town did look dreamy in the light, the green dome of the Cathedral and its pair of flanking turrets like an Ottoman relic washed up on western shore. The bay was still and on the far side of the waters the stony hills sparkled like fool's gold.

'Yes,' I said dryly. 'The view is fantastic.'

Leonard Crotty would have no need to enthuse about the view to his customers; they'd do it for themselves, mouths and cheque-books open at the prospect of owning a flat up here in the Spinney: "The town's last prime site, with spectacular views of the bay area", or some such builder-speak. The translation of this developer-code meant only one thing: money, profit, loot, moolah and dough.

'I haven't been at lectures for a week.' I heard Kelly say.

I followed her gaze towards the university. The old stone quad was radiant in the sunshine. 'What are you studying?'

'Commerce,' she shrugged. 'It seemed like a good idea at the time.'

I said nothing. I wanted her to go on talking. I wanted someone's voice to soften the pain I was feeling up here. Perhaps the pain began with Dolly. I didn't really think so. Perhaps it began up here, long ago, before I ever knew Dolly or even Jean, watching Prince and Mutt race along the home-made track – 80 yards only, squeezed between the boulders and the bushes – that my father had stepped out in measured paces along the stony soil. Perhaps that's why I was here. Dolly's revelation had seemed like a blow to my heart; some instinct of self-protection had driven me to College Court, as if I knew that I did not dare to walk alone here. Not now, with all that I knew and did not know about myself.

Kelly talked on. She eased herself into a sitting position, one leg bent, her arms wrapped around her ankle, her chin resting on her knee; her other leg swung slowly in time to some beat that she heard in her head. It was an image of artlessness and yet I wondered, listening to her words, if even that image was not also carefully designed.

She had a grant, she said, but it wasn't enough to keep going; you couldn't live on rice and lentils forever, and make-up would rob you: sometimes she stole her lipstick from Roche's or Dunne's. She'd taken a weekend job as a waitress in the bar of the Skeffington Hotel. She didn't mind the work, it was a bit of craic anyway; she didn't like the way the fellows in the bar, mostly students, felt they could lay hands on her mini-skirted bottom when they had enough drink taken, but strangely enough these fellows were not ungenerous with their tips.

'At least I didn't have to steal my lipstick anymore,' Kelly said, her denimed leg still swinging in tune with the music in her head.

Jean had sat like that, on the same rock, in the long-ago. There had been music in my head then but the tune had left me; now, watching and listening to Kelly, I could only try to remember the melody.

You didn't expect to find someone like Leonard in the Skeff, on a Friday night, Kelly was saying. I could see him through her words, his work-out muscularity straining against the three-piece suit, walrus-like among the shoals of student mackerel who swam and darted in the packed bar, hunting for drink and craic and sex. What had Leonard been doing there, ensconced with a couple of other suits at the corner table? Cast a cold eye on any profitable business: you never knew when you might decide to buy it. Or destroy it.

Kelly brought drinks to the table in the corner. The suited drinkers were polite: each time she put their drinks on the table, they said keep the change; the pound or so was always welcomed. When the men were leaving, Leonard sought her out, thanked her by her name – he had already asked what it was – and pressed a folded tenner into her hand. "For the service", he had said. "You looked after us well', he had said.

'I didn't do or suggest anything, honest!' Kelly said to me. 'Only what I was being paid to do, serve drink.'

When Leonard returned the following night, he was alone. He stayed half-an-hour, and drank two gin-and-tonics while he leafed through the Irish Times. It was the quietish hour around teatime and the bar was not busy; she found herself telling him things about her life when she brought his drinks to the table. Leonard pressed another ten-pound note into her palm as he was leaving.

She was disappointed when he failed to show up at the Skeff the following Friday evening and relieved when he arrived on Saturday evening, looking as if he had just stepped off the golf course. 'He stayed only about ten minutes.' Her voice sounded almost wistful. 'One drink, but I got my tenner anyway.' The foot went on swinging. 'I wondered when he was going to make his move . . . I knew he was going to do something . . . ask me out, or something, and I didn't know what I was going to say. He was nice to me, but he was so, so old.'

I waited for her to continue. I can't claim it was because of any concern for Kelly Carpenter. My concern was Leonard Crotty.

She was taken unawares, she was saying, when Leonard finally approached her. It was Saturday night, close to closing time; the bar was heaving with drunken, sweaty students. 'My feet were killing me. I was dying just to get home. Sometimes on Saturdays I used to go on to the nightclub after work, but that night I was just knackered.'

And then there was Leonard, I imagined, pushing his leviathan-like way among the puny, T-shirted students.

She saw him coming towards her as she was stooping over a table clearing glasses, wishing she had the nerve to empty the dregs of drink on top of the two leering fellows who were loudly discussing the color and texture of her bent-over knickers. She felt his hand on her shoulder and was glad that her pair of drunken customers saw this huge, well-dressed businessman smiling at her, saying "Hello" in a friendly fashion. The conversation about her knickers abruptly ended; Leonard whispered that he'd run her home after work, the car was right outside the door: "the black one".

The black one was a large Mercedes, filling most of the bus stop outside the Skeff. She'd reached her end-of-shift chores; emptying the ashtrays, stacking the chairs and stools, vacuuming the floor, but it was still nearly 1am by time its passenger door swung open and she sat in beside Leonard. When they reached the wooden chalet she shared in Newcastle she asked him in. 'My flatmate had gone home for the weekend,' she explained. Leonard drank his instant coffee and left without laying a finger on her. He asked her about her studies but made no comment about the shabby, freezing wooden hut where she lived in the back garden of a suburban house. After he had gone, she found a twenty-pound note on the chipped worktop, behind the jar of Nescafe.

Kelly's tale both fascinated and repelled me. The Spinney was, for me, a kind of sanctuary; the echoes that lingered, here on this sloping acre of rocks and bushes, were from a different world. It was a music that now seemed not only innocent but also old-fashioned; the panting of the hounds on the homemade track, my father's roars of encouragement, and my own childish yelps of delight and especially – *oh, God, how especially* – the half-seen dreams that Elizabeth and I had tried to shape with words and jokes in our springtime air. Listening to Kelly's story of money and seduction made me conscious even of what Leonard himself had lost: not long after I'd met him, I'd given him a hiding on this rocky slope. I'd sat on him, cuffed his already-bleeding nose with the back of my hand and told him I'd pull all his greasy hair out by the roots if he ever again called my mother a skivvy. "Is it all right to call her a domestic servant?" he'd panted, as I sat on his chest.

I wondered what he considered Kelly Carpenter to be; a bit-on-the-side; his young but available pussy; his girlfriend perhaps. Hardly his mistress; Leonard was too devious to contemplate the permanence of a mistress.

'He came back to the chalet a few days later,' Kelly continued. 'We went for a drive in the country and stopped for a drink in Kinvara. He couldn't have been nicer to me. I suppose I knew what he wanted but I pretended to myself that he wasn't really like that . . . Afterwards, I told myself it didn't matter, that I had a nice place to live and there was more time to study because I didn't have to work weekends anymore.' She looked at me for a moment before she looked out again over the town: her eyes, I felt, were seeing nothing now of the cityscape below us. 'Anyway, when we got back into town from Kinvara, Leonard pulled up in College Court. For a moment or so, I thought he was taking me home, to meet his family . . . I knew he was married, he'd never tried to make a secret of it . . . But when we stepped inside I knew I was just kidding myself. The flat was empty then . . . I mean, nobody was living there, but I thought it was just fabulous. Leonard said he owned it.' She tossed her head with a kind of pride. 'He owns houses and flats all over the town, you know, and when . . . When he handed me the keys and said I could live there as long as I liked, I . . . I just started laughing and crying together.' The leg had stopped swinging; the music in her head had stopped, or changed. 'Nobody had ever been nice to me like that before. My old man spends his time in the pub and my mother is more often in the church than she is at home. When Len did that . . . When he handed me the keys of the apartment, I just put my arms around him. He was like . . . like a . . .'

Like a father, or a sugar daddy, I thought, watching her to compose herself. 'Why are you telling me all this, Kelly?'

'He doesn't want me to have the baby.'

I waited while she wiped her eyes and blew her nose.

'He said it was a bad idea, bad for both of us.'

I said nothing; there seemed nothing to say.

'He'll pay for the abortion, flights, hotel, the clinic, everything.' She waited for me to speak, but still I held my tongue. 'Haven't you anything to say to me?' she demanded.

'What did you tell Leonard?'

'I told him to go fuck himself.' Her laugh was harsh. 'He said he'd prefer to fuck me any day.'

Her words were like a wound in the afternoon. I'd kissed Jean up here, more than once, sometimes on rare afternoons like this when she was able to get away from the hospital; more often on summer nights, while the lights of the town blazed below us like our personal arrangement of chandeliers.

'What can I do?' I could hardly hear her, so broken was her voice. 'I want to keep this baby, but I can't go home . . . they'd just throw me out. Len'll be the same. I know he's going to throw me out, when he realizes that I'm serious, that I really am going to have the baby. What am I going to do?'

'I'll help you.'

I hadn't meant to say that, but when I said it, I knew I meant it. I don't know why, I still don't. Perhaps it was the place, or the spirit of the place and if I had to put a name to that spirit, I'd call it love.

Chapter 10

'What on earth could you have been thinking about, Daniel, dumping all that stuff on Beatrice? She's sixteen, for goodness' sake and still at school!'

It's impossible to interrupt my ex-wife, when she's in full, indignant flow.

'How could you do that to her? Hadn't you any *idea* of the consequences of such . . . such . . .' For once, Elizabeth seemed lost for words. 'Such *irresponsibility*, Daniel?'

'It wasn't irresponsible,' I blurted into the phone. 'For Christ's sake, I was trying to help!'

'Your notions of being helpful are somewhat peculiar,' Elizabeth said acidly. 'And please don't swear. You know I don't like it.'

I bit my tongue, chastised: it wouldn't be helpful to remind her that I had about two hundred other habits which also didn't appeal to her English sense of propriety.

'I'm sorry,' I said. 'Just tell me if Bee is okay . . . Better still, let me talk to her.'

'And have you upset her again?'

'Please, Elizabeth. I need to talk to her.'

'No. I gave her a sleeping tablet and sent her to bed.'

For a moment the kitchen in Paternoster dissolved and I was back again in Bee's bedroom in our flat; Elizabeth's and mine, in St John's Wood, smoothing the Garfield duvet around my daughter's tiny body, marveling at the wonder of this beautiful creature that I had helped, without thought, to create, and promising to leave the hall light on and the bedroom door ajar.

'Maybe I should come over and see her?'

'No, Daniel.' Her response was swift. 'You've done enough harm as it is.'

'You don't understand, Eliza –'

'So you used to tell me.' Her tone was dry. *'Ad nauseam.'*

Only once or twice, I wanted to say. I tried to tell you once or twice, Elizabeth, but I gave up because you weren't listening. And maybe you weren't listening because I couldn't find the right words to tell you. I still can't.

'Tell her I'm sorry,' I said. 'And that I love her.'

'I seem to have heard that before too.'

For a long moment there was silence on the line between London and Galway. It was like that other silence between us, the one that lasted for years, when Bee was starting school and Elizabeth and I were learning the pain of sharing a house without love and a bed without loving.

'I'm sorry,' she said at last. 'There was no need to say that.'

'I'm sorry too,' I said. 'I thought telling Bee would help her to . . . to come to terms with the way I am.'

'I'm sorry you've got . . .' She hesitated. 'I'm sorry about your illness, Daniel, truly I am. Beatrice didn't say much about it when she came back home tonight, and at first I had no idea that her . . . her running away from school had anything to do with you. Sure, she was quieter than usual when she got back from Galway but I didn't think much of it: she's always like that after visiting you. She seemed her usual self that next morning and we chatted about hockey and stuff while I was driving her to the station. She gave me a kiss when I dropped her off and she looked like any other girl going back to school after half-term. When the school phoned on Tuesday to say she was missing, all I could think of was that she'd run off with some boy and that she was pregnant. I was beside myself, Daniel. I didn't know what to do. It was such a relief when she phoned that night and told me not to worry. Not to worry! Can you imagine it? She wouldn't tell me where she was staying, she just said there was something she had to figure out, and would I please be patient and to tell them at the school not to worry either. I made her promise to telephone me every evening and thank goodness she did. I couldn't even find out the number she was calling from. And then . . . When she walked in here tonight I was just so glad to . . .'

I heard the swallowing noises on the phone; I could imagine Elizabeth, sitting at her little writing bureau, pulling herself together as she had been taught to do at the same boarding school where she had insisted on sending Bee.

'She looked exhausted, poor thing, and I didn't think it was the right time to start asking questions, but after a while she told me about you and your . . . your illness and how school made no sense anymore. She said to me "How can I be there studying Pliny, Mum, when I know that my Dad will be dead in a year?" and I didn't know what to say.'

Once more, silence filled the distance between us.

'Beatrice loves you, Daniel,' she said quietly, to end it.

'I just thought it would help.' I looked despairingly around the kitchen where, only a week before, I had given Bee the sketchiest outline of what lay in store for me, but here too there was only unhelpful silence from the table and chairs and electrical machines. 'I was trying to prepare her for it, I thought it was the best thing to do.'

'Daniel,' Elizabeth spoke with a welcome tenderness in her voice. 'I don't doubt that you meant well. I think you always meant well but you were never really sure of what you wanted and so you sometimes jumped into situations with your eyes closed. Just think a little, that's all I'm saying, especially now, when things are as they are.'

Her softness, so unexpected, disarmed me. 'I'm sorry,' I whispered.

'I'm hoping that I'll be able to take her back to school on Sunday,' Elizabeth continued. 'I'll remind her to phone you before then, although I don't think she'll need reminding . . . But please try to remember what it felt like to be a teenager yourself, Daniel.'

There was also a long-forgotten warmth in the way we said goodbye to each other. Elizabeth's lecturing tone – she taught Communications, whatever that might mean, at a North London further education college – would normally, in other circumstances, have roused me to an argument. Now, given the upset caused by what Bee had done, arguing seemed pointless.

I could hardly begin to imagine that she had played truant, holing-up for almost a week in some God-forsaken numberless guesthouse, hovel or squat and yet, as Elizabeth had implied, it was my own words that had precipitated that flight. Perhaps, I was not, after all, such a master of those words. I remembered my impulsive promise to Kelly that afternoon at the Spinney. Perhaps I did go barreling in where angels feared to tread and perhaps I should button my lip; switch off the computer.

And then again, perhaps not.

Back in those adolescent years, that Elizabeth wanted me to remember for the sake of our daughter, back then the trouble was finding words, any words, to describe the maelstrom of feelings that churned inside you.

Chapter 11

'Let it down now . . . easy . . . towards me a bit more, Danny. That's it.' Jeff was directing operations in Crotty's kitchen.

I watched anxiously as Jeff tilted the kitchen cabinet towards himself, walking backwards, palming the cabinet floorwards until he had to step aside and allow it to rest flat on the floor.

'Now, we need to turn it on its side.'

Leonard Crotty made no move to help as Jeff and I levered the blue cabinet up and onto its side.

'Are you just going to stand there admiring us, Len, or d'you think you might give us a hand?' Jeff asked.

Like me, Jeff was eighteen; like me, he lived in a little house with a door that opened onto the street; unlike me, he felt no need to be careful with his words in front of Mrs Crotty.

Len laughed. 'This job needs a real man, I suppose,' he said, finally taking his hands out of his pockets.

'Real man!' his sister, Nuala snorted. 'Real brat, more like! Expecting to be waited on hand and foot just because he's supposed to be a man and he's home from Clongowes – '

'Nuala!' Her mother's voice, as always, was mild, but it was enough to silence the girl.

I wondered how my mother was taking this minor display of squabbling in the ranks of her employers but, when I glanced across the kitchen, I saw only that her face, as usual, gave nothing away.

Leonard was smirking as he brushed past his sister. 'Let me show these weaklings what real muscles look like,' he said.

Jeff spluttered with laughter. He took a wild, well-telegraphed, swing at Leonard but Leonard caught him by the wrist and then the pair of them grappled in a swaying bear-hug. Their careering bulk seemed to fill Crotty's kitchen as they laughed and pushed against each other.

My own amusement was tinged with envy. Jeff had, for as long as I could remember, been my best pal; I had introduced him to Leonard Crotty a couple of years ago, during summer holidays from school. They hit it off instantly. Afterwards, while Jeff and myself remained as inseparable as ever during term-time, we became, for all of Leonard's holiday periods at home, a more fluid threesome which often left me feeling as if I were on the outside looking in.

'Mind the cabinet, boys!' Mrs Crotty called but neither Leonard nor Jeff seemed to hear her.

The shouting and commotion drew the two younger Crotty sisters to the kitchen. They stood giggling in the doorway, looking from the grappling pair to their mother. Jeff stumbled against the sideway-turned cabinet; Leonard leaned over him, his two hands loosely clasped around Jeff's neck.

'Beg for mercy, pleb!' he hissed between gulps of laughter.

The redundant kitchen cabinet wobbled precariously under the weight of the two fellows.

'Boys! *The cabinet!*' Mrs Crotty's cry was only half-hearted; you could tell she was trying not to laugh.

'What's going on here?' Mr Crotty's bellow filled the already-crowded kitchen. 'What kind of bedlam is this?'

Leonard took his hands off Jeff's neck. He was smiling as he looked across the kitchen at his father. 'I was just teaching this heathen a lesson, Dad,' he said easily.

Jeff snorted. 'You couldn't even teach your grandmother,' he said, pushing off Leonard's hand.

'That's enough out of the pair of ye!' Mr Crotty looked stern. 'There's no need to wreck the house and break up every stick of furniture in the place.'

'Sorry, Mr Crotty,' Jeff said. 'But sure we'd build you another house anyway.'

John Crotty looked at Jeff with something like affection. 'I've no doubt you would, Jeff,' he said. 'No doubt at all.'

I felt his eyes turning towards me. 'The job is still there for you, Danny,' he said. 'There's still a couple of months to go before you start college and you'd make better money working with these two lads than you do in that slot-machine place or whatever they call it.'

'Thanks, Mr Crotty,' I said. 'But I promised the boss I'd stay until October.'

I liked my summer job, emptying the steel trays of pennies into my blue plastic bucket, making sure that the machines kept on working and the holiday-makers kept on putting their coins in the slots. Nor had I any wish to join Leonard and Jeff labouring on Crotty's latest building site on the north side of the town.

Jeff laughed. 'Our Danny is learning the tricks of the casino trade, so that he can break the bank at roulette in Las Vegas and Monte Carlo.'

'Slot machines and roulette.' John Crotty's tone was dismissive. 'You might as well be throwing good money after bad on the dogs.' He was looking at me as he spoke but then he dropped his gaze, like a child who has said something improper. An odd silence, deeper for the noise and commotion that had gone before, seemed to settle upon Crotty's crowded kitchen.

'Bad cess to the same dogs, that's what I say!' a voice suddenly broke the silence.

It was my mother who spoke. She was standing beside the tall fridge, her arms folded, wearing the tie-around, floral-printed housecoat that, years before, she had adopted as a uniform for her post as cook and housekeeper in the Crotty household.

'You're right, Mrs Best, as usual,' Leonard's mother said.

My mother hadn't finished. 'Are you boys going to stand there with your hands in your pockets for the rest of the evening, or are ye going to carry out this nice piece of furniture that Mrs Crotty is after giving me as a present?'

My mother could still astonish me. Ten years had passed since she had first brought me to this house and, through some sort of sorcery that I still didn't understand, leveraged a job out of my dead father's employer. During that decade a kind of sullen speak-when-you're-spoken-to silence had settled upon our house, which I had grudgingly come to accept as normal. Only in odd moments like this did she allow me to see that the fire had not died in her; it still glowed, but she hid it even from herself.

Without further chat we carried my mother's prize out through Crotty's back door and eased it onto the flat bed of the handcart I'd borrowed from a neighbour. Leonard's sisters were still smiling as they stood around the small cart: I had come to know them well over the years and, despite my own childish confusion in the beginning about our relationship, I had grown to like them, especially Nuala, who was just a year younger than me.

'Who's going in front?' I heard her ask now. Her brother announced that he'd take charge of the back of the cart, just so he could keep an eye on the two of us in front.

Mr Crotty, who had also stepped outside to watch our progress, nodded as if in approval of his son's remark. 'You'll have plenty of men to keep an eye on when you take over after me,' he said.

Taking care not to be seen by his father, Leonard winked at Jeff and myself. He planned to take a civil engineering degree; he wasn't even displeased when we razzed him about walking into a job after college.

'You too, Jeff,' Mr Crotty seemed intent on his own train of thought. 'You'll have to be able to take charge of all those nurses and . . . and porters and so on, who'll be under you at the hospital.' I knew I was next. Jeff knew too; he was already grinning at me. 'What about you, Danny? Are you still set on teaching? Surely you could do better than that?'

'I'm not going teaching.' I felt the others looking at me; further back, unbidden in the mist, came the memory of the bullet-head in the dark car at the Sportsground, the small eyes dismissive of the excited boy who held Prince's leash. Mr Crotty wasn't interested in what I studied and we both knew it. 'I'm just going to study English and History.'

'Sounds like teaching to me,' Mr Crotty pushed on. 'Don't you think so?' He turned to this wife.

Mrs Crotty smiled, shrugged, and said nothing.

'It sounds like dreams and . . . and more words and dreams to me.'

Every head turned to look at my mother.

'Dreams and words,' she said dismissively. She shook her head, her lips set in a thin line, before going on. 'Dreams. Just like Tom Best before him.' Once more the grey head shook, snapping back to the present. 'Be careful with that cabinet goin' down the hill, boys.' She turned away and went back inside the house.

Leonard and Jeff threw sympathetic glances at me. Mr Crotty cleared his throat. The girls giggled, but nervously now, as if unsure of themselves. My mother's tone and words had disturbed the calmness of the August evening, as though a shadow had crossed the sun.

'Let's get this show on the road.'

I was grateful for Leonard's heartiness. Jeff and I took a shaft each at the front while he steadied the cart from behind, lest it tilt and tip out its precious cargo. The wooden wheels of the cart crunched on Crotty's graveled drive as we made our way towards the gate. The girls walked with us, exhorting us cheerfully, my mother's words forgotten.

Yet her words stayed with me, as we hauled our load down Taylor's Hill and down the back lane behind the Crescent and into Paternoster. Why had she chosen to mention my father for the first time in years, and in such dismissive tones? The wedding photograph – he in dark shirt, regulation suit and brylcreemed hair – still hung in our front room, but I had not heard my father's name on my mother's lips in years. Why today, of all days? Was it, I wondered, something to do with Mr Crotty's remark about throwing money away on the dogs?

'Whoa!' Jeff's shout brought me back. 'Don't you know when you're home?'

I opened the door of our house and the three of us manhandled the Crotty's old kitchen cabinet into its new home in the kitchen of Number 1, Paternoster Lane. When, years later, I took over the house, it was the first thing I threw out.

Chapter 12

In the first week of October 1968, along with Jeff, Leonard and perhaps a thousand others, I signed on at University College, Galway. In that same week I met, for the first time, Jean Martin.

Afterwards, Jeff would sometimes remind us, teasingly, when we were all together, that we were both indebted to him, since it was through him that we had met. "Although I'm not too sure you should be too grateful, Danny", he'd say, or something like. "The woman's intelligence is suspect. She could have had me but she picked you". And we'd laugh, all three of us. The world was young then and, in Jean's company, I was learning to be sure of myself.

It was different at out first meeting. I spotted Jeff as soon as I stepped inside the door of the coffee shop; from the corner table he waved at me with such extravagant assurance that it was impossible to believe that he was, like me, a mere first-year student, on his second day in college, as indeed, were the five or six others gathered around the table.

'Danny boy, come and join us!' he shouted. 'Our Danny is only a miserable Arts student but we'll let him sit with us,' he announced, laughing, as I squeezed my way between the bentwood chairs. 'Just this once, mind!'

'Illiterate med,' I said, easily.

'Sit yourself down beside Jean there, Danny.' Jeff grabbed an empty chair and pulled it between him and a dark-haired girl I had never seen before. 'She's able to read books and she understands big words . . . I know, because she's been explaining the timetable to me.'

Even now, years later, I can recall that moment in the crowded, cramped coffee shop. Everything seemed to fade into an out-of-focus haziness behind the girl; the chipped, Formica-topped tables, the green, nondescript walls, even the animated huddles of smoking, laughing, gesticulating students. The medley of noises around us receded. It was as if the sea had suddenly ebbed and left only us two on a narrow foreshore. I remember still, as if she were seated now beside me, the soft waves of dark hair that fell around her oval-shaped face; the blue eyes that looked with interest into mine; the mouth lovely, soft and red; and speaking to me, telling me her name – Jean Martin – and that she also was a pre-med student, like Jeff and the others at the table.

Where was she from, I heard myself ask.

From town, she said.

She saw my surprise. I wouldn't have seen her around, she said, as she'd asked to go away to boarding school for the last two years of her schooling. She didn't think she'd be able to work hard enough at home and she wanted to be sure of getting into medicine.

And did the plan work, I asked and wished I could think of something more interesting to say.

'Well, I'm here,' Jean Martin said gently. 'Am I not?'

I tried not to blush.

'You work at the casino,' she went on. 'I've noticed you inside when I'm going out for a swim.'

I never watched the summer crowds spilling along the promenade outside the gallery of one-armed bandits. You were expected to keep your eyes peeled to the inside happenings, not for pickpockets or their like – the casino was not too concerned about protecting its customers' money – but instead, for the sharp operators who tried to slip their bets onto the roulette table long after "Last bets!" had been called, and the less sharp ones who tried to take the backs off the slot machines to get at the stuffed craws inside.

'I never saw you,' I said, embarrassed.

'Do you like the job?' she asked.

'I'll have you know, Jean, that this fellow is a notorious gambler.' We had not, after all, been alone on our tideless shore: Jeff had been following our conversation and took great pleasure in interjecting his observations. 'Just like his father, and all his people before him,' he continued. 'Have nothing to do with him, Jean, I'm telling you, he'll bring you nothing but grief.'

Jeff's mocking words are a part of that scene that is printed indelibly on my memory. They came back to me afterwards but, when they did, their mocking lightness was gone, leaving behind only their prophetic grimness. I used to wonder then – I still do – if Jean also remembered those words.

'Is it your dad's business then . . . the casino?'

'No,' I answered her. 'My father died a long time ago.'

'D'you remember him well?'

'Yes,' I said, surprised by the turn of our conversation. 'I remember him very well.'

'Good.' She was looking thoughtfully at me, as if deciding something in her mind. 'I'm glad.'

Our eyes met. Something, I wasn't sure what, had been said and was being said.

'I'm so glad myself,' Jeff said loudly. 'That Jean is glad about something or other. Now, are you two at *this* table or would ye like to go off and sit somewhere else by yourselves?'

Everybody laughed. My heart seemed lighter as I turned back to the rest of the group around the table. I said hello to two of them, classmates from school who were also doing medicine, and shook hands with two fellows from Donegal whose accent was a wonder to me. Talk and laughter washed over and around the table. We were allowed to remain for another half-an-hour or so until finally ejected by Mrs Craven, the bespectacled manageress who ran the coffee shop like a slave galley that would surely go to the bad if she didn't crack her whip a dozen times a day. 'Haven't ye lectures and libraries to go to?' she'd admonish us. 'If your fathers and mothers only knew the half of what goes on up here, they'd be savin' their money and not shellin' it out on wasters and layabouts.'

We poured out onto the open space beside the tennis courts, delighted with ourselves and with the truth of Ma Craven's accusations. We held the world in our hands back then, and we knew it; and lovely, smiling, dark-haired Jean Martin had told me that, yes, she would be at the Fresher's Dance that night, and she'd never speak to me again if I didn't come and dance with her.

Some moments in a life are destined to stick in your memory and that night was one of them. The sheer vibrancy of the feelings that washed over me can still lift me out of myself after all these years and that one night, when I danced with Jean Martin at the Fresher's Dance, seemed to cast a different light upon the years that had gone before and the endless tight-lipped days and nights in our house after my father died. There was no kaleidoscopic scattering of the pieces of my life to leave a new and unexpected pattern – no, Jean was too gentle for that; Jean's way was to listen to your story, to muse over the pictures you handed her, and then to give your story back to you, its pages neither defaced nor re-arranged, but somehow different. You listened to your own story, but it was told in a different voice. You looked through the same window, but inside the images wore different lights, different shadows. Jean taught me a new way of looking at the world.

'Your mother must have loved him very much,' she said.

I stole a sideways glance at Jean: it was almost impossible to believe that this girl with the wide-set eyes and the dark hair was walking beside me in the lee of the high wall of St Mary's. Any second now, from across the roofs of the houses on our right, I would hear my mother's voice, flat and unforgiving, demanding to know what was I doing out walking with a girl I didn't know at half-past-twelve at night when all right-minded people were sound asleep in their beds. It wouldn't have mattered, anyway: Jean would have inclined her head towards her in that characteristic way of hers, and she'd have said, with her little smile: "We're sorry if we've upset you or caused you to worry, Mrs Best, but you can be sure that no harm will come to Danny while he's with me", or something similar. Often I saw her say and do such things in the years that followed and always, in her presence, my mother's frown softened. Jean's honesty was a weapon at once innocent and irresistible.

'To change like that,' Jean was saying. 'To be full of life one day and then to have to turn in on yourself. . .' She shivered, her fingers tightened around mine. 'It must be awful to lose someone you love. It's no wonder your poor mother changed so much.'

Her hand in mine was precious. Although she had danced with a dozen other fellows in Seapoint and nothing overt had been said, it had somehow been understood between us that I was walking Jean home after the dance. Outside the dance-hall she'd slipped her hand into mine with as much naturalness as if we'd known each other all our lives. It was a windless bright night, as we walked along the empty streets, past sleeping shops and houses, it seemed to me that I had known her all my life. Only afterwards, when I looked back over all that had happened between us, did I realize the skill with which Jean drew me out on that first night, and the love with which she listened to my boy's tale of two greyhounds and a father, and of a mother who had literally steeled herself against the loss.

'You lost him too, Dan.' Again, my hand was squeezed by hers as we left St Mary's behind us, crossing the road at Cooke's Corner and heading on towards the hospital. 'Listen to me . . . going on about losing someone and you know all about that, better than anyone. Forgive me.'

'It's not just the losing.' The strangeness of the night, the touch of her hand, the smell of her skin, the very gentleness of her words, emboldened me to say aloud what I had never dared to say before, not even to myself.

'He never even said goodbye to me!' My own anger was a

surprise to me, as if it belonged to someone else. 'Christ, I never even got to the funeral . . . they sent me away while they buried him.' I gulped back tears, unable to continue.

I heard her shushing noises, and I felt myself being drawn back into the shelter of a grey, stonewall. She drew my head down onto her shoulder and her fingers stroked my head. 'It's all right, Daniel.' I heard her say. 'It's all right.'

When the trembling died in me, I was embarrassed. What would she think of me now, this girl with the gentle touch and the gentle words? Now that I'd made a fool of myself, sobbing like a sissy, she surely wouldn't want anything more to do with me.

How little I knew you, Jean! How could I know then on that first walk through the streets of our town, that yours was a life that you had already marked for giving? How could I know then, when I glanced at your face made radiant in the glow of the streetlamps, that for you it was neither the destination not the scenery that gave meaning to the journey but the traveling companions you found along the way?

'Tell me,' she said. 'I'd like to hear about it. I'd like to know more about you.'

Haltingly at first, and then more quietly and confidently, I told her about those last days; the smell of embrocation on Prince's haunches; the jibes of the fellows in the Sportsground; that other starlit walk with my father; Granda Flanagan's wheezing and whining; the empty morning and the sodden journey to Athlone; the empty homecoming and the emptier years that followed. The streets and the buildings fell behind us as I talked and Jean listened – the dirty, creamy, flat-topped bulk of the hospital on our left, the trees and the grey softness of the university on our right. We were silent as we approached the turning for Greenleas, the suburban estate where Jean lived. The road was deserted; the entire town seemed asleep.

'Where did everybody go?' I asked, in a kind of a whisper. 'Was there nobody at the dance tonight except the pair of us?'

She laughed, leading me on past the row of sleeping, pebble-dashed semis. 'Maybe,' she said. 'There wasn't.'

We sat on the low wall outside her house. It was like all the others, the garage converted, the car on the concrete driveway. The quietness of the night made us speak in conspiratorial whispers. Her thigh pressed against mine, scorching me with its heat through her white-cotton dress. My hand rested in hers, held close to the warmth of her skin. From behind us came the sound of a door opening, and then a man's voice, calling her name. She looked over my shoulder and gave a little wave with her free hand.

'It's late, Jean,' the deep voice said.

'In a minute, Dad.' She waved again. 'Just give me a minute.'

The door closed behind us.

'I have to go in, Daniel.' My hand was gently squeezed, her blue eyes searching out mine. 'Thank you for walking me home.' She leaned towards me, and her lips brushed gently against mine. 'Good-night, Daniel.'

'Good-night, Jean.'

When the door closed behind her, the night was still rich with the wonder of her; the streets had a magic I had never sensed before and the pavements, humming beneath my dancing feet, a music I had never heard before. I cut down by the college and then turned at Ward's shop, along by the canal: the still, dark waters were alive with reflected stars and I saw her face there, bathed in their silver light. Part of me wanted to shout my good fortune to the sleeping streets, yet another part of me wanted to hug my secret to myself. My hand and mouth quivered with the remembered touch of her.

I turned the key as quietly as I could in our front door but it made no difference: the crack of light under the kitchen door told me that my mother was still up. Her face was set in its habitual, unsmiling expression when I went into the kitchen.

'You're late,' she said. 'I thought you said the dance was over at twelve.'

'It's early yet, Mam.' I didn't want to let her quench the lights that were dancing in my brain. 'Sure it's not even one yet.'

'I'll make you some tea –'

'Don't!' I interrupted her, as she stood up. 'I couldn't drink tea at this hour,' I added more gently.

'A cup of cocoa'd be good for you.'

'No . . . no cocoa . . . I don't need anything, Mam, thanks.' I looked at my mother's head of white hair, saw the furrows in her wide brow and I remembered Jean's words with a surge of pity. 'Go to bed, Mam. You've to be up early in the morning.'

'At my age you don't need a lot of sleep.' My mother was 50, I knew, but she looked years older than Leonard's mother, whom I guessed to be about the same age, or possibly even older. I watched her, bending stiffly over the range, making sure that the dead fire would not engulf the house in a conflagration during the night, before, satisfied, she turned towards the door. 'Don't stay up too late, Daniel.'

'I won't.'

'Goodnight so.'

'Mam?'

'Yes?' She half-turned, standing in the doorway. 'What is it?'

'D'you miss Dad?'

'What kind of a question is that?' She half-closed the door and then opened it again. 'Did you meet a girl tonight?'

'I did.'

I'd have told her more if she had asked but all she said, looking at me across the room, was: 'Why wouldn't I miss him?'

I said goodnight then, and stood still in the silent kitchen, listening to her climb the stairs. I heard the door of her bedroom open and close, and I knew that she'd be on her knees for a quarter of an hour, the mother-o'-pearl rosary beads sliding through on her hardened fingers, before she finally got into bed. She'd be up before 7.00; after a gulped-down cup of tea she'd be off to prepare breakfast at the start of another day in the Crotty household.

I hadn't told Jean about my mother's job. I didn't know if Jean even knew Leonard Crotty. At the moment I didn't care. Mine was the hand that Jean's had held; mine were the lips she had kissed. Later in bed, I treasured the taste of her as I drifted into deep, deep sleep.

Chapter 13

I hoped the hammering on my front door would stop if I resolutely ignored it. Perhaps the ache in my head would also disappear if I just sat immobile on the kitchen chair. I'd had another sleepless night, hurt and brooding: no writing on the ceiling this time, just images of Bee that lingered through its long hours.

And silent. She hadn't called me over the weekend.

The banging on the door didn't stop and whoever was there now had the other hand firmly pressed on the doorbell as well.

When I'd phoned Elizabeth the previous evening, I'd got through only to her answer-machine. I hung up without leaving a message. Calling the school after that hadn't been a good idea: "You do realise what time it is, Mr Best?". I'd met the housemistress on one of my visits to the school: short, muscular and athletic, with the kind of cut-glass voice that could unman any errant parent with a single syllable. I'd pleaded extra concern because of the "problems" my daughter had been having of late, but it was no use: the girls were not allowed to receive telephone calls after 11.00pm. She'd let Beatrice know that her father had called: "In the morning, Mr Best".

A morning that was long in coming. I hoped Bee had slept anyway and that she was no longer angry with the father who so clumsily told her that he wasn't going to be around forever. Unlike, it seemed, the caller at the hall-door. I didn't care who might be there, or how angry they were, hammering with the brass knocker and pressing on the white bell. It couldn't be Bee, and nobody else mattered.

'*Daniel!*' The shout came through the open letterbox. 'Open the bloody door, Dan! I know you're in there!'

Go away, Jeff, I thought. Leave me here in my kitchen with my lumps and thoughts of my absent daughter.

'I'm warning you, Dan!' I could hear the anger in his voice now. 'The guards will break the door down for me if I tell then I have a patient inside who might have passed out unconscious.' There was silence for a moment, then the frustrated flapping of the letterbox. 'I mean it, Dan . . . I'm going for the guards.'

He would too and I had enough hassle in my life without having to look for a new front door. I got to my feet and made my way along the narrow hall. The rawness of the November morning hit me when I opened the door.

'Christ, Dan!'

I knew I must look a mess to Jeff: unwashed, unkempt, still in my dressing gown at nearly 10.00 in the morning.

'I didn't mean to wake you.'

'You didn't, Jeff. Now come in before you waken the whole fucking street.' From the corner of the Lane, Paudge Lydon raised his hand: he had grown stooped and white-haired, all these years leaning against the walls of Paternoster. I waved over to him as I closed the door. 'So what couldn't wait?' I asked, following him into the kitchen. 'Has someone found an overnight cure for the big C?'

He didn't answer at once but busied himself placing his bag carefully on the table, beside my half-drunk cup of tea. I watched the characteristic, almost comical way his mouth twisted and turned as he marshaled his thoughts. He used to do the same thing when we were schoolboys, wrestling in this same room with a particularly vicious geometry cut or a piece of calculus.

102

'I couldn't wait for you to come to me,' he said at last. 'I know my job, Dan, and I'm good at it . . . I work hard at it and I don't like losing my patients.'

'I know,' I said. 'It's tough giving up all these fees.'

'Fuck you, Dan.'

'I'm sorry,' I said. 'I didn't mean that.'

'Didn't you? You're always fucking sorry, Dan, and you . . . you were always a smart alec, especially where I was concerned. All those nights we slogged over homework here . . .' He half-turned, as if expecting to see the two of us seated with open books at the table while my mother went on with her knitting beside the range. 'D'you think I didn't know then that you thought I was thick? I wasn't thick, Dan, just not as quick as you, that's all.' Jeff was holding a brown A4-sized envelope in his hand and rolling it into a tight cylinder as he spoke. 'But I knew what I wanted, Dan, and I got it. That's . . . that's why I'm here. That's why I'm your doctor, banging on you door in the morning when I should be visiting patients who appreciate it.'

'Maybe you can do something for them,' I said.

'I could do something for your too, if you'd let me.' He gave a dry laugh and smoothed out the large, coiled envelope. 'I dug out some literature for you,' he said, handing me the envelope. 'Read it, think about it. Go to another doctor if you like . . . In fact, maybe you'd be better off with somebody else. But read that stuff. It'll help you to understand your problem.'

'My problem is called cancer, Jeff.'

Jeff snorted. 'There are treatments, Dan and sometimes remedies'.

'And are there remedies,' I asked, as I watched him take his bag and move towards the kitchen door. 'For what's happening up at the Spinney?'

He seemed to freeze in the doorway.

'What about the Spinney?'

'I hear Crotty Developments are going to build some glorious, executive-style apartments up there.' I didn't need to add that we both knew Jeff had been an investor in Leonard Crotty's development business ever since he'd left his father's builder's providers outfit to go it alone.

'For God's sake, Dan, don't start worrying about the bloody Spinney. You have enough on you plate right now.'

'So it's true then, it's in the pipeline.'

'What's true,' Jeff said. 'Is that I'm your doctor until you tell me I'm not . . . and I want you to read that fucking stuff I gave you.'

'They'll build apartments up there over my dead body, Jeff.'

'Maybe that's exactly . . .' He stopped, and we stared at each other, realizing what had been said and not said.

Long after the front door had closed behind him, I still stood there turning the brown envelope over and over in my hands. I knew that I was scared of what I would find inside.

'There's nothing to be afraid of,' Jean said. 'Nothing in the whole wide world! How could there be, on a day like this.' Her sweeping arm took in the town and the bay, sparkling below us in the May sunshine. 'With the whole world at our feet?'

She was laughing as she leaned towards me, her mouth puckered for kissing, but for once I drew back from her. I wanted to finish my point – I always did, as Jean sometimes told me with mock exasperation. 'I don't mean anything in particular . . .' I went on, trying to tease out in words the feelings of unease that sometimes seemed to overtake me on the blind side, up there, in the Spinney. 'It's just a feeling, you know, when everything is going so well you've got to be prepared for the unexpected.'

'So when you're winning you should be thinking of what it feels like to be losing?'

'That's not what I mean . . .'

'And when you've just passed your second-year medicine exams you should be trying to imagine what it feels like to have failed?' Jean was laughing at me, without malice: that alone was enough of a reason to love her.

'Okay, doctor,' I said. 'You win . . . as usual.'

'You should always trust your doctor.'

'Maybe I'll get a second opinion.'

'Would you settle for a second kiss?'

On the rough path that ran around the edge of the Spinney we stopped to embrace and kiss. The touch of her still enchanted me as much as it had done on that first night, almost three years previously, outside her house. Even then, in 1971, not yet 21, I was conscious of the inexorable passing of time. Blink, and you're a year older. In the batting of an eye-lid, empires crumble and nations are born or re-born. You walked out the door of a dance hall with a girl on your arm and before you draw breath nearly three years have passed and you know you're going to marry the girl. She's still there on your arm, a mystery, like the blur of years.

It was the unraveling of the mystery of that blur that drew me to history. When I started university, English had been my first choice and history was no more than the necessary second subject that had to be taken for a degree. It had been a slow dawning for me, the realisation that the ordering of the past had become more real to me than the yarns of novelists and the lyrics of poets. I found a comfort in this trawling of dates and places that, despite all that that has happened, still remains with me. Otherwise, why write down this account of deeds done and promises broken? I used to argue with Jean that the only lesson to be learned from history is that there are no lessons: people will still go on making the same mistakes that people everywhere have made since the world began.

The irony is that, deep down; I go on searching for some meaning, some new lesson, amid the minutiae, history and debris of my own life. These words will, perhaps make no difference to Bee, or to anybody else for that matter, but they are mine and as I tap them out on my keyboard, I still hope somehow that their ripples will touch some other life beyond my own and make a difference.

On that phantom-summer Saturday in May I knew with certainty that my own life was bound up with Jean's. She was in the heart of me. We had spoken our words of love to each other more than once and the previous Easter, on a rare occasion when Jean's house had been empty, we had made love for the first time, in the room she shared with her younger sister; a gallery of chewed and much-loved teddy bears on the window-sill looked down on us as we kissed and touched and fumbled in Jean's narrow, single bed. Afterwards, after the tears and smiles, under the unblinking gaze of the teddy bear line-up, she slept in my arms in the hot sticky bed and I knew that we would love each other always. Perhaps the silent, non-applauding teddies knew better; perhaps they were the true historians.

Amid the semi-wilderness of the Spinney, you had to believe that Jean was right: here there was nothing to fear, whatever echoes of dogs and other animals I might sometimes hear inside me. In a few months, in September, I would take my final degree exams and given the way I had coasted through the first two years, I was expected by many to get a First Class honours. I even expected it of myself: studying had never seemed as easy as when you knew that you'd be seeing Jean that evening or maybe for a hurried coffee between her own lectures and practicals. Her timetable was fuller than mine and in a way this suited, as I was content to pound the books in the library and be with her when she could see me.

Sometimes Jeff would join us and he'd tease her in front of me: "Why did the best-looking bird in his class have to give herself up to a bloody Arts student, when she could have her pick of the next generation of money-making medical specialists?" and "Are you going to settle for a bloody school-teacher?" he'd demand loudly, his huge frame draped across a couple of chairs in the college's new cafeteria.

"Not a teacher" she'd say, smiling: "Daniel is my scholar, Jeff, my historian, my intellectual, my rock . . . if you can understand me".

"Bloody fairies and nancy-boys! Give me a prop forward any day, that's what I say" Jeff would answer.

"Amen to that", or some such, Leonard would add, on the

infrequent occasions when he joined us. Mostly he stayed with his engineering mates in their old building beside the tennis courts where they seemed to deliberately cultivate their image of hearty drunkenness and boorish machismo. Only in Jean's presence did Leonard allow himself to be different, although you wondered which face was the mask; his everyday, obscenity-mouthing one or the gentler appearance he presented when she was around.

"He's not so bad", Jean said to me once, when I said something dismissive of him: "There's a bit of refinement in there somewhere, although Len does his best to hide it".

I thought it wiser to drop it. Maybe Jean was right. Since the time I had given him the schoolboy hammering in the Spinney, Leonard Crotty and myself had held a wary regard for each other. We often had a pint together, but always with Jeff, and although we sometimes disagreed violently over everything from the Beatles to modern architecture, we never came to blows. He never again mentioned that my mother worked in his house.

'So what?' Jean said, when I eventually told her where my mother worked. 'You have to admire her going out to earn her living.'

I learned to be at ease in Jean's house. I loved the life that was in it, a house that seemed always to be bursting with the energy of her clutch of brothers and sisters, all younger than her. Sometimes I fancied that I caught a look of bemusement on her father's face, lifting his head from some book or report, as if he were astonished to have fathered such a brood of boisterous offspring. I rarely heard him raise his voice and when he did, it was without vehemence, like that first night when he told Jean that it was late. It wasn't hard to see why he had fled the hurly-burly of the classroom for the more predictable life of the school inspectorate. When he did, occasionally, ask for silence so that he could get on with this reading, you'd see the children exchange a look of embarrassment that was mixed with indulgence: he asks for so little, they seemed to be saying, why do we make him ask for it at all?

Jean's mother was different. Perhaps, with such a husband and with so many children, she had to be and was obliged to run her household with all the vigour of a Napoleonic general trying to make sense out of the Russian winter. This was brought home to me early when, on my first official visit for tea, little Una, all flying pigtails and winking dimples of her, sent a full cup of tea flying to the floor with a careless elbow. Mrs Martin barked at the child with such fury that my own cup trembled noisily on its saucer. I looked anxiously across the table at Jean but I needn't have worried. Her father looked up, and with just one word, spoken so quietly that you could barely hear him, he restored calm. "Hannah", he whispered and that single word, spoken with his thin eye-brows raised just a little and a tender heart, was enough to make his wife blush and, in the look she flashed him from under her own dark brows, I fancied I caught a glimpse of – of what? Of love, I figure now, although back then I was too young to know that the faces of love are many.

'Thank God for Dad,' Jean said to me later, when we were walking together to the cinema. 'We'd never able to manage Mammy without him.'

I reminded her of it now, climbing the path between the mossy rocks to the top deck of the Spinney. She laughed, hanging on my arm. This acre of semi-wilderness had become a place of pilgrimage for us. Up here, we fed each other rare wild raspberries, from delicate shoots between the rocks, and in the autumn I had kissed her mouth all purple from the abundant blackberries, big and juicy on the heavy bushes.

'Promise me,' she said. 'Promise me, Daniel, that you'll manage me like that when my hair is grey and I'm cross with the kids.'

'You're the one who manages me,' I said. There were kids playing hide-and-seek around the rocks but I didn't care, I kissed her anyway.

'Promise me, Daniel Best,' she said, drawing back from me.

'But you'll never be cross anyway.'

'Promise me!'

'I promise.'

All life was rich with promise in that dreaming time. Even my mother's unsmiling face, still closed against the wounds of the world, could not darken the languorous light that seemed to bathe all my days. Between Jean and me, nothing had been said and yet everything was understood. Second-year medicine, reckoned to be the toughest of her exams, was behind her since the spring and soon she'd be mixing hospital rounds with their regular university classes. Three years to qualification did not seem so long to go. After my own degree finals in the autumn I planned to take a Master's degree in history; I'd work at the roulette table for part of the summer, enough to lay some money aside for the following year when, I figured, I would be able to earn a little also from giving tutorials to first year students. Jean knew that I didn't want to stop at a master's; she knew that I wanted a doctorate.

'Poor me!' she'd groaned. 'I'll be a working girl by then with a penniless post-grad on my hands!'

Beyond all the exams, beyond all the degrees, beyond it all lay life; unseen but tangible; as real as heaven.

'How many?' Jean said, as if she were reading my thoughts.

'How many what?' I asked, but I knew.

'Kids, you daft historian.' Over her shoulder the water was suddenly silver in the sunlight. 'How many kids are we going to have?'

'Lots,' I said. 'And a dog for every single one.'

'Greyhounds if you like.'

The breeze from the sea stirred her hair and I was, for a moment, speechless, as though it were the first time she stood close to me. 'We'll see,' I said at last.

'We'll take it in stages, Daniel.' Her lips brushed against my forehead. 'We have all the time in the world and we can take it all in nice, easy stages.'

Were those really her words? Or is memory playing its tricks on me again? Or perhaps it is fear that is playing the tricks on me now as I turn the pages of Jeff's uncoiled photocopies and it churns inside me.

I begin to read:

> *Staging is a way of describing the extent and*
> *spread of the cancer in your body.*

The words blur on the page and I press my palms on the kitchen table to steady myself. I read on:

> *It is very important because the type of treatment*
> *you receive depends on the stage of the disease.*

Did Jean really say those words on that sunshine Saturday in the Spinney, or am I dreaming them now, when the stages are not nice and easy and all the time in the world is beginning to run out? I forced myself to continue:

> *Stage 1:* *One group of lymph nodes affected and*
> *the disease is only on one side of the*
> *diaphragm.*
> *Stage 2:* *Two or more groups of nodes affected*
> *and the disease is only on one side of the*
> *diaphragm.*
> *Stage 3:* *Disease in lymph nodes on both sides*
> *of the diaphragm.*
> *Stage 4:* *Disease spread beyond lymph nodes, for*
> *example to sites such as the liver,*
> *lungs or bone.*

There was a diagram of the human body: the lymph glands ran like veins of barbed wire from the neck to the groin and under the armpits, down to the spleen. I'd never known what a spleen was – I still didn't, but I could see it now, a small outline below where I imagined the breast to be. The diagram had no face, but it didn't need one. It was your own frightened, angry face that stared back at you. It showed no heart. Perhaps the author thought you couldn't get cancer of the heart. I had news for the author.

I flicked backwards and forwards through the pages, at once repelled, at once fascinated, by this description of what was happening inside me. It was like looking at yourself in the mirror and being terrified by what you saw there, but you went on looking anyway, unable to shut your eyes against this image of yourself that you wished was a lie:

> *The first symptom of a non-Hodgkin's lymphoma*
> *is usually a painless swelling in the neck,*
> *armpits or groin – other symptoms may include*
> *any of the following:*
> *Excessive sweating or fever, especially at night.*
> *Persistent itch all over the body.*
> *Loss of appetite, weight loss and tiredness.*

Why had Jeff chosen to uncoil this stuff on my kitchen table, on me? Was it to excite my fear and my anger and send me running to the surgery? In the kitchen I could smell my own fear and taste the anger in my bitter-dry mouth. The array of cupboards and kitchen gadgets seemed to crowd around me, like some resurrected Berlin wall confining me to a country of one. The wall was strung with bullwire, garlanded with thorny lymph nodes that could tear the flesh and rip the unknown spleen. Beyond the wall was life, remembered hands, and echoed voices. I gasped for breath, clawing at the innocent table. I ached for the touch of those hands, the music of those half-lost voices. I wanted the juice of those fat blackberries on my tongue and the coolness of Jean's lips on my forehead.

The phone was ringing; I groped for it, still drowning, gasping and frightened too. I half-expected to hear Jean, calling to me across the wall. At first I didn't recognize the voice. She was weeping and the words were spilling out; the words barely audible above the background sound of traffic.

'You'll have to speak up and more slowly too,' I said. 'I can't make out what you're saying.'

'That fucker locked me out! Leonard-*fucking*-Crotty locked me out.' Kelly Carpenter sobbed. 'I went home yesterday, just for the night, and when I got back this . . .' I heard a rumbling noise, like a lorry whooshing past and I missed some of her words. '. . . had changed all the locks. The rotten fucker, I've no place to go.' Her wracked sobbing spilled into my ear.

'Where are you, Kelly?'

'In a phone box near the flat . . . I don't know what to do, the . . . the bastard left all my stuff outside in bags.'

'Listen to me, Kelly.'

'You said you'd help me!' It was like an accusation.

'Listen to me,' I said again. 'Just listen to me.' I heard a swallowing, gulping noise as if she were trying to pull herself together. 'Just stay where you are, Kelly, and I'll come and get you.'

'When? When will you come?' she began to weep again. 'I can't believe the fucker threw all my stuff out on the doorstep!'

'In a few minutes,' I said. 'Just stay where you are and I'll be there in about five minutes.'

'Promise.' Her voice was a whisper. 'Promise *me* you'll come.'

'I promise,' I told her.

I felt a rush of relief inside me as I put the phone down. I pushed the photocopied pages away from me and grabbed my set of keys. Life still went on, outside my walls, and I wanted to remind myself that I was still a part of it.

Chapter 14

Her wave of acknowledgement was half-hearted as I pulled up at College Court. She was sitting on the top step outside the door of the apartment and behind her, sweating in the light rain, half-a-dozen black refuse sacks leaned against the wall. I parked the car at the foot of the stone staircase and made my way slowly up to join her. She made no move to stand up.

'C'mon, Kelly,' I said gently. 'You'll get soaked.'

'What does it matter?'

'Never mind that now. We need to get you fixed up with some place to live.'

'Maybe you should dump me and my stuff on Leonard's doorstep.' The idea seemed to revive her. 'Not forgetting my little extra, of course.' She stroked her midriff with a circular motion. 'I'm sure Mrs Leonard-fucking-Crotty would find a spot for it.'

I could have gone on looking at her there, wet and beautiful in the rain, but I had promised her to help her. 'Help me with the bags,' I said. 'Are these are all yours? I mean, this isn't rubbish left out for the bin-men?'

Her laugh was small and bitter. 'Obviously it was rubbish as far as Leonard was concerned, just like myself.'

'You're not rubbish,' I said firmly. 'Now let's get your stuff in the car.'

Half of the bags we crammed into the boot; the remainder we piled on the back seat. I let the engine idle when we were both sitting in the car. The slow, rhythmic action of the windscreen wipers was almost hypnotic; I switched them off, trying to concentrate.

'Where are we going?' Kelly, too, was trying to focus on the next move.

'Home,' I said at last. 'My home! You can get dried off while I'm making some phone calls.'

I was glad of her silence on the short run back. The blue jeans and dark, loose-fitting jacket could not conceal her sexuality: clothes clung to her tiny, perfect frame in a way that seemed to undress rather than clothe her. I tried to fix my mind on the road, easing the car along the docks, then over Wolfe Tone Bridge and up into Henry Street. Our arrival in the Lane would, in the old days, have been watched by eyes from every window and half-open doorway of the street; now only Paudge was interested enough to observe us, zipped and buttoned against the drizzle in his olive-green German army surplus greatcoat, his cigarette cupped in his right hand, the other raised, almost surreptitiously, to acknowledge our arrival. I wondered, as we got out of the car, why Paudge stood there in the drizzle, day after day: the house was his now, his sisters married with grown-up kids somewhere in England, and yet still he did not surrender his post at the corner of the street.

'Who's that?' I could hear the shudder of distaste in Kelly's tone as she glanced across the street.

'A neighbour,' I felt suddenly, inexplicably, protective of the scarecrow figure in the rain. 'The only one left in the street.'

Inside the house she seemed hesitant. 'I shouldn't have called you.' She was turned away from me in the narrow hallway. 'I panicked . . . I can go and stay with some of my friends.'

'You don't have to be scared. It wouldn't be . . .' I searched for the words. 'It wouldn't be the best for anybody if you stayed

114

here.' Still her back was turned to me. 'I'll find you a place . . . Now go up the bathroom and get yourself dry.'

She did what I asked and I stood a moment, watching her haul herself up the fourteen steps before turning away, wondering how someone so young and fresh could move like an old woman. I was still thinking about it as I turned the pages of the directory, digging out the phone number. The girl put me on hold; bland, lounge-style music tinkled dawn the line as I waited for Brian.

'Dan, it's good to hear from you . . . and a surprise too. I haven't seen you out walking for a while.' Brian Murray spoke with the practiced ease of an estate agent.

'I've taken to walking in the mornings,' I said. 'While you're in there, wheeling and dealing.'

I hardly knew Brian: we were acquaintances on the Salthill promenade walk. Once, shortly after I came back to Galway, he had stopped me, apologetically, and while the sea stirred and his wife smiled indulgently, he told me how much he had enjoyed *The Prince of Morning*. The book had moved him, he said, it reminded him of his own childhood in Ennis. His eagerness, humility even, touched me; thereafter we greeted each other almost like old friends and sometimes he and his wife would stop to chat a while.

'How can I help you, Dan?' he asked.

It took only a moment to explain what I wanted. There was, Brian said, no problem; he didn't handle lettings himself, it was his son's responsibility, but he knew they had taken on a new development beside the Spanish Arch, mainly two-beds but there were also a few smaller apartments.

He laughed when I asked if it would be possible for my friend's daughter to move in today. They were quick, he said, but not that quick. Give him a day to fill in the details on the lease and to organize the deposit.

What name, he wanted to know, on the lease.

Mine, I told him.

And payment? Would a standing order be okay?

And so it was done. I was now committed to a twelve-month

lease on an apartment I had never seen for a pregnant girl I barely knew. Daft, probably, or maybe it was just a gesture of defiance.

Kelly still seemed ill at ease when she came downstairs. She'd fixed her mouth and her eyes; she looked very like one of those waifish models you might see on the cover of Vogue.

'It's all arranged,' I said. 'You have a flat in that new block beside the Spanish Arch, and . . . and you can move in tomorrow.'

She was taking wary stock of the kitchen; the pile of newspapers on the chair; the pile of books on the table, and went to stand closer to the photograph of my father and myself and the two dogs. 'Is that you?'

'Yes.' My mother had taken the picture with a little Kodak outside our front door; Prince had turned away from the camera to look up at me. 'It was a long time ago.'

'And is that your Dad?'

'Yes.'

'He looks nice.' I could hear the longing in her voice and in that longing I could sense the cold house she came from: the coldness from which she wished to escape but which still drew her back. 'I wish,' she hugged herself, shivering. 'I wish that –'

'I know,' I said, stopping the pain.

She looked at me then. 'Why are you doing this, getting me a flat and all?'

I shrugged. 'I'm not even sure myself, it's just nice to able to help.'

'You're funny, you know that?'

I shrugged again. 'Would you like tea or coffee?' I asked, turning away to fill the kettle.

'I haven't told you everything,' I heard her say.

'You don't have to.'

'But I think . . . I think I want to.'

'About what?'

'About me and Leonard.' Her full lips worked together, pouting. 'About the apartment in College Court and about . . . about Eileen.'

'Who's Eileen?'

'The girl I shared with. The other girl in the flat.' I remembered the scattered blouses and underwear, seen through unclosed doors on that first day at College Court. 'She sometimes works in Dunne's, as a check-out girl.'

'What about her?' I asked.

There wasn't much shape to the way Kelly told her story. She went backwards and forwards; she'd realise she'd left something out and she'd go back to fill in the gaps. I could fill in some of them myself, as it wasn't difficult to divine the direction of her yarn; the frailties of mankind are pretty much the same everywhere and the smell of lust and power don't alter between decades or continents. Some of the gaps were Kelly's own silences: she'd look away from me and stare out the window into the backyard, wordless, too choked or embarrassed to continue. In its essence, Kelly's story was no more and no less than a common-or-garden tale of money and adultery; sex and business; power and weakness.

A couple of weeks after she'd moved into the apartment, Leonard had told Kelly she'd be having a flatmate. At first she'd been glad of the company when Eileen moved in: nothing had been laid down but Kelly knew that she was not at liberty to entertain any college boyfriends at College Court. Leonard had, in any case, made sure that there was no boyfriend before he installed her in the flat. When he got into her bed that first night – she was studying the window at this point – it was like the sealing of a bargain. She didn't mind that Leonard couldn't stay long on his visits, in some ways she was relieved, but she was lonely.

She'd have gone on working at the Skeff but Leonard didn't want her to; there was no need for her to do so now, he said, she had a nice place to live and he didn't leave her short of money. The money and the clothes, however, somehow didn't compensate for the absence of *craic*, especially in the evenings, away from her own crowd. When she was told of Eileen's imminent arrival, therefore, she was sufficiently pleased to set about cleaning and polishing an apartment that was already immaculate.

The two got on well at first. Like Kelly, Eileen was from out of town and was the same age; unlike her, Eileen was extrovert and liked to drink a lot. Kelly went to the pub with her but found out she couldn't keep up with Eileen's frantic pace of downing vodka-and-white. The third night she was expecting Leonard to call; what she hadn't been expecting was that he'd arrive with a friend, a solicitor, who obviously already knew Eileen. Nor was she expecting Eileen and the solicitor to disappear into the other bedroom, with much laughter and giggling, while she and Leonard were still sitting apart on the white leather couch.

The solicitor was gone before morning but he was back again a week later. Marcus Whelan, solicitor, wasn't the only one who came calling to the apartment in College Court. So did Eamon McCarthy, hotelier and entrepreneur. So too did Jeffrey Reynolds, physician.

'Jeff?' I couldn't keep the astonishment out of my voice.

'Yes.' Kelly turned her head. Then looking directly at me, explained, 'Eileen said she liked him better than the others, he was nicer to her.' She was silent a while, engrossed in her recollections. 'He never bothered me but . . .' The beautiful mouth was downturned with distaste. 'The other fuckers tried it on with me, calling when Leonard was away. I threatened Leonard on them and it didn't happen again.' She shivered once more, remembering. 'It didn't stop them looking at me though. Like I was a piece of meat, like . . .'

She began to weep then, and her small body went on shivering. Her shoulders shook so much I wanted to reach across and comfort her but I was afraid to. Perhaps I was afraid of myself. Perhaps that was why I hated so much what she had told me, because I feared that, deep down, I was no different from these business and professional mullahs of the town who slipped adulterously in and out of College Court under cover of darkness.

'And then the fucker throws me out on the side of the road like I was trash!' Rage and hatred had made the beautiful mouth ugly now. 'Who do these people think they are, fucking around with people's lives like that? Who do they think they are!'

It took a while before the sobbing subsided, before she groped in the box of tissues I pushed across the table to her.

'You have to do something,' she said at last. 'They can't get away with this.'

'Adultery, is not a crime.'

'It's not just that . . .' she hesitated.

'You mean Eileen? Different men visiting her?' I was thoughtful. 'Believe me, nothing would please me more than being able to name Leonard Crotty as the owner of a brothel but I don't think that's possible.'

'But he owns the apartment!'

I shook my head. 'Penny to a pound,' I said. 'Some company owns the place and Leonard will have no connection whatever with that company. He's just . . . just too cute to be caught out like that.'

'You could try.' She picked up a copy of *NewsTruth* from the chair beside her and half-waved it at me. 'You could put it in your magazine.'

'And if you could prove he was the owner of a brothel,' I asked her gently. 'Where would that leave you . . . and your baby?'

'I just think the fucker shouldn't get away with it.'

'No,' I said. 'He shouldn't.'

'So . . . you'll do something about it?'

'I'm flattered by your notion of what I can do but . . .' I laughed. 'All I write is a column in a magazine.'

'But people take notice,' she said doggedly. 'It's not like you're nobody.'

There was at least a grain of truth in what Kelly said. *NewsTruth's* circulation in Ireland is tiny, less than a 1,000 copies a week, I think, but its readers are movers and shakers: journalists, of course, checking on stories and angles they might have missed; intellectuals and academics; a few internationally-minded entrepreneurs; the small handful of priests and politicians who can manage joined-up talking and writing. The magazine inevitably wields an amount of influence that far outweighs its readership. What this means is that Irish leader-writers and pundits often refer to its content and line: like people everywhere, we are fascinated by what others think of us. Since I am *NewsTruth's* own resident writer here, my pieces are often picked up by the *Irish Times* and *Independent*; I have on a few occasions been included in television chat-show line-ups for an examination of Ireland's spiritual and moral belly-button although, more usually, my comments are sought at the end of a line for radio phone-in programmes. As Kelly put it, it's not like I'm nobody, although you might wonder if this is the same as saying that you're somebody.

'You can stay here tonight,' I said, changing the subject. 'It's only for the night,' I added hastily. 'The apartment will be ready tomorrow.'

'You're sure it's okay?'

'Why wouldn't it be okay? I'll make up the bed in Bee's room for you.'

'Bee?'

'My daughter! She lives in London with her mother.'

'Oh!' The look on her face was almost one of shock. 'I didn't know you had a family.'

'Even a fellow like me, can have a family,' I said gently.

'I didn't mean . . .'

'It's a joke.'

'Sorry.'

She went out soon after that, saying she'd be back in time to cook dinner. She waved my protest aside; it would do her good to get dinner ready, she said, she'd feel like she was repaying me in some small way. She took the key from me, but also waved aside my offer of money for groceries. We'd have dinner on Leonard, she said; with any luck, his own dinner would choke him. Her frailty seemed at odds with her defiance; I wondered, watching her close the hall-door behind her, how she'd cope in six months or so with the arrival of her baby.

I was glad to escape for the afternoon into my *NewsTruth* piece. Thomas Nalty is an award-winning furniture-designer who has built a stone-clad round-house a few miles outside Galway; the house has, naturally, a look of our old monastic round towers and has already become something of a tourist, rubber-necking, camera-clicking, halting-spot. What makes this gifted, often-sullen carpenter worth a column, however, is his eccentricity: when, some years ago, he lost a leg in an alcoholic road-accident, he disdained the use of a modern, artificial limb. Instead, he fashioned a leg for himself from some ancient Irish bog-oak and now, rangy and red-raised, he has become a dramatic, even alarming, figure in the streets and pubs of town. He wears his leg of bog-oak naked, his trouser-leg folded and pinned above the knee, like some latter-day Ahab at large in our taverns; sometimes, kids on the street tease him, but they do so at their peril. More than once I have seen Thomas collar a terrified teenager in the crook of his walking stick and I have heard him threaten to set Beelzebub upon the offender. Beelzebub is the mongrel, which accompanies Thomas on his pub-crawls and is notable for having just three legs. Lucifer, the black cat which Thomas keeps at home, is also short of a leg and there is also a pet duck called Mephisto: this creature has a complete pair of legs but has only one wing.

I spent a happy afternoon in Thomas's lop-sided world. It's the kind of "human interest" piece I enjoy doing, like the moving statues in Ballinspittle a couple of years previously or the doe-eyed teenager in County Mayo who drew huge, fee-paying crowds to witness her invisible encounters behind the hay shed with the Blessed Virgin; the crowds – and financial offerings – dried up only when her very pregnant belly made it obvious that some other, more earthly kind of encounters were also taking place, possibly even behind – or inside – the hallowed hayshed. I am, as I pointed out to Gabriel all those years ago in that pub near Paddington station, no newsman. "Give me what interests you," he'd said: "The funnies, the freaks, the . . . the world is full of guys who can give us the heavy stuff. This," he went on, twirling his copy of *The Prince of Morning* above his head; "Is different. Just be yourself, Dan and give me more of it. Just do it on time, every goddam week".

Now more than ever I was grateful to my eccentrics and funnies, and to my countrymen's obsession with the sideshows of existence. Hysteria is rarely marked absent on this island of saints and scholars. It calms you down when life threatens to become too serious. Like now, like this almost languorous afternoon, when, for at least a brief period, I could forget about the state of my lymph nodes and the continuing silence from Bee. And I could almost forget that Kelly, childlike in her womanly beauty, would be sitting down to dinner with me later that evening. For the moment, Thomas and his physically challenged sidekicks were my world, and I was glad of it. I knew he wouldn't be displeased with my column: his design fees grew in proportion to his notoriety. And yet I was not without some misgivings: the more outlandish Thomas's fees, the more he drank and the less work he actually did. It was not hard to foresee that, in a few years time, Thomas's one-legged world would be all drink and no work. Was it Oscar who said that nothing succeeds like excess? Or was that Elton John?

Gabriel himself acknowledged the safe arrival of my copy. His cheery e-mail response flashed up on the screen only minutes after I'd finished sending my words down the line. With it came his assurance that he'd be making his annual flying visit to Ireland inside a couple of weeks: I THIRST. HAVE THE BLACK STUFF READY. When I lived in London, I used to pour Gabriel into the Departures area at Heathrow at the bleary-eyed end of our annual, so called review; his more recent excursions to Galway have been somewhat tamer, but only a little. He retains still his huge zest for work and play and when he gets pissed; he likes to reminisce about the flower-power days when he produced soft-porn comic books in Berkeley. "The pussy was endless, man, just endless" he'd say, playing with the now-greying beard that still reaches to his belly: "Like the Garden of Eden before we were all kicked out to hell".

He's an odd mixture of ruthless businessman and sentimental visionary, is Gabriel Jankowski, founder and publisher of *NewsTruth*. I owe him a lot and I like his company, yet now I almost fear his arrival. I cannot hide my sickness from him and I dread the pity in his eyes. And the anger too: Gabriel will rail against the iniquity of fate and then he will try to take over my life, summoning both specialist and alternative quacks with his usual bullying gusto. Gabriel will try to imbue me with his fierce energy for survival, and yet I have no wish to be overwhelmed. My die is cast, my Rubicon crossed.

It was almost 7pm when Kelly came back. She didn't volunteer where she'd been, apart from the supermarket and nor did I ask. I was content to take myself into the front room, as she'd instructed, while she cooked our dinner. I wanted my sense of contentment, fragile as I knew it was, to linger a while longer, so I drank a glass of red wine and managed to eat more than I had for some time. I felt her eyes upon me as I declined a second helping.

'You don't eat much,' she said.

'Never had much of an appetite,' I told her. 'But it was delicious.'

I sensed the question on her lips but I said no more: I had no wish then to offer explanations as to why I too had been in Jeff's surgery on that day. For now, too, her sexual presence seemed muted or perhaps it was just that I was tired and sluggish after the wine. I was content with her company, conscious of her nearness as she thumbed through my shelves of books and music, exclaiming as she came across something that she had read or meant to read.

She said goodnight before 10.00; her perfume lingered in the kitchen after she had closed the door. I was still, listening to her movement overhead, on the landing, in the bathroom and then the click of Bee's bedroom door closing behind her. She was still awake when I went upstairs a little while later: my eyes were drawn to the chink of light under her closed door as I was going into my own room.

Lying in the darkness, waiting for the nightly sweats to come,

I thought I heard my own blood steaming through my veins and arteries, relentlessly searching out all the reaches of my body. There was no escape from your own blood, from your cells, from your bloody lymph nodes. My barbed-wire lymph glands imprisoned me as surely as the barbed fencing confined the miserable inmates at Auschwitz and Belsen. It was time, I thought bleakly, to get a prescription for some sleeping tablets.

Perhaps I slept, perhaps I only dozed but as I drifted on the dark-brown streams of my own blood, the creak of my bedroom door opening brought me fully awake. In the gloom Kelly was gliding soundlessly towards my bed. In the half-light from the landing she seemed like a moving statue; the long pink T-shirt seemed moulded to her body and fell like drapes against the gleaming flesh of her thighs.

I shivered when she laid her hand against my face.

'I'll stay with you if you like.' Her voice was a throaty whisper.

'There's no need.' My own voice was broken, pierced by the bullwire of the night.

'I know that but . . . but I don't mind staying.' She leaned over me; her pointed breasts pushed against the flimsy stuff of her T-shirt.

'I'm flattered . . . and I'm grateful.' I longed to draw those breasts to my lips, forbidden fruit overhanging the dark-red rivers, but there were other voices insistent in the darkness. 'Go back to sleep, Kelly.'

'I can't sleep.'

'Try.'

I felt her breath, sweet and hot on my face. The breasts stirred on the sheet. 'You're sure you don't want me to stay?'

'It's better if you don't,' I swallowed. 'You and I have to stay friends.'

She sat upright on the edge of the bed; I knew she was staring down at me. 'I'd like that,' she said at last.

'Goodnight, Kelly.'

She bent over me again and for a long moment her lips were pressed on my forehead. 'Goodnight, Daniel.'

I followed her gliding passage towards the light of the half-open door, my eyes drinking in the sculpted beauty of the T-shirted body, the delicate shoulder blades and the draped firmness of her buttocks. As the door closed, the room once again filled with darkness and I knew that the night would be long.

Chapter 15

Long, too, that other night in the long-ago.

Not that I could remember much of what I had done after Jean and I had parted. I'd walked to Salthill, along the promenade in the November evening but seeing neither waves nor the hills across the bay. A fine, drizzly rain began to fall; I knew I was drenched, bareheaded and wearing only a sweater, but I didn't care. Perhaps the road beneath my feet would take away the weight of Jean's words, lift them up and scatter them over the grey sea. I plodded on, past Knocknacarra Cross, on the darkening, deserted road, seeing and hearing nothing except her words in my heart.

And my own words, spoken so fearfully that afternoon in the Spinney.

'But how can you be sure, Jean? How can you know for certain?'

'I just know, Daniel, that's all . . . I just know.'

At Barna crossroads I turned left, away from the lights of the pub, down along the narrow road that led to the sea. Night had fallen with the rain; standing on top of the old pier in the pitch-blackness, I could hardly see the waves beating against the dark stone at my feet. It was enough to know that the sea was there, like an open pit, black and inviting.

Later I had turned away almost reluctantly, heading back towards town in the black, drizzly night. The road was pathless but I stuck doggedly to the edge of the tarmac, heedless of the cars that passed with flashing lights and honking horns. What did it matter now if one of these angry drivers tossed me onto the greasy, mucky margin? No speeding car could break or batter me more than Jean's words had already done in the grey afternoon.

'I just know I'm right,' Jean had said. 'Trust me, Daniel.'

The rocks and bushes of the Spinney seemed to dissolve as she spoke. Below us, the quiltwork of the town seemed to disappear. The university quad, that had sparkled and shimmered for my graduation just a week earlier, darkened in the afternoon. The world was crumbling under my feet. How could I trust Jean when I could not even trust my own tears?

'I can't believe this. I can't believe you're telling me this.'

'D'you think it's easy for me to say this, Daniel?' Her eyes were filled with tears and yet she had never seemed lovelier. 'I wanted to tell you before but you conferring was coming up . . . I didn't want to spoil it for you.'

'And it's okay to spoil it now, is it? Just to let me know that everything up to now was a lie.'

'Please, Daniel, please don't!' A single tear trailed down her cheek. 'Everything wasn't a lie.'

'You just said you wanted to say all this before conferring . . . I suppose I should be grateful for your pity.'

She'd worn a cream-coloured, collarless suit with gilt buttons; I knew, looking back at her as I returned with my first-class scroll to my place in the crammed, vaulted Aula Maxima, that she was the loveliest woman in the hall and that I was the most fortunate fellow in the world. Even my mother, new-hatted and new-coated for the occasion, had managed a grim smile for the *Connacht Tribune* photographer; she also managed a reluctant reprise when the photograph of the three of us appeared on the front page of the paper the following week. A framed copy of the picture soon found its way onto the wall of our front room, as if my success and Jean's smile had somehow engineered a chink in my mother's wall against the world.

All through that long afternoon, through the gowned and be-ribboned ceremony, throughout the posed photographs on the lawns of the quad and the teas-and-cakes in the coffee shop and the handshakes in the Archway, it was Jean's smiling serenity that overlaid the day like the promise of a long spell of sunny weather. When she leaned against me for our own separate picture on the steps of the Aula, I knew that we were on our way. Already, in the weeks since the degree results had been published, I had been promised a steady diet of tutorials for freshmen; the intimation of a future was made real in the softness of Jean nestling in my arms and her hair nuzzling against my cheek.

'Was all that a fraud?' I tried to halt the tears welling in my voice. 'All the pictures and all the lovey-dovey of just a week ago?'

They'd fallen like ninepins around us at Graduation Ball in the Great Southern Hotel; bow ties undone, jackets discarded and hair-structures collapsed, they'd danced on the tables before getting sick in the lavatories, and elsewhere. I was drunk enough with the nearness of Jean. In her off-the-shoulder, ankle length gown she seemed to me like some fabulous goddess who had strayed into a drunken pantomime. Her skin, pale as alabaster, was real to my touch and so was her mouth, parting under mine, as we danced close together in the heel of the night. Afterwards we walked arm-in-arm and hip-to-hip up past the Square and down to Eglinton Street. We had declined to go to a couple of parties; to be together was enough for us. Past the Cathedral we took the short cut through the grounds of the college, deserted now after the ceremonial busyness of the day. The moon was huge over the old quad; the ivy on the old, grey walls gleamed like ancient laurel leaves. In the afternoon, as Jean and I had smiled for my mother's and her father's cameras, I has sensed my future here; now, in the white silence of the night, I felt that I could almost touch the past that gave substance and foundation to that future. We paused to kiss in the shadow of the Archway and our bodies trembled together in a long delight.

'Tell me!' I demanded again. 'Was all that a lie? Have you been lying in my face for the last three years? Have you? *Have you?*'

Her crying was uncontrolled now, her face almost ugly with pain and weeping. 'I never lied to you, Daniel, never . . . Honest, never!'

The Spinney tumbled about me.

'Then why are you saying all this stuff to me now? Why? Why?'

'*You're hurting me!*'

I had not known my fingers were fixed vice-like around her wrist; shamed, as though her wrist had scorched me, I dropped her hand. I could not let go of my pain, my anger. 'Why?' I demanded again. 'I don't understand.'

'Try to understand, Daniel, please try.' Her shoulders sagged; her arms were crossed loosely under her breast, like some supplicant lost in the wilderness of the Spinney. 'I just want to have some time to myself, Daniel, that's all.'

'Then why can't we just cut down on meeting? We don't need to see each other during the week.'

'No.' Jean straightened herself; when she went on, there was a hint of resolve in her tone. 'I need time alone, Daniel. I'm over 21 but I've never known what it is to be on my own.'

'And whose *fault* is that?' I demanded bitterly. 'Whose idea was it to meet up at the dance?'

'It wasn't anybody's fault, Daniel, it was just the way we were –'

'Thanks,' I interrupted her. 'I can see it's not the way we are now.'

She was silent a while. A cloud slid across the November sun and the Spinney was suddenly cold. 'I fell in love with you, Daniel, and I don't regret that . . . I never will. I think I'm still in love with you . . . I hope I am . . . but I want some time for myself, some space so I can get to know myself and what I really am.'

'Then take some time,' I said desperately. 'We won't see each other for a month, or six or seven weeks, and we can arrange now to go out together for Christmas. We can have a meal together and you can tell me all about whatever . . . whatever you figured out while we were apart.' I stopped; my own tears made it impossible to continue. I looked, pleading, at Jean but there was no relenting in her face or in her voice.

'I'm sorry, Daniel,' she said. 'But it won't work, putting a timetable on it like that. I have to feel completely free, otherwise it's no good, don't you see that?'

'Free to do what, Jean? What is it that you want to do?'

'I don't know, that's the trouble. I'm over halfway to being a doctor and yet everything is mapped out for me. You and me, and us, and a job and . . . and everything! I don't want it like that, not now. It's all just too serious and I just want . . . I want to have some fun for a while!'

'And we don't have fun together?' I was angry. 'Is that what you're telling me?'

'You're twisting my words, Daniel.' Her voice was firmer now, as if she had made up her mind. 'All I'm saying is that I don't want to feel hemmed in all the time. I've realized that I hardly know the rest of my class. I meet them in lectures, we do the rounds in the wards together, but outside of that I don't know them. They go drinking together, they have parties in flats and sometimes in the hospital and when I hear them talking about it I feel like . . . like I'm left out if it and my time as a student is passing me by.'

'So you want to go to parties and fool around, is that it?'

'That's not what I said!' She flung the words at me in exasperation. 'But so what if I do!'

'There's nothing more to be said then, is there?' In the distance a dog barked, and then felt silent. I waited, listening, but no dog answered from the fields and gardens spread out below us. 'The rest is bloody silence.'

'It doesn't have to be,' Jean said. 'I don't want it to be.'

'When?' I asked. 'When is this . . . this period of space, going to end?'

'When it ends,' Jean said. 'It will end, when it ends.'

'Are you going to go out with other guys?'

'Is that what you think this is about? D'you think I don't love you?'

'Then answer the question!'

'It is not a question you should ask.'

'I'm asking it anyway.'

'Maybe,' she said at last. 'Probably . . . but it's not important. You have to trust me on this.'

'Trust you!' I snorted, betrayed by my despair, my disbelief and my anger. She looked hurt. I didn't care. In my mind the rain was falling and I was staring into the backyard at Paternoster, taking in the low, stone, wall and the empty spaces where the kennels and the wire fencing used to be.

'Trust is for children,' I said, turning away downhill towards the gap in the Spinney wall.

'Daniel!'

When I turned to look up at her, she seemed rooted upon the rock, smooth and moss-covered, where we had so often sat together.

'Are you going to leave me like this?' she called in a broken voice.

'Is there ever a good way to leave?'

'Can't we be friends from now on?'

'What for?'

'Because we meant . . . we mean so much to each other.'

'You have a funny way of showing it.'

'Please, Daniel.'

I remembered my mother's stony face staring down at me as I passed into the empty yard. 'You expect me to wait for you until you decide you're ready to come back? Right?'

'I still care for you,' she said. 'More than anybody in the whole world.'

"Tell that to the marines", Granda Flanagan used to say when he was pronouncing upon something completely ludicrous. 'Tell that to the fucking marines!' I said.

Her head was bent and I could not see her face, but I knew she was crying. Her body trembled and I watched her fold her arms tightly about herself as if to quell the spasm of shuddering. I longed to go back up the path to her, to comfort her, to stroke her hair and dry her tears, but my own pain and rage and jealousy held me back.

Even after all these years, that image haunts me: Jean, on the rock, her body racked, her head of brown hair bowed under the weight of my words, my fury. Afterwards, in the days that followed that Saturday afternoon in the Spinney, I would wish more than once that I could have undone some of the pain of our parting. I did not know then, stumbling blindly down the hillside, that within a few weeks my behaviour that day would seem almost meek, at least by comparison with what I soon would do.

Perhaps the madness in me; that madness that is in all of us, erupted that day for the first time, as I walked unseen around the docks and the back streets of the town. Or perhaps its origins began much earlier, in the days of our, my father's and mine, apostolic procession and had until then been suppressed. I have only the murkiest recollection of that afternoon; if I did meet anyone I knew, I have no memory of it.

As night was falling, I found myself in Salthill, and thereafter plodded on towards the terminus of Barna pier. Perhaps it was fear that drew me back from the edge of that stone mole which jutted out into the black, angry waters or perhaps it was just tiredness: I had already walked miles and my brain had gone beyond the point of making decisions. Like a lost dog, it was mere homing instinct that drew me back through the rain and the night to our house.

My mother was still up when I got in. At first she was angry over the late hour but her anger abruptly changed to clucking and fussing over "the state of you". She shooed me up the stairs to dry my hair and "get out of those wet clothes". A little while later she came into my room with a mug of tea, standing by the bed to make sure I drank it. After a while, I heard her say "Goodnight,

133

son" and, for the first time since my father died, I felt her hand stroking my face before she left. Her alien touch made the darkness seem deeper, the night even longer. I lay there, staring into the blackness, waiting for my father to call me to walk the dogs, and to hurry up because Jean was coming with us.

Chapter 16

Kelly was up and about early next morning. I could smell the rashers in the grill when I went into the kitchen; she immediately cracked a couple of eggs into the frying pan. 'How d'you like them?' she asked, flashing me a smile. 'Hard, soft or sticky?'

'Whatever way you're having them yourself.' I looked at her with wonder. Her unmade-up face glowed with health; her body was perfect as ever in its sheath of tight, black jeans and skinny, mauve sweater. She looked like a woman whose only care in the world was putting up a perfect breakfast of bacon, sausage, egg and tomato.

'What's the point in going on as if it's the end of the world?' she said, as if guessing my thoughts. 'That's what I said to myself this morning when I woke up. Okay, I'm in the club, the father is a complete wanker who doesn't want to know me, but so what?' The plate of food she placed in front of me would have fed a crew of hungry dockers. 'The baby . . . My baby is going to come, and I have to get ready for that, don't I? And I have to be thankful for my good fortune too,' she went on, pouring tea for me. 'I mean, I met you, Daniel, and you've been more helpful to me than anybody could expect.'

'You don't have to . . .' I pushed a piece of sausage around my plate. 'What I mean is, I'm glad I could help.'

Her huge eyes stared at me over her teacup. 'You're a funny man, you know that? But you're a nice man too.'

'There's no need –'

'There is,' she cut in. 'Look, I meant what I said last night. If you want me to, I'll stay. I don't care what the neighbours say . . . anyway, who gives a fuck these days? You don't have to pay for a flat for me. I'm fine here. I'll cook for you and run the house and I promise I'll be quiet, so you get on with your writing and things. And . . .' she hesitated. 'You don't have to sleep with me, or anything like that. I'll stay in your daughter's room and I can get out whenever she's coming to visit. I won't leave a trace of myself behind, she'll never know anybody was here, I promise.'

'Don't.' I put my hand up to stop the torrent of words. 'Please don't. Let's just stick to the plan we made yesterday.'

'But . . .' she was staring down at the table, as if afraid to look at me. 'Don't you want me?'

I laughed. 'Have you any idea,' I asked lightly. 'Of just what a knockout you are?'

'Then why . . .'

'Then nothing,' I said firmly. 'You and I are going to be friends and I'll visit you in your flat if you'll let me.'

'Won't you . . . won't you have a key? I mean . . .'

I could hear the catch in her voice; I could guess at the rasping memory of keys turning in the lock at College Court and doors closing in the early hours of the morning as our wayward professionals headed for connubial nests in the suburbs.

'The keys to the flat will be yours,' I told her gently. 'You decide who comes and goes, okay? How old are you, Kelly? Nineteen? Twenty? Get a life of your own, baby or no baby. This is your time, don't you see that? Have your baby or don't have your baby. Get your degree or don't get it. It's your life, not someone else's, just yours. Get yourself the space to live it and . . . and . . .' I finished lamely, waving my knife and fork about. 'Just be yourself.'

I felt exhausted after my outburst; in a curious way, I felt even angry with myself, as if I ought not to be spending energy and emotion on this young woman who had strayed into my life. I felt, literally, hot under my collar; it occurred to me that, incredibly, I was blushing under Kelly's wide-eyed gaze.

'Your eggs are getting cold,' she said, and there was an edge of wonder in her voice.

I didn't tell Kelly that my helping her had something to do with my last day with Jean, and with the events that followed. It was too personal and, besides, she might not understand. I didn't fully understand it myself; it was more of a feeling than anything else.

In the weeks after that last afternoon with Jean at the Spinney, I went through the motions of living as if I were run on batteries. I took my meals; I gave my tutorials; I went to the library. I engaged with nothing and with nobody. The sheer effort of getting through the present moment made it impossible to remember the one that had gone before or to plan for the one that came after. I mumbled excuses when a couple of other Post-Grads in the History Department invited me for a pint. My mother looked strangely at me when I told Jeff in our kitchen that I was too tired to go out with him; her look grew more searching when, not five minutes after Jeff had left, I put my coat on and told her I was going for a walk.

My walks grew longer. The mechanics of putting one foot in front of the other seemed simple enough for me to perform, and exhausting enough to stifle the memory of Jean; at least for some minutes at a time. Once, unthinkingly, I walked to Spiddal; when I realized that I was faced with a ten-mile hike home, I felt almost pleased. It was nearly four o'clock when I crawled upstairs to my room; the light still shone through the crack in my mother's door.

Only once, too, as the weeks passed and November turned to December, did I see Jean. It wasn't surprising; by now she was spending almost all of her time in the hospital while I moved between the library and the classrooms in the great ugly block of cement and glass that had been raised beyond the quad. I was turning the corner of the canal, on my way to give yet another uninspired tutorial, when I saw her; she was with two other girls, heading for the college gate, coming from the direction of the hospital. All three of them wore long coats and boots; they walked with a nonchalant swagger. Although they were at least a hundred yards away, their laughter was clear and loud in the raw December afternoon. I drew back into the doorway of Ward's shop; thankful I had not bumped into her on the pavement.

I could not imagine what I might say to her if we did meet face-to-face. Five days after the Spinney I had swallowed my pride and my anger and had written to her, begging her to come back to me, promising her all the space she wanted, whenever she wanted it; by return had come a brief note, asking for my trust, and saying that she was still trying to figure things out. Rage and hurt swelled inside me as I stared at the signature: "Yours always, Jean". Twice afterwards I phoned her house. On the first occasion her father answered but it was Jean herself who picked up the phone the second night. I held the receiver to my ear in silence, listening to that familiar voice saying over and over: "Hello? Hello?" There was a long, sibilant pause when I thought I felt her breath in my ear and when she said: "Daniel? Daniel is that you?". I hung up and stepping out of the phone kiosk in Eglinton Street, found the night was sharp with winter.

I might have coped if I had not seen her a week later in the coffee shop. I might have coped, yes, and it might not have changed the course of her life and mine. And I might not have spent the rest of my life trying to forget what I had done.

It was the second week of December; there was a hint of snow in the bitterness of the afternoon. For once, the archway was empty of idlers or chatting groups; the old buildings were murky in the winter gloom. I hurried on towards the steamed-up windows of the coffee shop, figuring I just had time for a warming cup before my class.

It was Leonard's deep voice that I heard as soon as I pushed open the door of the coffee shop. He has a loud rumbling voice; the sort that says you cannot ignore it. Through the clouds of cigarette smoke and steam I could see him clearly, sitting at a corner table with his back to me. The white coffee-cup looked tiny in one of his huge hands; his other arm was draped lightly across Jean's shoulders.

There were others at the table but I had no eyes for them. I saw only that brightly sweatered arm and the huge hand at the end of it, and the thick fingers of the hand close to the face that I had kissed so often, the head of dark hair that I adored.

'Shut the fuckin' door,' someone shouted. 'Or you'll freeze the joint.'

I saw Leonard's fingers idly stroking her hair before I pulled the door shut behind me and stepped back into the December chill. I hurried along the rough track between the trees towards Mahomet and I just made it in time to vomit into the ancient, chipped lavatory bowl.

'There was nothing to it,' Jeff said when we met-up later. 'Sure they're only pals, just hanging around together.'

'Its not the way it looked to me,' I leaned on the garden wall of Jeff's house to steady myself. 'Not the way it looked at all.'

'It's not like you, Danny, getting pissed as early as this,' Jeff said. 'In fact, it's not like you to get pissed at any time.'

'It is the cause, *it is the cause*, Jeff,' I quoted darkly. Was it Othello or Macbeth? Leaning on the counter in the Cellar it had seemed like a good idea to come to Jeff's house but now I wasn't so sure. Fair Hill seemed to tilt beneath my feet; the open doorway of Jeff's house was angled oddly against the night sky.

'The cause is drink,' Jeff said easily. 'And quite a lot of it by the look of you.'

'*Frailty*,' I said. '*Thy name is woman*.' I could remember quoting the line repeatedly to a fellow in Cullinane's until he told me to fuck off and let him drink his pint in peace.

'Sure what about it anyway?' Jeff was in his shirtsleeves; he seemed not to notice the cold of the night, sitting on top of the grey cement wall. 'There's more than one fish in the shaggin' sea . . . Don't tell me you haven't a cracker or two in those First Year classes you're supposed to be teaching. Tell you the truth, Danny boy,' he added, laughing. 'The last woman in the world I'd want for a girl-friend, is a feckin' female med student. They think they know it all and they never shut-the-fuck-up.'

I shook my head. It hurt. 'All is dross that is not Jean.' Shakespeare? Who cared? She had let him touch her hair with his puddingy fingers as if she didn't care that I loved her.

'Look,' Jeff said, taking my arm. 'There's a party tonight up at the hospital, mostly interns, but myself and a few of the lads are asked. Why don't you come along with me? There'll be plenty of drink and plenty of nurses too. What d'you say? Get the taste of some fresh fruit, Danny boy, and forget about this long romance stuff. Are you on?'

'A party? In the hospital?'

'Exactly! Nurses and drink and beds to hand. Are you on?'

Was this what Jean was missing? A grope in the corridors? A fling in some intern's cubicle? Leonard's hands upon her? I had to leave.

'Danny! Wait!'

'Can't.' I didn't turn around to answer him; it was difficult enough to steer a straight course on the pavement.

'What'd you say?' he shouted from behind me.

'Then must you speak of one that loved not wisely . . .'

'Come back, Danny!'

'But too well,' I hiccupped. 'Poor bastard! Poor black bastard, I know how you felt!'

Old Othello at least didn't have to face his mother when he arrived home pissed. She threw me a withering glance when I stumbled in that night but I was too far-gone to care. When I woke the next morning I was still in my clothes, curled foetally on my bed. My head rang with an echoing pain and the room stank with the stench of stale alcohol. The house was silent and I knew that she had already left for work in Crotty's. I washed quickly and put on clean shorts and socks. Minutes later, when I passed Paudge at his usual sentinel post, he opened his mouth as if he would speak to me but something in my expression must have stayed him and we passed each other in silence. I wouldn't have been able to speak to him anyway, not without a fresh drink to still my thumping head.

Keeping track of them was easy. You couldn't miss Leonard's Mini Cooper, the little technicoloured car was a permanent fixture for most of every day at the corner of the handball alley, next to the Engineering Building. When it moved, I moved, following along a safe distance behind on my old Humber bicycle.

Speed and distance didn't seem to matter: from my high perch on the bike it seemed impossible to lose sight of the Mini. I had travelled in it more than once, crammed into the back seat with a couple of others while Len and Jeff swapped rugby yarns up front. Back then, the car's flamboyant colour scheme had seemed no more than another example of Len's swaggering arrogance; now, as I pushed my bike in its wake, I grew to loathe the bright, crimson roof, the green doors and side panels, the deep, yellow bonnet. Easy to follow though!

I tried to keep my eyes fixed on the scarlet roof but, sometimes, rounding a corner, I'd see the car close ahead, in a short line of traffic or maybe pulled up outside a shop, and I couldn't help but catch a glimpse of them inside. I didn't want to see his hand inclining towards hers. I didn't want to see her turn towards Leonard and see her face crease with laughter at something he had said.

Truth is, as far as I can tell, I didn't know what I wanted. I knew I wanted Jean, yes, but I also understood I couldn't have her, not right then anyway. But I didn't want to be skulking in corners, watching for a sight of the technicoloured Mini Cooper. I didn't want to be watching, or be seen watching, him collect her at the hospital each evening. I didn't want to see him drop her off at home in Greenleas. I didn't want to see the car at the side of the Estoria cinema and know that they were inside, together in the darkness, perhaps watching the images on the screen.

Or perhaps not.

I didn't want to feel that I was going out of my mind and that I was powerless to prevent my fall into the pit. Alcohol had always seemed a pointless kind of pleasure to me, yet now I drank steadily through the afternoons and nights, gulping pints down greedily whenever I knew they were indoors and the Mini would be parked for a spell. Alcohol still seemed pointless but now it was also irresistible.

'Are you trying to kill yourself or something?' my mother asked me late one night, when I was fumbling with the bike in our narrow hallway.

'Would anybody even notice?' I answered, trying to shut the hall door behind the bike.

My mother's face grew white. For a moment I thought she would strike me. 'God forgive you,' she said. 'God forgive you!'

She turned away then, climbing the stairs with a creaky gait. I could see the years in her stiffness, in her snow-white hair. Stubbornness and pride kept her at her job in Crotty's even though there was no longer any need for her to work; my grandparents had died within a few months of each other and the Flanagan nest-egg, although never quantified to me, was, she'd said, "more than she'd ever expected or needed".

I was astonished, therefore, when she came into my room the next morning, carrying a mug of tea. I guessed, without looking at my watch, that it was around mid-morning and was sure, or fairly sure, that it wasn't her day off.

'I left after their breakfast. I told herself I had somethin' to do in town,' my mother said, seeing the question in my expression. 'Anyway, I'll be back in plenty of time to have their lunch ready.'

I said nothing, hoping she'd go.

She told me to drink the tea while it was hot.

I sat up reluctantly in the bed, accepting the mug of tea from her hands. She waited until I had taken a sip before she spoke.

'There was a row above in Crotty's this morning,' she began.

'The dining-room door was open and I could hear it in the kitchen. One of the girls was giving out to Leonard; she said it wasn't right for him to be carrying-on with Jean, because she's your girl. His mother wanted to know if it was true, and Leonard said it was nobody's business but his own. Mrs Crotty said it was her business too, that you were a friend of the family, Daniel. She said Leonard had no business coming between you and Jean after you were great with one another all these years. He back-answered her and then the girls started at him and the whole lot of them were at it hammer-and-tongs until Mr Crotty came in and told them all to be quiet, that they were shouting like "a bunch of tinkers".' She was silent a moment, as if remembering the scene, and then she added, 'When I brought Mr Crotty his fresh pot of tea, sure I didn't know where to look.'

I sipped again at my own, not knowing where to look.

'Is it true, Danny, I mean about yourself and Jean . . . and about Leonard?'

'What if it is? Aren't they welcome to each other?' I could hear the sour bitterness in my own voice.

'If you think she's right for you,' my mother said. 'You have to fight for her, and . . . and if she's not, then you have to forget her.'

'I'll do my best,' I said sarcastically. 'And you can tell your precious Crotty's not to be worrying about me. I don't need their pity, or anybody else's either.'

'The Crotty's treat me fairly.' There was anger in my mother's voice now. 'And they've always been nice to you too. You'd want to be blind not to see that the girls up there have always doted on you and I don't want bad blood between us and them.'

'Isn't it a bit late for that? I was there remember! Holding your hand when you ambushed old Crotty into giving you a job!'

'That was a long time ago.'

'What was all that about anyway?'

'That was a long time ago,' she said again.

'I don't care,' I said. 'It was really something, watching you put that oul' fucker in his fucking place –'

'Stop it!' she cried. 'I won't have that kind of language in my house! Your father never used a word of bad language in this house and I won't have it from you either!'

'My father isn't *fucking* here, is he?' Her face was grey with pain but I was unable to stop myself. 'He's not fucking here anymore, is he?'

My mother stumbled, sobbing, from the room; I lay there, listening to the sound of her unsteady steps on the stairs and along the hall, and then the front door was opened and slammed shut. The sobbing noise went on and I realized that it was my own sobbing I was listening to. My body shook; great gobs of hot tears running down my cheeks.

Years later, sitting beside her as she died, I would recall that scene with horror and wish that I had been able to take the hand that, for the first time since my father's death, she reached out to me. By then, it was too late, just one more entry in a lifetime's catalogue of regrets. In the moment when she tried, I scorned her help and reminded her of her own pain. I could not see beyond my own. Jean was gone. The dogs were silent.

'Oh . . . Just dump it anywhere, Daniel.' There was a lilting excitement in Kelly's voice; in the new flat she seemed like a small child surrounded by gifts on Christmas morning. 'And sit yourself down! I'll make us some coffee, okay?'

I propped the black plastic bag against the other refuse sacks in the middle of the living-room floor. I was glad it was the last of them; I felt out-of-breath after the repeated trips up-and-down to the car. While Kelly busied herself in the kitchen alcove, I surveyed the apartment I had contracted to pay for; ubiquitous magnolia walls, two-seater couch, a couple of armchairs; a small dining-room table and four chairs at the other end of the room; a nylon-haired rug in front of the electric fire; two tall windows that looked out at the squat monstrosity that filled Spanish Place. There was a bathroom and one medium-sized bedroom with a double bed.

'It's great,' Kelly said, coming back with two mugs of coffee. 'I can't believe it's mine! I don't know how to thank you.'

I said nothing; I was still trying to get my breath back.

'You look tired.' She looked at me over the rim of her mug, her eyes huge.

'The coffee is great,' I said. 'Just what the doctor ordered.'

'Are you okay, Daniel? I mean, you never said why you were at the doctor's that day when . . . when we first met,' she finished lamely.

'I'm fine,' I said. 'Just a bit out of condition.' Or contrition, I thought.

'It seems a lifetime ago, doesn't it?' She was teasing out some thought, some feeling, of her own. 'But, it's only been a few weeks.' I watched her hands, cradling the coffee-mug, and I found myself wondering what it would be like to be touched by those pale fingers. 'I wish Leonard could see us now,' she said.

'Fuck Leonard,' I said quietly.

'Hardly!' She stood up, and began opening the refuse bags. 'Here it is!' she cried, pushing deep into the belly of one sack. 'Remember this?' she asked.

I looked at the picture in the gilt frame, the spreading fan of cracked glass, the remembered face in the photograph.

I nodded.

'I can't believe I did that,' she said wonderingly. 'I never threw anything at anybody in my life.' I felt the full force of her billion-watt smile then. 'Am I forgiven, Daniel?'

'Of course,' I told her, trying to cover my confusion.

But who, I wondered, would forgive me?

Hardly a day passes that I do not go over and over the events of that last afternoon and night. My action replays make no difference. They cannot change the outcome. An old life ended on that wet day in 1971, a few days before Christmas. No amount of re-running of my tapes can alter that.

I started drinking at lunch-hour that day, in the gloom of

Stoney Carty's pub in Dominick Street. Old Stoney was his usual irascible self but I stayed beyond the range of his sour-tipped barbs, sucking my way methodically through pint after pint at the chipped, red-topped table just inside the door. The alcohol only deepened the despair I felt. The previous night I had supped for a couple of hours in Ward's Hotel while the Mini Cooper sat outside the Estoria; from the door of the bar I'd watched them emerge, arm-in-arm and laughing. I'd tried to follow the car through the rain but had given up, cold and drenched, at Cooke's Corner, unable to figure out which way the car had gone. The night before that I'd pedalled manically to keep the car in sight, all the way from the Skeff to Greenleas. I'd noticed, clutching at straws under a dripping tree that Len was not invited into Jean's house but I also noticed, with mounting anger and bitterness that a quarter of an hour passed before Jean got out of the parked car and Len drove off in a noisy cloud of spray.

'Are you sure you're all right, young Best?' Stoney asked, ancient eyes narrowed, as he placed yet another pint in front of me.

He'd known my father; more than once he'd talked about him to me but I was in no mood now for reminiscences of days that were gone. I put my money on the counter and went back to my place on the soiled, leatherette seating where I nursed my hurt with my pint, scraping and scratching at it until my rawness was bleeding.

It was still seeping out of me as I finished my drink, stood up and left Carty's, to wheel the bike, unsteadily, along the street towards the Galway Arms. Outside once more, the blinding rain was almost welcome. The cold and the wet gave me something else to feel. Or maybe they just numbed me. I left the bike there and buttoning my coat up to my chin, pushed on across O'Brien's Bridge. For a moment I was puzzled by the piles of pine-trees stashed forlornly against the parapet of the bridge: I had forgotten that it was only four days to Christmas and that even in the rain of my misery other people were living lives, buying presents, selling Christmas trees. I wondered if Leonard and Jean were together somewhere on the sodden streets. The university term was over: the technicoloured Mini would not be outside the Engineering Building today, nor had it been parked on Crotty's' drive when I had cycled slowly past earlier in the afternoon.

I stood a while in the bucketing rain outside my old primary school, trying to figure out where to go – or rather, where to drink. Without my hallucinogenic quarry I was lost in the rain and after that, I lost track of myself. On automatic, I probably, was in the Cellar, the Tavern, the Skeff, but the journey into hell is jumbled, the sequence uncertain.

I do remember when it finally dawned on me that I was utterly pissed; I found myself standing outside Patsy Glynn's pub with a pint bottle of Celebration ale in my hand, standing shakily on the corner, trying to steady the wavering lights of Mary and Abbeygate streets. As far as I could make out, I was alone on the road, as if abandoned by the entire town. Focusing with difficulty, I wondered why I had bought the large bottle of ale. I never normally drank the brew but I did now, swaying back and forth on the rain-lashed pavement. I have the haziest recollection of making my way along Lombard Street, past the frozen portraits in the windows of the *Connacht Tribune*, and back again to O'Brien's bridge. The Christmas trees and their marketeers were gone. Across the road, the Galway Arms was closed. How long I stood outside, debating whether I should attempt to ride my bike home, I don't know.

It was the bottle of ale that decided it: I'd surely drop it if I attempted to get up on my bike. I took a long swig, deliberating.

My scrambled mind made up. No matter what the hour, as if that really mattered, it was time to have it all out with Leonard Crotty. The fucker wasn't going to ignore me, just as his bullet-headed father had done so long ago, glancing dismissively at me from the dark interior of his idling car. And so, fortified with drink and numbed with rain and cold and jealousy and rage, I lurched onwards towards Crotty's and my personal date with destiny. Perhaps it was all written in the stars but you couldn't see them, not even if you were sober, hidden up there behind the banks of clouds, at almost midnight, four days before Christmas.

I hardly noticed the few cars that sloshed past me along Sea Road and along the Crescent. I was dimly aware of fairy-lights twinkling on Christmas trees in curtainless windows; I stopped outside one house to blink back at them before pushing on doggedly, bareheaded and sodden. I wondered if the Mini would be there on Crotty's drive.

It wasn't. I knew the big, black car outside the door to be Leonard's father's, the smaller one beside it his mother's. I hung back inside the entrance to the driveway, screened by a large tree, to stare at the lighted windows, remembering how I had first seen Leonard's face grinning out at me from behind the big bay window to the right of the door. I tried to imagine the conversation my mother had overheard in the dining room of the solid, white house. The more I remembered, or imagined, the more I raged. In those pain-drenched moments, standing on his lawn under the big tree, I wanted to strangle Leonard Crotty.

I was slugging the last dregs from the bottle of Celebration when, I finally heard the throaty growl of the Mini Cooper coming up the hill. Leonard cornered into the driveway with his usual, speedy flamboyance and I watched as he came towards me, ploughing psychedelically through the gravel. Suddenly, I took the bottle from my lips and hurled it at the approaching car. Hidden behind the tree, I watched the dark bottle somersault through the darker air, tumbling over and over until it struck the windscreen with a shattering noise. Immediately the car skewed crazily before, in an almost slow-and-gentle motion, colliding with a smaller tree on the other side of the lawn.

The engine's throaty roar was choked; for a moment an eerie silence settled upon the night. The passenger door popped open a little with the impact and the internal reading-light automatically came on. From where I hid behind the tree, it was like looking at a faded, old, sepia photograph. There were two faces in this yellowing picture. One of them moved: Leonard's, frightened, and blurred through the white-frosted glass of the damaged windscreen. The other face was hidden, slumped over the dashboard, but I would know that head of dark hair behind a thousand fractured screens.

And then there was the slow-motion nightmare in the wet night. Leonard pushing open the driver's door and the horn of the car blaring urgently and endlessly through the darkness. I watched his head turn frantically from Jean to the still-silent house as he kept his hand on the horn. I whimpered in the darkness, unable to move or help him. More lights went on in the house. The front door flung open and Mr Crotty was standing on the porch, peering into the darkness.

'What's going on out here?' he shouted.

'An ambulance!' I heard Leonard call. 'Jeanie's hurt! Get an ambulance.'

In a blur I watched as Mr Crotty took command. He came charging through the rain, dressing-gown flapping about his huge bulk, his wife and daughters flapping after him. One of them was immediately dispatched back to the house for umbrellas, another for the keys of his car. Frightened now, lest I be seen, I buried myself against the rough trunk of my sheltering tree and strained to hear what was being said. A stone on the windscreen, Leonard said, or maybe a low-flying bird, he wasn't sure. It didn't matter now, his mother said, the important thing was to get Jean to the hospital.

Mr Crotty pulled his car down alongside the Mini and then, with surprising care and gentleness, he and Leonard manoeuvred Jean out of the passenger seat. The girls swung the black umbrellas above them as their mother cradled Jean's head in her hands. My heart pounded louder than the rain on the umbrellas. Jean's head suddenly moved and in the light of the headlights I saw Mrs Crotty smile down at her. My knees threatened to give way for I knew then that I had not killed her. They put her in the back seat of Mr Crotty's car, between his wife and one of the girls, and the big car moved slowly out towards the road. Leonard and his other two sisters piled into his mother's car and sped off in pursuit.

I waited there, until silence had settled again before I stepped out from my hiding-place. I could barely grasp what I had just witnessed, what I had done, and almost done. Instantly sober, I was betrayed by a kind of self-preserving cunning, a survival trait, which, for years afterwards – perhaps still – filled me with a sense of shame. I began to search among the sodden shrubs and flowerbeds for the fragments of the Celebration bottle; I found, instead, the dark-green bottle whole and undamaged, gleaming on the slick grass. I could only surmise that it was the thick, heavy base of the bottle that had collided with the windscreen, rebounding unbroken onto the lawn. I stuffed the bottle into my coat pocket and conscious of the glare from the house of left-on lights slunk out onto the sloping escapeway of Taylor's Hill.

I didn't go home. I headed for the hospital and stood opposite, shamed and shivering, in the doorway of Kelehan's pub until Mr Crotty's car exited from the entrance, followed a few minutes later, by Leonard at the wheel of his mother's car. Only then did I step inside the phone kiosk and dial the hospital switchboard. I waited while the number went on ringing somewhere in the silent building across the road; when, eventually, a tired voice answered and I enquired about Miss Jean Martin, admitted that night as a casualty patient, I was asked to hold again until I was put through to the ward. A different voice answered; again, I stated my inquiry.

'Are you a relative?' the voice asked.

I hung up, the receiver heavy in my hand as I stared across at the dark hospital. No, I wanted to immediately confess, I'm the fellow who put her there.

I held the bathroom door ajar, listening to the voices approaching in the corridor outside. A couple of nurses, discussing plans for their Christmas. Two ward attendants pushing a high, metal trolley laden with rattling cups and plates that almost drowned out their rough voices. Getting ready for lunch, wishing they were somewhere else.

Like myself, I thought, a criminal drawn into his victim's

orbit. To my left, a guilty face stared back from the bathroom mirror; red eyes hollow under long, dark hair. I'd washed it and taken a bath but no amount of scrubbing in the tiny new bathroom in our house could wipe away the hung-over, hung, look on my face. Like Cain, I thought, turning away from the reflection, my own rage had marked me forever.

I stepped out into the corridor of the long ward. From the nurses' station at the end of the corridor came the sound of a phone ringing, and then a low, indistinct voice. I had headed straight to the visitor's bathroom on reaching the ward, propelled by the urgency of my fear. "She is in St Mary's ward", the receptionist downstairs had informed me, yielding reluctantly to my garbled protestations that I was Jean's brother and hadn't heard about the accident until this morning. "Room 9", he'd added, looking at me distastefully, before reminding me that visitors were not allowed until the afternoon.

I pushed open the green door of Room 9 tentatively. The second bed in the room, by the window, was empty but in the near bed Jean was sleeping, propped up on pillows, her hands resting outside the covers. I hesitated. Her face was pale and her breathing sounded heavy through her parted lips, but it was the bandage that made me swallow and gulp nervously, a thick swathe of it, wound around her head, covering her right eye completely. I stood in the doorway, afraid.

'You can go in if you like.'

I jumped at the facilitating intrusion.

A small, fair-haired nurse was standing behind me, a pair of sheets draped across her folded arms. 'It's okay,' she said, smiling at me. 'We won't bite you.'

I shifted nervously from foot to foot, searching for words. 'Will she . . . will she be okay?'

'She'll be home for Christmas dinner . . . She was just a bit shook up, concussed, you know.' There was a hint of laughing mockery in the pale, blue eyes. 'Are you the boyfriend?'

I shrugged, closing the door, looking for an exit, anxious to be gone. 'I'll come back after dinner,' I said.

'She'll be awake by then. She's still out after the sedative.'

'Thanks, so.'

'For nothing at all.'

She turned away then, a small, stout figure on flat-heeled shoes and for a moment I envied her the confined horizons of this ward, with its rounds and routines and comforting sedatives. I knew what I must do and the knowledge did not cheer me.

'Nurse!' My own voice sounded loud in the deserted corridor.

She turned back to me, a smile still on her lips.

'Will Jean . . . will she be marked?'

Her smile broadened, compassionate. 'She has a few stitches and they had to cut away some of her hair to dress the wound on her head.' She walked back to stand beside me before continuing. 'She might have a little mark beside her eye when the stitches come out . . . Just a teeny-weeny one, mind. But sure won't that just make her more beautiful for you!' She laid a hand on my sleeve, amused by her own notion. 'Sure, you could even kiss it better if you wanted to.'

Her creamy-skinned innocence was too much. I had no right to these well-intentioned sallies. I knew what I knew. I turned away, from her and from Room 9, muttering my thanks as I almost ran along the corridor. Her cheerful "goodbye" followed me down the corridor and down the stairs but it could not blot out the image of Jean's shaven head and the teeny-weeny mark that she would bear for the rest of her life.

'And what about your studies?' I had just told my mother I was going away. 'Are you just goin' to throw everythin' away like that after all the work you've put into it? Is that what you're goin' to do, Daniel?'

'There's nothing else I can do, Mam.' I wanted to be gone from the kitchen. Upstairs, out, anywhere that I didn't have to look at the panic in my mother's face. 'I have to go. I can't stick it here any longer.'

'But what will you do in London?'

'I'll get a job . . . Don't worry. There's always work in London, you know that.'

'I didn't raise you to go labourin' on a buildin' site!'

I turned to leave; I couldn't bear the open wound in her words. 'I have to go, Mam, I have things to do.'

'It's Jean, isn't it?' she said. 'And the accident. But . . .' I felt her eyes upon me. 'Glory be to God . . . But sure you had nothin' to do with that, had you?'

I couldn't meet her pleading eyes. 'I'm going now, Mam.'

'If you won't talk to me,' she said, almost weeping. 'Wouldn't you at least talk to somebody else? Would you not go and have a word about it with Mr Crotty or even Mrs Crotty . . . Please, Daniel.'

It was her mention of the Crotty's that made me decide to leave that evening and not to wait, as I'd planned, until the following morning. Mr Crotty would see through me at once, in his bullying way; so, in a kinder way, would his wife. The thought of being confronted by either of them galvanised me into panic-stricken action.

Heedless now of my mother's pleas, I hurried upstairs and began to pile clothes and books into a blue tote bag that I'd used to hold my swimming gear and a smaller duffle bag that I used for college. Packing didn't take long. When I was finished I stood at the chest of drawers, beside the window overlooking our backyard, and I started my letter to Jean. There was so much I wanted to say to her, so much to explain, but looking down into the empty space, where once old Mutt and Prince had drenched my face with their pink tongues and my father's rough hand had tousled my unruly hair, the words deserted me. I stared through the window into an abyss that was beyond forgiveness, into a past that was beyond recall and the few lines I did manage to write to her seemed trite, inadequate and cowardly.

From downstairs, my mother shouted "goodbye", and that she was going back to Crotty's. 'I'll talk to you when I come home,' she pleaded. 'Okay?'

I said nothing and moments later I heard the front door open and close. When I came downstairs, I checked the clock in the kitchen. It was almost 2.50 and there was just enough time for me to make it to the bank. I tried to close my eyes against the familiar objects of my life; the enamel teapot with the dented lid, the red-and-white tea cloth on its hook by the sink, the narrow hall with its floor of shining linoleum, the Sacred Heart-topped holy water font inside the door. I tried to erase the images, but knew I would carry them with me always, in my baggage-laden heart. When I finally pulled the door of the small house on Paternoster Lane shut behind me, it was as though I were saying goodbye to a part of myself.

On the corner of the Lane, Paudge eyed my bags. 'You're off on your travels, Danny boy,' he asked.

Impulsively I burrowed in my pocket, my fingers searching among the loose change. Paudge looked curiously at me, then back at the half-crown I had handed him. I hardly knew why. A penitential offering? A sop to angry gods? 'Have a drink on me, Paudge,' I said, taking up my bags again.

'Have a good Christmas, Danny,' he said. 'Wherever you're off to.'

Even when I turned the corner I felt his eyes upon my back.

The bank was full of queues. Shopkeepers heaved fat sacks and dog-eared lodgment books onto the shining counter; cashiers in shirtsleeves cracked jokes. You could smell the Christmas frivolity in the booze-laden breaths of the customers.

'You want it all?' the teller asked when I handed him my deposit book. He was sandy-haired, about my own age, with a residue of teenage pimples around the corner of his mouth.

I nodded at him. Over two hundred pounds remained in the savings account, harvested through a long summer of late nights at the casino.

'You must be going on a mighty piss-up for Christmas.' The teller grinned at me as he started to count out the notes.

It was 3.30 when they let me out of the bank but there was still time, more than enough time, to do what I had to do.

I turned my collar up against the biting wind that had

followed in after the previous night's rain and hurried as best I could along the street. The sight of my bike, still leaning against the wall of the Galway Arms, defiant, unmolested, astonished me. I pushed it ahead of me into the dimly lit porch of the pub.

The bar was crowded with Christmas drinkers but Tommy caught my wave and came to the corner of the bar.

'You're looking the worse for wear,' he said, laughing.

'My bags, Tommy,' I said. 'Can I leave them here with you for a little while?'

'No problem,' he said, taking the bags in behind the counter.

'And my bike,' I went on. 'Later on, can I leave it in the porch? Ask Jeff to take it away with him the next time he's in.'

I saw the curiosity in his eyes and the question on his lips, but he merely nodded: perhaps it was the long years as a barman that lent him his discretion, or perhaps it was just indifference to the idiosyncratic behaviour of students.

'Sure.'

I cut up through Nuns' Island on the bike, then out behind the grey-green bulk of the cathedral, the newish pseudo-classical building known to students and wags of the town as "the bishop's last erection". Passing its granite tumescence, I recalled an earlier time and purple-draped shoulders inclining towards me in front of the altar of the old pro-cathedral, fat lips moving in a puffy, disdainful face and a hand on my cheek and stickiness on my forehead. Choosing Thomas as my confirmation name had been easy. I didn't know it then but the bishop would soon be called to the happy hunting grounds where, no doubt, he has been provided with appropriate quarters, far removed from the likes of Tom Best and his pair of optimistic greyhounds.

I was a sorry soldier of Christ. I hadn't set foot inside a church in years, yet now, pedalling on towards the hospital, I almost wished I could enter again that dark, cool world of whispered sins and murmured pardon. I knew however, that I had gone beyond that easy pale of promised redemption; to a state of exile and mind, where forgiveness did not, would not, come calling.

It was visiting hour at the hospital and I hung back on the

landing of St Mary's, watching for the little blonde nurse while keeping an eye on the closed door of Room 9. I had almost given up hope when at last she emerged from the multi-bedded section at the far end of the corridor. I waved at her, almost furtively, and she came breezily towards me, a smile on her mouth in recognition.

'What are you doing skulking out here?' she asked. 'Jean's awake . . . her parents went into her a while ago. I'm sure –'

'I can't stay,' I said quickly. 'Will you give her this? Please.'

She turned the envelope over in her hands, examining it. 'You don't want to give it to her yourself?'

I shook my head. 'I can't stay,' I said again.

She raised a penciled eyebrow. 'Okay,' she said. 'I'll be the postman.'

'And . . .' I hesitated. 'Will you wait until her visitors are gone?'

'And there's nothing in this mysterious letter,' she waved the envelope about with a laugh, 'that could upset my patient?'

'No,' I said, trying to smile. 'Of course not.'

She folded the envelope then and put my letter away in the pocket of her uniform. We said Happy Christmas to each other and I hurried down the cold stairs, still anxious lest I bump into any of the Crotty's or any members of Jean's own family.

My face was wet from windblown tears as I pedaled back into town. Perhaps it was the wind in my eyes or perhaps it was my heart, trying to steel itself against the image of Jean in that antiseptic room, her wounds wrapped in bandages, her family about her. There was no place in that gathering for me, but there was no other place I wanted to be.

Tommy was busy when I got back to the Galway Arms and parked my bike in the porch. One of the other barmen gave me my bags and I left quickly. I had to cross O'Brien's Bridge but after that I took the back streets. I met no one I knew, shouldering my bags along the darkening streets. When I rounded the corner of Merchant's Road I could sense the crowds and the gaiety from the top of the Square so I turned away from it, heading for the quietness of Forster Street. The small, gloomy bar I went into was unknown to me, but it would do to kill the time in before the evening train to Dublin. The few drinkers at the counter looked at me with unconcealed curiosity at first, but after that they ignored me, seated in the darkest corner of the pub. I barely touched my pint: maybe it was my own bitterness that made the dark stout taste even tarter than usual.

Ahead lay a journey that I had no stomach for, but it was one, which seemed unavoidable. There was no longer a place for me in this town where I had grown up; the quicker I was gone, the better. The train to Dublin and a B&B overnight stay before taking the bus to the airport the next day. "There'd be no problem getting a flight out", the travel agent had said, "Sure wasn't everybody coming back home at this time of year".

Jean would be home for Christmas, the little, smiling nurse had said. At least she wouldn't forget me. Every time she'd look in the mirror she'd have the marks of my madness staring back at her. And she could always re-read the handsome apology in my letter:

Dearest Jean,
I am deeply sorry for all that has happened.
All of it is my fault and mine alone.
Believe me, I would give anything to be able
to undo all that has been done. Please believe that.
I'm going away for a while. I don't know yet
when I'll be coming back – if at all.
Please forgive me.
You were always the whole world to me.
Yours,
> *Daniel*

A masterpiece of cowardly evasion, garnished with a generous dollop of self-pity. Perhaps Jean would read my so-called apology just once before tearing it into tiny pieces and flushing it down the lavatory of St Mary's ward, discarding it as irrelevant as I was discarded.

Nobody turned to look when I stood up and walked out of the bar. It was as if I had never been there.

Chapter 17

Rafe O'Hanlon's office is on the first floor of City Hall. The pictures are pretty much what you'd expect to find in the office of the Chief Planning Officer; framed prints of street-plans showing the development of the city from those terrified days when Cromwell's storm-troopers marched through the town and taught the cowed natives that the meek do not inherit the earth. Not that there had been much by way of development for a few hundred years: potato markets and fish markets seemed the pinnacle of industrial achievement until the 1960's when the town finally stirred, like a beast waking, prodded into life by the new storm troopers, the new roundheads preaching a new gospel of dollars and development.

The Chief Planning Officer didn't really need to refer to the hand-painted charts with their antique spelling to study the town's accelerated, sprawling growth. All one had to do was look through the windows of Rafe's corner-office to see the living; and the dying, enactment of the story. Through the clear glass behind him I could see the old hulk of the Grammar School, derelict on the hill, windows smashed or boarded over, its walls peeling in the morning rain and, all around the decrepit building, the yellow, executive-style homes blooming like triffids eyeing up their prey.

'So,' I said at last, after we had exchanged civilities about the dreadful weather and traffic. 'You are going to tell me that this rumour I'm hearing is just a load of old cobblers.'

Rafe fingered his moustache thoughtfully. The moustache is jet-black, which is odd, because Rafe's hair and eyebrows have been near-white for as long as I can remember. Maybe that's why he strokes it so often, I thought, to remind himself of the man he used to be.

'As you well know, Daniel,' Rafe said. 'This planning office deals only in facts, not in rumours.'

'I'd be glad to hear that this particular rumour is not a fact.'

'Be specific,' he demanded.

There's preciseness about Rafe O'Hanlon; maybe it comes from having to deal with so many lawyers and architects intent on blasting highways through your most carefully crafted prose.

'Exactly the same location as the last time I sat in this office, Rafe.'

Once more the delicate fingers set about stroking the black moustache. 'I figured, when you phoned, Daniel, that's . . . that's what you wanted to see me about.'

'Just tell me it's only a rumour. Tell me we sorted the Spinney planning-issues out last time around: recreational and amenity use only. It's all up there,' I said, gesturing towards the maps on the walls. 'In the city development plan.'

'Yes, we did sort it, didn't we?'

'And you helped, Rafe, we all know that.'

It had really been more of a skirmish than a campaign. At the time, five years earlier, it had almost seemed that Leonard Crotty's advisors had been slipshod in their planning and half-hearted in their efforts but Rafe's help had made our – an ad-hoc group of anti-development campaigners – job easier in stopping any development on the Spinney. The suddenness of Leonard's capitulation had left us slightly stunned but it had left me uneasy too. Perhaps, I thought at the time, the Greeks were quietly building a wooden horse in the shelter of the nearest headland. "No chance", Rafe had said then, when I'd voiced my misgivings to him: "As long as I'm planning officer here, nobody will ever get permission to build on the Spinney". I believed him, partly because I had come to know him for being an honest man but partly also because I wanted to believe him. Yet inside me I was being reminded by a small insistent voice that people like Leonard Crotty did not shell out huge sums of money to the heirs of an old spinster for land that could never be built on.

Now, however, Rafe looked at me across his large, immaculate desk and said: 'It's true, Daniel. There's planning permission for a development of flats on the Spinney.'

In the silence that settled on the office the rain was insistent, drumming with erratic fingers on the big windows; farther off, up the hill, a loose door flapped and clattered in the dead school.

'You can't be serious,' I said into the silence.

'I wish I were not.'

'Then why did you give the *fucking* permission?'

'I didn't,' Rafe said. 'I mean, *I didn't*.'

'If you didn't, then who did? You're the head honcho here, aren't you?'

'It's a long story, Daniel.'

'I've got time for a long story.'

So long as it's not too long, I thought. So long as you finish it this morning, before the tiredness engulfs me, before the rain drowns us all in watery possibilities and the wind chokes us with barbed regrets. On my way up to City Hall that morning I'd slowed almost to a standstill outside the small, pokey pub in Forster Street where I'd spent my last hour in town in that vanished life; although I'd been back for years I'd never set foot in the place again. Perhaps Kelly had ventured into it, in search of atmosphere: it wasn't far from Leonard Crotty's love-nest in College Court.

'After all,' I said. 'Stories are what my life is all about.'

'Is that what this is about, Daniel? A story for *NewsTruth*?'

I'm a magazine columnist, not a newspaperman, but even I know when somebody wants to talk off the record.

'I doubt if the great American public wants to hear about planning intrigues in the West of Ireland,' I said drily. 'Anyway, if there's scandal here, surely I'll be reading about it in the local papers?'

'You think they'll jeopardise all those pages of house-advertising by the great and the good for the sake of a story?'

Rafe's deadpan expression reminded me of yet another reason for liking him: he belonged to neither clique nor club in town. Before his appointment here, he'd worked as an assistant in the planning office in his native Belfast; he'd come south with his wife and kids in the 70s and, in the almost hysterical hands-across-the-border welcome for northern refugees, had been the surprise choice as Chief Planning Officer for Galway. I'd been in London then, trying to survive; what I knew of Rafe O'Hanlon was gleaned from occasional sightings in the *Connacht Tribune* and the little he had told me about himself during our dealings about the Spinney. He did not play golf, nor was he known to frequent the clubhouse. He kept a small boat with an outboard on the lake and sometimes I'd see him and his wife – small, neat and dapper like himself – marching briskly along the prom.

'Maybe I'll write about it,' I said. 'But anything you tell me will remain unattributed.'

'Outline permission for a development of flats on the Spinney has been given to Prospector Enterprises Ltd.' Rafe's thin lips seemed to curl downwards in distaste. 'It was a fix but the permission is legal.'

The rain went on hammering on the windows. I tried to speak but my throat was dry and constricted.

'And that's it,' Rafe said. 'End of story.'

I found my voice. 'Tell me the fucking story, Rafe!'

'It's a pathetic story, so pathetic you won't believe it.'

'Try me.' A lifetime's trawling through a landscape of pregnant virgins and three-legged dogs had given me a somewhat generous view of the frailties and deviousness of my fellow-humans. 'I'm all ears.'

'You need to know how our system works in here,' Rafe

began. 'We get applications in here from different kinds of sources: sometimes from owners who want to build on their sites, or maybe extend or rebuild entirely their existing buildings. Sometimes the applications come from builders who are going to do the job. More often than not, for major projects, the application is sent in by a firm of architects acting for the developers.' The moustache was stroked again. For a moment Rafe's dark eyes met mine but then he looked away, as if he could read something in the bucketing rain. 'That's what happened with the application for the Spinney. The planning application was made by Healy & Heffernan, Solicitors acting for Prospector Enterprises,' Rafe said with sudden savagery. 'And then the application disappeared.'

'Disappeared?'

'As in dropped out of sight.' Rafe made a face. 'Every application we get is given a registration number the day it arrives and the application is assigned to one of my staff for processing. The applicant is legally entitled to a response within one month. In this case, the Healy & Heffernan application for Prospector Enterprises, that didn't happen. Seven days after the expiry date we had a letter couriered to us by the architects pointing out to us that we ourselves were in breach of the Planning Acts and that their clients were going to exercise their statutory rights.'

Rafe fell silent. I could guess the answer but I needed to hear it from him.

'What rights?' I asked.

'The legislation is clear on this point.' Rafe's tone was flat, emotionless. 'Where an applicant is not given a reply within a calendar month, then the planning authority . . . meaning us . . . is obliged to allow the applicant the permission for which he applied.'

The rain was running in shapeless rivers on the windows.

'So,' I said slowly. 'You fuck up on your own internal procedures and Leonard Crotty walks away with permission to make money out of the Spinney.'

'Not Leonard Crotty . . . Prospector Enterprises.'

'D'you think there's any difference?'

'It's not the point, though, is it?'

'No,' I said. 'It's not. The point is just too impossible to believe . . . I mean, how could a file like this just go missing, especially when everybody knows the consequences?'

'That *is* the point, Daniel, isn't it?'

'So how could it happen?'

'We're overworked,' Rafe said. 'I kid you not. The town is booming, there's a flood of building applications in here, but I don't have even one more person on my staff now than the day I took this job.'

I could no longer contain my anger. 'Your office makes a monumental cock-up like this and that's all you've got to say about it? That you're overworked and understaffed!'

'We're even more understaffed now than we used to be. When the Spinney application came in, my department had three planning assistants and three clerks in our general office. As of last week I still had my three planning assistants but I'm down to just two clerks in the department.'

I looked at Rafe, puzzled, wondering why he was so specific in giving details about staff numbers. It suddenly dawned. 'Someone left last week?' I asked.

'Someone got fired last week,' Rafe said with loaded implication.

'So, off the record, you are saying Leonard got to somebody,' I prompted, not having to be a genius to work out what had transpired. 'He had a friend at court who'd lose the file and conveniently re-discover it when it was too late to do anything about it.'

'You have to draw your own conclusions,' he said, with a learned political evasiveness.

'So, tell me, Rafe,' I looked long and hard at him, 'who had to leave your department?'

'You remember Stephen Conroy? Thin, timid –'

'Of course I remember him,' I interrupted. Five years

previously Stephen had lingered beside the photocopying machine in the general office next door, trying to delay me in nervous conversation after he'd handed me copies of some planning procedural documents. I'd sensed his loneliness; at the time I'd put it down to being a middle-aged clerk, without hope of promotion, in an office that was run by two younger women. 'There was something about him!'

'Stephen's wife is wheelchair-bound; she's been suffering from MS for years. He has three daughters, all of them at home. Two of them are at university and the youngest is still at school.' He was looking out at the rain again. 'God knows how they're going to survive now.'

'But you sacked him anyway.'

'There wasn't anything else that could be done. His fingerprints were all over this; he was the one who issued the receipt for the application, who issued the registration number for the file and who, six weeks later, suddenly remembered that the application was lying in the bottom drawer of his own desk.'

'But the whole thing is so obvious . . . so childish, I mean . . .'

'I did warn you that it was pathetic, didn't I?' Rafe made a face. 'As soon as I found out about this, I had to take it to the City Manager. Although there was no doubt about Stephen's involvement when we confronted him he admitted nothing. He just kept on repeating that he'd forgotten the application was in his desk. I almost felt sorry for the poor sod; it was like he had no spunk left in him, probably never had it, anyway, now that I think of it. So we couldn't not give permission, not without some evidence that Stephen hadn't just screwed up all on his own.'

'But why? Why would he do this?'

'You tell me.' Rafe's laugh was bitter. 'He didn't even object when he was told he was being fired for gross negligence.'

We were both silent for a while. I imagine Rafe's thoughts were much like my own: the Spinney scarred, wounded, a weak man on the slagheap of life; the rich get richer and the poor get fucked.

'How will he manage?' I asked at last. 'I mean, d'you think

Leonard will give him some kind of a job . . . look after him in some way?'

Rafe snorted. 'Unlikely! D'you think the Leonard Crotty's of this world look after the Stephen Conroy's of the world when they're finished with them?'

I saw the wetness at the corners of Rafe O'Hanlon's eyes and I wondered if his tears were of rage against Leonard Crotty or of pity for an unemployed local government official, whom now had to explain to his sick wife and three young daughters why he no longer had a job. Perhaps both. In the keening of the rain on the windows I could hear my mother's voice, wounded but uncowed, asking old Mr Crotty for a job.

I stood up and shook hands with Rafe, thanked him and told him I'd keep in touch. I'm not sure he heard me. When I looked back at him from the office door, he was still staring at the rain-lashed windows. I wondered if he, too, could hear voices in the rain.

'He's not here right now.' The voice on the phone was adult and confident. 'Who's calling?'

'I'm an old friend of Stephen's. I've been out of touch for a while.' It wasn't much of a lie. 'Is that Mrs Conroy?'

'No, this is his daughter, Karen.' One of the girls at university probably, I thought. 'Dad's at work. You can call him there if you want to.'

'At work?'

'City Hall.' There was laughter on the line. 'You know, the bunker on the hill.'

'City Hall,' I repeated.

'Yes, or call him here this evening. Dad's usually home around 6.00.'

'I'll do that.'

'Can I tell Dad who called?'

'Best,' I said. 'Daniel Best.'

A pause then, followed by an audible intake of breath.

'The writer?'

'That's me,' I said, hating what I was doing and myself.

'I read your book, Mr Best. It was lovely, just lovely and . . . and warm. I really liked it.'

'Thank you.'

'I'll tell Dad you called. D'you want him to phone you back?'

That wasn't necessary, I told Karen Conroy. I thanked her again and then hung up quickly. The girl's words of halting praise made me feel guilty. Sometimes I wished I had never written the bloody book. I hadn't opened it in years, except to sign a copy for somebody. Trouble was, I didn't need to open the damn thing. The whole thing was still there in my head.

Now Karen Conroy was in there too. I wondered what she looked like, this student with the engaging telephone manner who still didn't know that her father had been fired from his job in City Hall. What did Stephen hope to gain by postponing the inevitable? His family would eventually have to be told the truth. Perhaps not: perhaps Stephen Conroy hoped to have a new job by then. We all have our personal methods of escaping from the truth. More to the point, what did I hope to gain by meeting Stephen? What was done, was done. It could not be undone. But maybe, just maybe, Leonard could be undone, even if only in some small way. He treated people, and places, like dirt to be disposed of, and he shouldn't be allowed to go on getting away with it. Just once, somebody needed to retaliate and perhaps it was unavoidable that weaklings like Stephen Conroy would get wounded in the process of retaliation.

Or so I tried to convince myself, staring out my front window at the greyness of Paternoster. It had been raining all day, without let-up since I'd left City Hall that morning. How could you get through such a day, dodging neighbours, enduring the sodden hours until it was time to go home and pretend you had punched another day at the office?

They start work at City Hall at 9.00 but I didn't know if Stephen

Conroy used go to work on foot or by car or bus, so I was in position next morning by 8.15. Better be sure than sorry was one of my mother's favourite maxims. I pulled my car in near the top of hill on which the Conroy's live; their house indistinguishable from any of the hundreds of others that make up the Tirellan area estate. Supporting a family of five on a minor local government employee's salary doesn't leave much over for extravagances such as conservatories or aluminum double-glazing. The Conroy garden was tidy and the wooden windows looked freshly painted but otherwise the house probably looked as it had when it was first built twenty years earlier. If Leonard had seduced Stephen with his filthy lucre, then his house certainly wasn't giving the game away, at least not on the outside. Neither was the car on the drive, an elderly Mirafiori estate car.

At 8.30, Stephen came out of the house carrying a black, attaché case. With him was a girl who had to be his youngest – about thirteen or fourteen, short and plump, dressed in the navy-blue coat and black stockings of the Mercy Convent. They got into the old car and I gave them a good head start before easing away from the kerb and following down the hill. I had the sensation of feeling trapped in a bad B-movie storyline, an unshaven, hung-over Sam Spade or Philip Marlowe trying to earn a buck. I'd had another rough night: Bee had neither phoned nor written and I was beginning to fear I'd never hear from her again. Whatever Stephen Conroy had done or not done, I could not help envying him the simple pleasure of ferrying his daughter to school along the Headford Road.

I wasn't used to this side of town, at least not in the morning. The two-lane highway was choked with bumper-to-bumper commuter traffic, the same commuters who fed the bottomless maw of Leonard and his like with endless deposits and even more endless repayments. Stephen Conroy's car was a hundred yards in front of me but it didn't matter. Yesterday's rain had given way to the bright clear frostiness of a November morning and anyway, if I did lose him, I now knew his first stop.

After passing the old Town Hall and Court House, the red

Mirafiori swung left into the narrow road by the river. I followed and pulled in behind where Stephen had parked; watching while his daughter leaned across in the front of the car and kissed him on the cheek. I watched as the car-door slammed shut and the girl give a final wave to her father. Then she was gone, skipping behind the rusting, metal railings of the school with an unexpected lightness.

The street was clear but Stephen made no move to pull away from the footpath.

Come on! I urged him. Move. Let me see where you spend your days. Where you while away the tedious hours until you motor back to your neat semi-detached house in Tirellan. Back to your womenfolk who lift their unsuspecting faces for your lying touch, your kiss of betrayal. Move, Stephen, so I don't have to go on sitting here, knowing and remembering that I am master of that kind of touch, that brand of kiss.

The red car moved at last. I followed, back around the block, then right into Eglinton Street, up past the still-closed doors of pubs, giftware shops, the GPO, the Cellar. When we turned onto the Square I thought, for one absurd moment, that he was, indeed, heading for City Hall and that he would sit there in the employees' carpark until it was time to go home again. I was trying to figure out what I would do when he swung right at the foot of the Square, past the front of the Great Southern hotel, then left towards the docks.

It was well after 9.00 now, and the traffic was thinning out. Only a few late stragglers held the roads, hurrying towards the factories and the industrial estates that have been spawned on the north and east of the town. Stephen led me away from the docks, swinging left by the old Dominican church. The few pedestrians on the street marched purposefully with windsailing arms but one young couple caught my attention. They dawdled by like hip-to-hip Gemini: you could almost smell the sweat and the semen of the night past from their locked hands and slow-motion limbs. Stephen didn't seem to be driving much faster than the strolling pair. Perhaps this was how he spent the day, driving in circles around the town, feasting his eyes on the green holdings and yellow cranes plastered with the name: CROTTY.

Cruising slowly along the Salthill prom, with the winter sea strangely still in the windless morning, I thought perhaps he was heading for the country, out along the coast road. Instead, he turned up Threadneedle, still barely breaking out of second gear. At the top of the slope Stephen took a right, heading down Taylor's Hill. The lights changed before I could follow him but it was of no importance now. I had a pretty shrewd idea where Stephen Conroy was headed. I remembered my mother approaching the Crotty home from the other end of the hill, on foot, my hand in hers. Stephen, I figured, was on a like errand, in search of work.

I was wrong and driving slowly, so sure of our destination, I almost missed him. I came round a bend on the hill, a really tricky one below Maunsell's Road, just in time to see the tail of the old, red car turning into a narrow lane. When we were kids, we called it just that, the Lane, but the blue-and-white street-plate declared its official title: Winchester Lane; a nominal reminder of "Olde England" for some forgotten freebooter who felt lonesome under the sullen glances of locals who had once owned the field and rocks that he so carefully re-christened. Maybe it was the same lonesome pirate who named the scrubby hillside patch where trees had never grown: the Spinney. The names lingered although the pirates, the foreign ones, anyway, had disappeared over the horizon of the twentieth century.

Stephen seemed not to notice when I drew up behind his car in the lane. He was standing with his back to me at the top of the Spinney, looking out over the town. His hands were sunk into the pockets of a cheap-looking, fawn-coloured Mac; the coat was short and narrow-shouldered, like a leftover from some 70s charity-shop. My feet crunched on the rough, frosted grass but still he didn't turn around. I wondered what he was seeing, beyond and below him.

Perhaps Stephen too was wishing he were in Winchester.

'Good morning, Stephen.'

When he turned towards me, I was, for a moment, shocked by the change in him. The clerk who had tried to detain me in chat at City Hall a few years ago had been a slim, thin-faced fellow with a slightly diffident air; the man who looked at me now was gaunt-faced, with furrows etched in his pale skin and in his eyes the look of someone who was hunted and frightened. There was no recognition in the eyes. Only fear.

'Daniel Best,' I said, standing beside him. 'I spoke to your daughter on the phone.'

'Ah.' The hollow eyes seemed to focus. 'Yes, Karen told me.' He looked suddenly from me to my car. 'Were you following me, Mr Best?' His eyes shifted and he went on, more meekly: 'I mean, how did you know I was here?'

'Daniel,' I said. 'My name is Daniel.'

'I have to go now.' He looked away but he didn't move. 'I'll be late for work.'

'Your daughter thinks you're still in the planning office.' He flinched with reality of my words but I pressed on. 'Why won't you tell your family you don't work there any more, Stephen?'

'What are you trying to do to me?' he pleaded.

It was my turn to flinch: the face that looked into mine was like an open wound. 'I only want to talk to – '

'Amn't I destroyed already? Why won't you leave me alone?'

'I only want to help you.'

'I heard that before and look where it got me!' He shook off the hand I had laid on his arm and stepped back from me. 'This is where it got me. No job and a family to feed and a mortgage to pay.'

He began to weep, thin shoulders twitching under the polyester coat, and I waited, watching for my opening. He took a white hanky from his pocket and in its crisp, folded neatness I could see the hands of one of his daughters, bent over the ironing board, helping out in place of her chair-bound mother. He blew his nose noisily and wiped his eyes and there was a spark of defiance in his voice when he spoke. 'It's none of your business where I'm working.'

He started to walk away towards the estate car and I knew – I wanted to believe – that I had to say it then.

'It *is* my business when somebody is fiddling the books and losing files and making a fortune from building fucking flats on the Spinney.'

My words halted him, but it seemed an age before he turned again to face me.

'Look at me,' he said. There was no defiance in his voice now. 'Do I look like I'm making a fortune? *Do I?*'

'We both know who's making the fortune. The question is . . .' I moved closer until I was, once more, standing beside him. 'Are we going to let the fucker get away with it?'

'What can I do about it? I haven't even got a bloody job.'

'Tell the truth, Stephen.' Just like I did, I thought, just down the hill from here, when Jean was lying slumped against the windscreen on a rainy night. 'People often take a generous view when they know someone's telling the truth. When they hear about your wife and her . . . her condition. And with all your girls still at school and college, I'm sure people will be very understanding. I mean, we all run into financial difficulties from time to time.' I stopped, wondering if I had gone too far.

'Financial difficulties?' Wonder was mixed with horror in Stephen's voice. 'Is that what you think? That I took money from that . . . that –'

From Taylor's Hill came the sound of a car-horn, angry and urgent. Further up, unseen but audible, the great mechanical diggers and shovels were clawing at the wounded earth along Bishop O'Donnell Road. Grey smoke wisped in the morning air from the hospital chimney to our left. All around us, men and women were bulldozing and building, living and dying. None of it touched us, up here on the Spinney. Here was only an open mouth, speechless with horror in a pale and furrowed face, and hollow eyes that accused me of – of what? What was it that I had done? I had, by implication, accused Stephen of stealing, pocketing a back-hander: bribes, baksheesh, commissions, whatever name you called it, was the easy money that greased the axles of the world's commerce, from Suharto to Saudi princes, from bent briefs to town-planning clerks. It was the reason the innocent earth was opened and the hospital furnaces were fed; yet clearly the very idea left Stephen Conroy aghast.

'I don't understand, Stephen,' I said gently.

'Nobody understands, that's the trouble.' He spoke so softly I had to strain to hear him. 'Joan understood, she always did, but now . . .'

'Joan?'

'My wife, she's . . . she's in a *fucking* wheelchair and she's never going to come out of it!'

'I know. I'm sorry. My grandfather was in a wheelchair . . .' I wanted to keep him talking. 'I used to push him in it, when we were walking the dogs. My father kept a couple of greyhounds. They used to call us the apostolic procession.'

'Are you taking the piss?' he demanded. 'Am I supposed to feel better just because your old grandfather ended up in a wheelchair? Am I?'

'I'm sorry,' I said, 'I just thought . . .'

'Don't think, don't fucking think . . . Not about me anyway.' He looked away from me and I knew he was searching for the white houses of Tirellan on the other side of town. 'Joan thinks about me and . . . and I think about her. But that's all too late now!'

'It's never too late,' I said. 'No matter what's happened.' If only Jeff could hear me now, I thought.

Stephen laughed sarcastically. 'D'you really think that? Do you?'

Something about his frayed earnestness silenced the glib response that was on the tip of my tongue. I knew what it was to lie awake in the comfortless embrace of regret. 'Maybe you're right,' I said. 'I don't know anymore.'

'Nobody can help me now.' He was brittle as the frost underfoot, angry one moment, the next full of self-pity. 'Nobody can help Joan and my girls now.'

'I'll try to help you if you'll tell me what happened.'

'Why should I tell *you*? You'll put my name in a book or a magazine or something. I know what you do, Mr Best. I saw Karen reading your book, she even talked about it last night when she was telling me you phoned.'

'I won't do that, I promise I won't.'

'Promises!' Stephen snorted.

'At least I'm not promising you money or . . . or whatever it was that somebody else promised you.'

I could see the struggle in his pale, etched features. I knew the faces of grief and rage. And hope too. I was all he had, and we both knew it. He started to talk about his arrival in Galway from Longford, his Leaving Cert in his pocket, to take up a clerical position with CIE. The work at the bus station was simple but boring: it didn't take long to master the art of filling out consignment dockets for parcels being dispatched to Claremorris or Ballinasloe. The other fellows in the digs on Prospect Hill did nothing with their time except drink and drinking didn't interest Stephen very much. Meeting Joan at the dance in Seapoint lent shape to his days and purpose to his life. He used to meet her at 5.30 outside the insurance office on the Square where she worked as a receptionist; if he were on the late shift, she'd be waiting for him on the steps of the station when he came out at 9.45. They were the same age, 22, when they were married in Joan's home parish in County Clare; they had two salaries and they stayed in nearly every night in their rented bed-sit, saving for a deposit on their own home.

I'm not sure Stephen even knew I was there as he talked about himself and Joan. I didn't interrupt; content to let him feel at ease with me as he ran through his familiar tale. And familiar it was, the carbon of so many other stories in so many towns: they saved for two years before they put down the deposit on the new semi where they still lived. Karen, their eldest, was born less than a year after they moved in. For a time, Joan stayed on at work, but there wasn't much out of her income after you paid for a child minder. It was tight, but they were just able to manage after Joan gave up her job with the arrival of their second child. By that time, what was increasingly noticeable was Joan's tiredness. Sometimes he'd come home from the late shift and find one or both of the children crying while Joan lay exhausted and half-asleep on the couch. It would be better, the doctor told them, if Joan didn't get pregnant again too soon. Stephen got a job in the planning office: the pay was a little better and there wasn't any shift-work. Joan's tiredness didn't leave her but at least she didn't seem to be getting worse.

She had their youngest, Siobhan, after a gap of four years. Afterwards, the doctor advised Stephen that he mustn't blame himself; the pregnancy and the new baby had nothing to do with Joan's condition. By then it was known that she had MS; very soon, reading the brightly-coloured brochures that the doctor handed to him, Stephen would know that there was no turning back for Joan. Nor for him:

"It got so we never touched each other anymore".

I knew that loneliness. In his poignant words I recognised his hunger and longing. In my youth, lying on my sleepless bed in Paternoster while my unforgiving mind refused to allow me to forget where Jean might be, I had thought that the world's pain was mine alone. The years had taught me different. Stephen had met Leonard Crotty a couple of years earlier, at a reception in City Hall.

'I knew who he was, of course, I'd handled plenty of files for Healy and Heffernan and I knew that most of them were for Crotty Developments. I should have known better.' He looked at me, pleadingly. 'I mean, I should have known Mr Leonard Crotty wouldn't be talking to the likes of me unless he had some bloody good reason. I suppose I was flattered. He invited me to things, parties, tickets for the Crotty tent at the Races, that kind of thing. He always invited my wife too and he always said he was sorry she couldn't come. They were never anything too big . . . just fairly small affairs. Never a dress-dance or anything like that. It wouldn't have looked right, I suppose, particularly if Mr O'Hanlon was to be there as well.'

'I suppose,' I agreed.

He fumbled in the pocket of his mac and produced a packet of cigarettes. 'I only started back on them a few weeks ago,' he said apologetically. 'And I can't afford it.' His hands shook as he struck a couple of matches before managing to light the cigarette.

I said nothing, waiting, willing him to continue.

'I started to drink a little. Not much, I don't really like the stuff but Leonard always paid, he was always pushing a drink into my hand. I used to get sick sometimes. Some mornings I'd be so bad I could hardly face going to work. But I liked it in a kind of way. It made you forget about things at home . . . God forgive me.' He dragged hungrily on the cigarette. 'God forgive me.'

'For what?' I asked.

'I'm not afraid . . .' He shuddered to a silence but then, after a couple of minutes, continued. 'I'm not afraid to tell Joan about the job . . . about losing it. I'm not afraid to tell her about the drinking either. It's the other stuff. It would kill her!' Stephen looked straight at me then. 'My wife is dying slowly, and we both know it. She just doesn't deserve the other stuff.'

'The other stuff?'

'In the apartment,' Stephen said. 'The apartment down in College Court.'

I don't remember his exact words after that. He went on speaking in his quiet, diffident way but I knew the story already. That apartment in College Court, where Leonard sometimes took a few of his pals back for late drinks; the two girls who lived there, one dark, one blonde. The blonde one, a student; the other a checkout girl in a supermarket. The blonde one seemed to be Leonard's own; he seemed different, less loud, when he was around her.

'The other girl, the dark-haired one, was . . . was a . . .'

Stephen didn't elaborate. He didn't have to.

'And he threatened to tell your wife if you didn't agree to lose a file for a month or so?'

He nodded.

'She mightn't have believed him,' I said. 'It's your word against his.'

'He has photographs.' His eyes were downcast now. 'He showed them to me. Disgusting photos. I was drunk, I . . . I can't believe I did those things with that other girl.' His voice fell to a whisper. 'But I did. They . . . they showed me the pictures.' He shivered. 'It . . . it would kill Joan.'

A watery sun broke through the cloud cover then, bathing the town below us in innocent light. The buildings, the waters of the bay and even the great cranes beside the docks sparkled. From the Spinney you could not see the apartment block where Kelly Carpenter now lived or the old apartment in College Court where she had refused to play hostess for Leonard and his mates. In my warped arrogance I had thought that that "mafia" contained only the great and the good of Galway; the builders and the bankers and the lawyers and the fee-professionals; I had not realised, listening to Kelly's sobbed-out story, that it had also included lesser, but equally useful functionaries, like the poor sod who now stood beside me. People like Stephen had far more to lose as they had nowhere to shelter.

'What am I going to do, Mr Best?' he asked.

'What d'you want to do?'

He shrugged. 'I don't know.'

'Can you go on like this for another while, pretending you're going to work, going through the motions?

'Yes.' He spoke with infinite sadness. 'I think so.'

'Then do it. I'll phone you in a few days, maybe in a week or so. Call me if you want to . . . I'm in the book.'

'What are you going to do . . . I mean, what can you do?'

'I'm not sure, maybe nothing.'

'But you think you can help me?' The note of hope in his voice was frightening, like a child's seeking reassurance.

'I'm going to try,' I told him.

He shook hands with me then and for a moment, looking into his beseeching eyes, I wondered at my own foolhardiness. Before he left, I had to promise again that I would not betray his secrets and that I would phone him as soon as I had any news. I knew, watching him drive away in the old Mirafiori that he would be on the phone to me within 24 hours, begging for information, frantic for salvation. Who was I, I asked myself, to be hinting at deliverance, to be playing at God? Maybe it was the last irony: I could not save myself but I could save others.

It was time to have a word with Leonard Crotty. But not just yet. For all my messianic notions, I was still not ready to come face to face with the ghosts of my own past. Not just yet.

Chapter 18

The next morning's post brought a letter for me. Now that it had come, I was almost afraid to open it. An end to my waiting, yes, but I sensed that here too there was pain that I could not run away from. I could see her hand, her long, elegant hand with long, slender fingers, shaping the neat script on the envelope. My own hands trembled, holding the letter, imagining; or trying to, my sixteen year-old daughter's misgivings.

The letter was dated two days earlier, 25 November:

Dear Dad,

I know my silence will have hurt you. All I can say by way of explanation is that I would have hurt you more if I had written to you sooner. I needed time to get all this clear in my mind.

It all seemed so easy to understand when we talked in Galway, there was a kind of sense to what you were telling me. You are seriously ill. You have decided not to go along with your doctors and have treatment. What must happen must happen, you said. I thought that it all did made sense and that you were very brave.

But when I came home it wasn't clear at all, Dad. You and I never discussed that so-called 'happening'. You left it all up

179

in the air. A time will come, probably sooner than later, when you will not be there any longer, Dad. What we didn't talk about either, Dad, is that I am going to be here. What am I going to do when my father is no longer here? Is that selfish of me? Or is it that selfish of you?

Do you know how many times I've started this letter? Can you guess how many different ways I've tried to ask that question – answer that question? I've made umpteen attempts. I've torn up pages. I've crossed out lines. None of it helps.

I don't want to be in this situation, Dad because I'm afraid I won't cope, to be strong for your sake.

Perhaps I'll pretend all of this is not really happening, that it is like the games we played when I was small. Remember how we used to think up really bad situations and then somehow, magically, find a solution. I don't want to do that either. I know you've got, what you've got but I want to make you proud of me, Dad; I want you to be around, to be there for me. That is my wish, my selfish solution.

I don't want this letter to cause you even more grief, Dad, but I'm asking you to think about it at least. Why not come to England and get another opinion? Don't give up, Dad. Don't give up on me.

I'm sorry about what happened at school. Running away like that was childish but I so wanted to run away. School and exams seemed meaningless. At the time it just seemed like the only thing to do. It won't happen again, Daddykins, I promise.

One month from now will be Christmas Day. Term ends a week before that and I've promised Mum I'm going to stay with her for Christmas, but you can expect me for the New Year. Even mum isn't objecting to me spending a bit more time with you, Dad!

Promise you'll think about this, Dad.

Hugs and kisses,

Your own busy Bee.

She'd drawn a smiling face beside her name and for a long

time I went on staring at the childish circle with the upturned mouth. No Latin here, nor Shakespeare, just a sixteen year-old's raw pain and unselfconscious hope. Hope in the shape of Christmas and the end of term; hope in her pleading words, that I should consider all the angles.

Why should I deny my daughter a glimpse of hope? She was the only person in the world who truly loved me: why I could not offer her some token of the currency that I so willingly held out to Kelly, whom I barely knew, and Stephen, whom I didn't know at all?

Whatever Elizabeth might say or think, I knew I had meant well in telling Bee about my condition and my decision about the treatment. But perhaps good intentions were not enough. I had wanted to spare Bee the sudden, world-ending silence that had fallen on myself, all those years ago, in this very kitchen. Perhaps you can never protect another human being, not even the one who was more precious to you than yourself, from the sound of closing doors and the empty silence that follows after. Perhaps the human heart can never be programmed for that level of pain but must find its own threshold in its own endurance, its own strength.

I could tinker with the lives of others but play-acting at being God was still no more than play-acting. Bee's best defense against everything that life might throw at her, or take from her, was her own character. Her openness, her ironic turn of humour, her refusal to mourn before death had come to sit in the room, her selfishness.

But her honesty too: her refusal to deny that disaster had a face and some day you would look into it. It was the kind of honesty that I had always managed to avoid.

That first year in London it was difficult to avoid looking myself in the eye but I did my best. At mid-day on Christmas Eve, 1971, I rang the Galway Arms from a bar just off the Cromwell Road, where the airport bus from Heathrow had disgorged me along with a handful of other travellers into a biting wind that threatened snow. My nerve almost failed me when Tommy came to the phone and I could hear, behind his cheerful voice, the familiar voices of the pub. What was I doing here in this unknown city when I could be leaning on the counter with Jeff rather than leaning my head into this plastic pelmet that covered the phone outside the gents in a pub I had never seen and had never wished to see? I nearly wilted, nearly surrendered to the call home but then recovered and stuck to my guns: I told Tommy only that he was to make sure that Jeff, or somebody, was to let my mother know that I was safe in London and that I would write to her in few days.

'Mind yourself, Danny boy,' he said before he hung up. 'And Happy Christmas to you.'

I fled from the pub, shouldering my bags, burrowing into the wind with gratitude: wind, rain and snow would be welcome, anything that closed my mind for an instant against the image of the bandaged head on the pillow and the rise and fall of her breasts under the hospital coverlet. And my mother's face too, marked with a grief that I could not fathom, I nevertheless knew that my going would darken and tighten that unsmiling face even more grimly against the world. Like my letter to Jean, my phone message for my mother was no more than a guilty and cowardly sop for my dishonest conscience.

I burrowed on as the afternoon darkened around me, drawing towards Christmas Day. Not until later, when I had grown more familiar with the terrain, would I realise that I had trudged north through Kensington and on into Notting Hill. In the gathering darkness the streets grew brighter with a brittle brightness and I hurried from the lights as from an enemy, like that night from the house on Taylor's Hill. On an impulse I boarded a bus that drew up at a stop where I had paused for breath and as the bus ploughed deeper into dark canyons of peeling, ugly terraces I knew that I had found the country I deserved.

I'm not sure that Westbourne Park did deserve me. In the years that I lived in the gloriously misnamed Eden Hotel, I gave nothing to the area except the rent for my room, the price of my weekly travelcard and the few pence I spent on a daily newspaper, at first *The Express* or *The Mail* and then, as I grew more accustomed to my new surroundings, *The Guardian*. In return for my ungenerous stipend the fading stucco terraces of Westbourne Park gave me the punishing anonymity I craved. Mrs Percival, flat-chested and shrewish, never attempted to move past the exchanges of daily civilities to any kind of intimacy from that first day when, seeing her "Rooms to Let" cardboard sign in the downstairs window, I rang her bell. I sometimes thought that she was merely grateful for the whiteness of my skin in contrast to the daily arrival of more and more of the commonweal's colonial cousins; "No Irish need apply", did not apply within that warped logic.

My continuing presence amid the transients of the Eden Hotel was probably a mystery to Mrs Percival's suspicious view of the world; she expressed her approval of my presence, or at least the regular payment of my rent, by moving me from room to room until, after ten weeks residency, I had acquired the Eden's most prestigious quarters. The room had the advantage of a washbasin, although the hot water tap was connected to no obvious source of any kind of water; better still, the bathroom was right next-door on the same landing. The room was at the back of the house, offering a claustrophobic view of dirty, yellow-bricked backs of the terrace behind us. I could have moved to better, more comfortable places but it never occurred to me: from my window I could look down into a tiny, cramped yard that was littered with bits and pieces of broken-down furniture: two decaying headboards, a mattress propped up against the door of an old privy, even the naked entrails of a couple of old television sets. Sometimes the wind would spiral up and down in the canyon of the yard and I'd awake in the afternoon with a start, hearing in the baying of the wind the voices of Mutt and Prince in the long-ago yard behind Paternoster. I'd know it was no more than a dream, my imagination turned by the wind, but sometimes I'd hurry from the narrow bed and peer into the debris-strewn well of the yard as though I might see in the afternoon light those elegant heads and the long pink tongues and the dark, creosote eyes. I never did see them but sometimes, when the afternoon was dark with slanting rain, I'd draw back from the window, sure that I had seen below me, huddled beside the bleeding mattress against the old lavatory door, a small boy that I had no wish to remember. Perhaps Mrs Percival, or one of her proprietary predecessors, had not after all been so crazy in the choice of name of this down-at-heel rooming-house: one way or another, we are, all of us, searching for the Eden that we think we once inhabited.

When I look back now at those years I spent in London, it seems to me that my life there hinged upon forgetting and remembering. Not long after my arrival, a few days into a freezing New Year, I found work as a porter at Paddington Station. A first-class honours degree in History seemed to fit me for nothing except teaching, a job that interested me not at all; the job at Paddington offered survival wages for work that I could have done in my sleep but, more importantly, it was night-shift work, which meant that I did not have to try to sleep my way through the tortured hours of darkness.

Instead my mind could sleepwalk its way through the night while my body bent, gathered and heaved sacks of mail and bundles of the next day's newspapers into trains bound for the West Country. Until around midnight there were late-night travellers to distract me; later, as the station emptied and the night grew chill, it was more difficult to fend off the faces that loomed at me out of my past. Yet each night passed with its own soporific rhythms: the patrolling constables moving the winos and vagrants from their drunken, sprawled sleep on the benches, the odd dinner-jacketed and evening-gowned couple catching a late-late train back to Oxford, the gaudily dressed hookers prowling hopefully for some stray client in the gloom of the almost deserted station. Somehow each night turned to dirty, streaky dawn and I knew I had survived another darkness. My whole life was an exercise in forgetting, right down to ignoring the ongoing grief caused to my mother by my continuing presence in London.

It was my own pain I wanted most to forget. I missed Jean with a rendering ache; an ache that left me empty but yet went on filling my emptiness with a deepening grief. What I had done, drunkenly but deliberately, had placed her, I was sure, forever beyond my reach; had I spotted her on a Paddington platform, as I sometimes dreamed of doing, I would have turned from her in shame. I had marked her for life and I was beyond redemption.

Nor did I seek any. I sought nothing more than the obscurity of the Eden Hotel and the gloomy precincts of Paddington. I longed for my shame to be erased but I took no steps towards mending or undoing the wrong I knew I had done and continued to do. Each morning, just before 7.00, I clocked off my twelve-hour shift and took the Hammersmith line for the short ride to Westbourne Park. There was a paper to read, a mug of tea and a bacon sandwich to while away an hour or so around the corner from the Eden: I lived in a presence that was stained with the grime of lives beyond mine and I welcomed it. The future I had dreamed of was forever lost; the only now that I deserved was one of greasy spoons, cracked cups and milk doled sparingly into your tea by a mustached virago who might have been Mrs Percival's better-fed half-sister.

When Elizabeth asked me, a couple of years later, why on earth I was living in such a dreadful place for, and why on earth I went on doing such cretinous work, I was almost surprised by the question. I was living the only life I deserved, the only existence I was capable of: her well-bred nostrils fairly flared at that and for two weeks afterwards, whenever I phoned her digs in Oxford, she was always "at the library", even at 11.00pm, just after we'd finished loading the Exeter train.

Elizabeth came later, two years later.

During those two years the days and the weeks and the months drifted by like random leaves. Each passing week was marked by the arrival of my mother's weekly letter, written with a fountain pen on small, ruled pages, each one beginning with the same opening that she, and her entire class, must have learned by rote at primary school: "My dear son, I hope this letter finds you as well, as it leaves me".

I don't think she ever fully understood the reasons for my abrupt leaving, or perhaps, more likely, she did not wish to have her suspicions confirmed: I would learn later that my mother was no stranger to the pain of sudden departure.

At first she used to ask when I'd be back; after some months, recognising that I refused even to acknowledge the question, she ceased to ask it. Instead, she fed me snippets of information about Leonard and Jeff; as if the morsels might tempt me back to the table I had left. And there was news of Jean. The accident had left her with an ugly scar: "but Jean is good with the make-up and sometimes you can't see the mark at all". I couldn't breathe reading that, sitting on my bed in the Eden, watching again the Celebration bottle somersaulting through the wet night until it hammered against the windscreen of the Mini.

Under separate cover the local newspaper also arrived every week. Once or twice I wrote to tell my mother not to be wasting her money in this way, and yet, truth to tell, the *Connacht Tribune* fascinated me. Its pages kept me in surreptitious touch with a life I had once lived for and now planned never to return to. In that life nothing seemed to have changed; Crotty's Builders Providers continued to advertise their wares and their excellence every week in the bottom right-hand corner of the front page; the same faces stared out of posed photographs at dinner-dances (rugby, the law, chamber of commerce) and socials (GAA, trade unions, supermarket staffs). There were graduation faces too at the University: the summer I had fled, the Crotty's had an extra presence on the front page of the *Tribune*, a large photograph of Leonard, flanked by his smiling parents and holding, at the traditional 45 degree angle, the scroll proclaiming the honours degree in Engineering which he had just been awarded.

I couldn't help but wonder if Jean had shared his big day with him. In her letter that week my mother made no reference to

Jean, remarking only that, for the Crotty's, "it was a great day and everyone was very proud of Leonard".

It was Jean herself who put me out of my misery, but only in a manner of speaking:

26 Greenleas,
Galway.
22 August 1972

Dearest Daniel,

I've just put off writing to you until now. I kept hoping to hear from you but not a word has come from you since the accident so I feel I've got to write. I don't wish to blame you for the long silence but all the same I can't help feeling unhappy about it. I was grateful for your note – nurse Kinahan delivered it to me as if it were some kind of message from Romeo to Juliet and I hadn't the heart to enlighten her about its real contents or meaning.

Nobody else knows about it either, Daniel. What I mean to say is that nobody else knows what really happened that night at the Crotty house. Len was telling some joke and paying too little attention to his driving when we turned off the road – it's a wonder he didn't ram the gates in the awful rain – but I saw you. I don't know how I knew it was you, the lights didn't catch you or anything, but just as we swung into the drive I caught a glimpse of someone crouched under the big tree and I just knew it was you. I don't know how. I just knew it. My heart went out to you at that moment. If I could have stopped the car right there I'd have taken you in my arms and told you that I'd had enough time, that I knew all I needed to know about being on my own and that all I wanted was for us to be together.

Len didn't see the stone or whatever it was that came flying at the windscreen – to this day he believes that it was some deranged bird that caused the accident and I haven't made him or anyone else the wiser. Yet in those few seconds I learned more about myself than I could ever have known if that night had not happened. What I mean is that turning to you in the rain would have been a mistake. What happened to me that night was a lesson that I welcome, one I intend to profit from, even do some good from.

I know now the unhappiness I caused you by ending, even temporarily, our relationship. I bear the responsibility for that night just as much as you do, perhaps even more so. You and I might have had a future – we certainly talked often enough about it – but in my selfishness I gambled with that future.

Now I know that it is impossible; I see more clearly than ever, where life is leading me. Forgive me, Daniel, for whatever I have unwittingly done to you. And forgive Leonard too, although really there is nothing to forgive him for. He wanted more, but he and I were never more than friends. He's not a bad fellow; just not as serious as you and he maybe takes too much for granted all the good things that life has given him. I caused him, I think, a lot of confusion but he never reproached me for it.

I won't be seeing you for a long time. I didn't lose any time over the accident and I got through my third medical exams okay. Anyway, I know now the road I must take and so I'm going away for a year and after that I'm transferring to Dublin to finish my course.

I wish you a long life of happiness, Daniel. From the day we met, you were precious to me . . . You still are. Always remember that.

Please don't remember me too unkindly. I am doing only what I have to do. You will always be in my heart. Keep me in yours, and also in your prayers.

Yours always,

Jean.

I don't how long I sat there on my bed in the Eden, holding her letter in my trembling hands. I'd seen it on the floor as soon as I wakened that afternoon, pushed there from beneath the door by Mrs Percival. I'd known the handwriting immediately and I'd torn the letter open with a hunger that I had not wished to know was in me.

In the slanting light of the August afternoon, Jean's words were both a whisper of love and an indictment of guilt. Even without my cowardly note, furtively delivered, even without that, she had known my shame. Her reproach was unspoken but I could feel it, my hands stung by the innocent paper, my heart skewered on the stake of might-have-been: "I'd have taken you in my arms", over and over I read her words, as though I might rewrite the events of that night and throw myself upon her mercy. There could be no revisions however; the paltry history of that night was forever marked upon her face.

No mention of the scar upon the face I loved: yet that silence too was but more reproach, staring in at me through the dirty window and the unwashed net curtain of my Eden residence. When I stirred myself at last, it was past 6.00pm and Paddington station would have to survive without me that night: I had no heart for its robotic labours and vaulted gloom. Jean's words were a reminder of the lilting light that had once filled my life and I longed for it, its touch and taste, the shape and sound of it.

It was too late to book a flight that evening but come the morning I would be in the travel agency on the corner of Harrow Road, looking for the first available flight home. It wasn't just the nightshift routine that kept me from sleep that night. Jean's cryptic words twisted and turned with me in the narrow bed throughout the night. What road was it that she spoke of? And could I yet walk that road along with her?

Dawn was breaking when I fell asleep at last. I was coming out of the bathroom, dressed and ready to go out, when Mrs Percival appeared on the landing.

'You're getting popular,' she said, handing me an envelope. 'Two letters in two days.'

The letter was from my mother. Jean had called, she wrote, to say goodbye to her; that very day she was leaving for Drogheda, where she had been accepted as a member of the Medical Missionaries of the Sacred Heart.

Chapter 19

My sense of attachment to the beliefs and rituals of Catholic Ireland had been tenuous, at best, since around the time I'd discovered masturbation; Jean's deranged decision finally cut me completely adrift from the ship of Rome. For me, her move to some convent sisterhood of doctors and nurses was clearly insane; it was clear that Jean's over-developed sense of personal responsibility had led her into the incense-fudged realms of cloud-cuckoo-land. Why should she take responsibility for my misdemeanors and Leonard's interference in our lives? I had never trusted the smell of incense, the chime of bells, the pale delirium of book and candle. Jean's madness only confirmed my suspicions. Any religion that could lure a lovely, intelligent woman on the brink of a professional career into some cloistered purdah surely was anti-life. The paradox of the Christian cross, the death-is-life stuff, had never been for me. I had lived with the consequences of death for a long time, and in its emptiness, I could discover no evidence of life. Jean's flight into a nunnery was just further proof of the madness of it all.

For a little while I thought the madness of her decision might be temporary, that she'd come to her senses and return to

Galway; perhaps then, I figured, things might work out for us, especially as she had made it clear that Leonard Crotty was no threat. It was a notion that I entertained only briefly: I knew her too well to imagine that she would reverse her decision without giving it her all.

My immediate response was to rail against the Mother Church that had supposedly nurtured me but I got over that, sloughing off my spiritual rearing like an old and useless skin. It was different with my hatred of Leonard. Only friends, Jean had written, but she has also written that he had "wanted more" and I could not forgive him that. He had been after all, a sort of friend; he and I were bound together by ties that were often uncomfortable to me but were undeniably real: why then had he attempted to come between Jean and myself? For me the answer was brutally simple: Jean was just one more thing he wanted, and whatever Leonard Crotty, or Crotty's Builders Providers, or *fucking* Prospector Enterprises wanted, they expected to get.

In the weeks after I heard from Jean I could feel the anger and the bitterness bleeding inside me, fouling the bland dullness of my down-at-heel Eden. The mindless routines of my job became almost intolerable; every Friday I swore that I would hand in my notice while collecting my wage packet. I never did: I was in the grip of a lassitude, which made any kind of decision involving change too troublesome to handle. For a while I toyed with the idea of registering at London University for a Master's but that too demanded thought and action that I was incapable of.

Today, I might be inclined to say that I was experiencing some kind of breakdown induced by stress and depression; back then, through the autumn and winter of 1972, I merely thought that the world was "weary, stale, flat and unprofitable", and that I was lonely, bored and fed-up. I was filled with anger too, of the righteous variety, and I fed off that anger with an intensity that even I could see was threatening to unbalance my miserable life altogether.

It was old Mutt and Prince, and my father, who pulled me back from the brink of that nervous abyss.

Finding it more and more difficult to sleep after my shift, I had taken to lingering longer over my mugs of tea at the zinc-topped table in Eve's Cafe before making my way around the corner to Mrs Percival's establishment. On one such Friday morning, remonstrating with myself again for not having given notice earlier when I collected my wages, I found myself staring at the card for that evening's meeting at Haringay Stadium, in a copy of the *Greyhound Express* left behind, no doubt in error, by some earlier patron of Eve's. Afterwards I could remember not a single greyhound's name from any of the eight races, but I read the short accompanying article and the tipster's pronouncements with real curiosity; for a few minutes I even considered skipping work that night and trying to find my way to Haringay. By the time I was climbing the stairs of the Eden to my first-floor room, carrying the *Greyhound Express* along with my bottle of milk and loaf of bread, the notion of going to Haringay had disappeared; instead I was filled with a profound sense of the presence of Mutt and Prince.

Their tongues, pink and soft and scaly, were wet against my face and hands. My room seemed filled with their warm animal smell. I could hear in my ears and in my heart their excited, high-pitched yelping as they waited in their kennels for me to come to them. And when I looked down into the wasteland of the Eden Hotel yard, the boy I saw there was not crouched in unhappiness but alert with love, fingers gripping the links in the netwire fencing around the kennels, and when I looked again I saw my father, standing beside me, his face creased with laughter under his dark crown of curls.

Along with those memorable minutes when I had first met Jean in the coffee shop in college it was, I think, the only moment of what might be called "epiphany" in my life. It was a moment free of insight of analysis; it was, on the contrary, a purely emotional experience. I knew that neither the dogs nor my father were there; I knew too that the boy I had been was not really there. Yet, for those seconds or minutes all of us were there, in the yard or in my room or in both. It's still not quite clear to me, nor do I want it to be.

What I also knew, or felt at least, was that I wanted to hang on to the warm, glowing feeling that was filling me. For almost a year I had detached myself from any heat that life might have to offer. Now, in an instant, my whole body felt warmed and lighted and I knew that I wanted to hug the feeling, and the firelight, to my heart.

I opened the foolscap pad that I used only for writing my occasional letters to my mother – there was no one else to write to – and sat down at the small deal table, pushing the bread and milk to one side. I had written nothing substantial since arriving in London but the writing fluency of a studious lifetime came back to me: I filled page after page with my recollections of life in the old house in Paternoster. It was noon when I laid the pen aside and fell gratefully into bed. When the alarm wakened me at 5.00 that afternoon, the first thing I did was read over the pages I had written that morning and I felt warmed again, reading over my own words. It was with regret that I left for Paddington but the following morning my bacon sandwich breakfast at Eve's Cafe was a more hurried affair that usual, I was anxious to get back to this past that I, like my mother, had buried so deep that I hardly recognised it at first as my own.

Christmas 1972 was my second Christmas in London. I felt no guilt about leaving my mother alone for another Christmas; by then the foolscap pad I had begun with had been replaced by another and that too was almost filled with my words. More than fluency had returned to me. At school and college I had been used to writing essays that had a recognisable beginning, middle and end; I soon realised that I wanted, needed, to impose some order on the material that seemed to be pouring out of me. I had no thought of showing it to anyone: what the pages represented to me were a way to hang on to the feeling of happiness that I had experienced on that first morning, but my own innate desire for order insisted that I put some shape on what I was writing. What I was doing would probably be described today as writing therapy, or some such; through those winter days of 1972-1973 I saw it as a door into a lost magic world that had once been mine and was now, magically, once more laid open to me.

I laid aside the first 50 or so pages that had seemed to flow out of me and did what I had been taught to do at school: I began at the beginning and worked my way from there. I found it a less constricting experience than writing history essays: this history was mine and I took liberties with it. I invented conversations between Dad and me, between Mam and me, between me and anybody and everybody. When I could only half-recall something, I drew pleasure from concocting the rest. I had "rules" of course: whatever I made up had to "feel real". And I found, as one pad gave way to another, that I was creating a world without 'baddies': there were contrary characters, of course, like Granda Flanagan, and mean-spirited creatures like my grandmother; even poor Paudge, who is the most harmless of men, assumed a certain cryptic inscrutability, as seen through my child's eye. But the world I wrote about was a world without villains; in my innocence I figured that to be a fair reflection of the kind of world that Paternoster Lane actually was in the '50s. More importantly, it was a world peopled mainly by heroes.

The greatest of those was my father. I chose the title as a kind of silly play upon the name of our less-than-speedy greyhound, but in my heart there was always only one *Prince of Morning*. I remembered him as a prince among men and that was how I wrote about him. His presence made our home a palace and our working-class street a kingdom; his good humour, gentleness and kindness ennobled everyone in that kingdom.

As the weeks and months drifted by, I added to my world of words: the dogs, the apostolic procession, my grandparents, our neighbours on the street, and the other boys at school. Winter became spring; summer came and choked the streets of London with dusty heat and then the leaves were falling again around Paddington Green and once more the dark of winter was settling over the city. Christmas was at hand again: I had been two years in the city, two years in which I had done little except eat and sleep and work and write. In all that time I had neither gotten drunk nor even asked a girl to go out with me; I just didn't meet any girls and I didn't go where I might have met them. Yet, I was not unhappy. My paper world gave me something to cling to.

I could see, but only afterwards, that creating my golden childhood kingdom did something else: put simply, it kept me from having a youthful nervous breakdown. Put more deeply, my exploration of that distant world held the more traumatic events of my more recent past at bay. In a nutshell, it saved me the bother of having to deal with them. I'm pretty sure I never did deal with them until now, when the leaves are falling again and yet another Christmas is round the corner, and when it's probably too late to mean anything, this belated setting straight of the record.

Around noon on some midweek day early in December 1973, I put the pen down for the last time. My father was dead in sudden, unexplained circumstances; Mutt and Prince had disappeared forever from my life. I knew that I would write nothing of subsequent events: everything that happened afterwards was but an imitation of life. The mere retelling of my small, personal golden age had kept me alive, even lent my life a kind of contentment.

Yet, when I got into bed on that last day, I couldn't sleep. What was there now to keep me alive in my narrow confines of my narrow world, a world that extended only from the Eden Hotel to Paddington Station, and back again, with an occasional film thrown in before the evening shift? Once more I was back in the yard at Paternoster, the kennels were gone and the future was a place you had no wish to visit. I even thought of going home but the fear of what I might meet there was deeper than the fear of what I might have to live with in Westbourne Park.

And then Elizabeth walked into my life.

Actually she came leaning into it, angled lopsidedly to her left over a huge suitcase while carrying a smaller bag in her right hand.

The 7.43am train from Oxford had just pulled in. I was making my way against the exiting crowds on Platform 4, trying to look as if I was actually doing something. After a few weeks on the job you developed a proper porter's knack of not looking anybody in the eye while you walked purposefully through the station towards some task that was simply demanding your most urgent attention. Everybody did it, even the supervisors; in fact the greatest stress you could inflict upon old Stowell, our night-shift supervisor, was to let him see you idle, in which case he felt obliged to find something for you to do when he'd much prefer that you simply loaded and unloaded the trains and stayed sensibly out of sight in between times. Being a porter at Paddington demanded neither Einstein's intelligence nor Hannibal's industry, but you did need to display some common savvy. Given the manner in which I fucked-up so much of my life, it's still a wonder to me that I'd been made permanent in the job after no more that the minimum three-months probationary spell. I must have displayed all of the required skills of avoiding the public.

Anyway, on this particular evening, I was swimming determinedly against the 7.43-from-Oxford arrival crowd, making their way towards the gate of Platform 4, when I almost collided with a lop-sided girl of about my own age struggling, as I say, with a leviathan suitcase and a smaller bag. In my two years as a porter I had never carried any passenger's luggage; I was content to hump mailbags and newspaper bales and forget about possible tips; we left that to a few of the older guys who hung around the Left Luggage office, practicing their lines in small talk and ingratiating smiles.

And now here was this tall, slim creature in a palomino-shaded afghan coat, the last of all her tribe on the 7.43-from-Oxford, coming suddenly to a lop-sided halt and smiling gratefully at my navy-blue British Rail porter's uniform. On any other occasion I would have muttered something apologetic and scarpered for the sanctuary of the staff lavatory on Platform 1. "Never engage the enemy", my fellow porters had warned, and "not to worry about it" as old Stowell never paid any attention to complaints from the travelling public. For once I was caught flat-footed. Partly, I think, because I had, just that day, finished my writing task but partly, too, because the girl in the palomino-shaded afghan coat was pretty and she was smiling a tired smile at me.

'Please.' The single word dripped with English breeding. 'Could you help me?' It had been a long time since I'd been this close to a smile, especially one like this, all white teeth in a wide mouth, hazel eyes begging me from behind squarish glasses. 'I'd be most grateful.'

I realised that (a) I was staring at her and (b) I had not even opened my mouth.

'Of course.' I reached out to take the suitcase from her. It was blue, piped along the edges in maroon. It weighed a ton. 'What've you got in here?' I tried not to sound truculent. 'Cement blocks?'

'Books.' Her laugh had a tinkling sound like a small bell. 'Full of good intentions for Christmas but they'll probably come back with me, unopened, in January.'

'You're a student then?' I managed a sideways glance at her, beneath the palomino-shaded coat: mauve high-necked sweater over a tartan mini-skirt, long legs in dark stockings. I wished I could manage something more interesting by way of conversation.

'Sort of.' The small bell tinkled again. 'I'm doing post grad work in English.' I felt her eyes upon me; I wondered if she was wondering if I knew what she meant.

'So you fancy being an academic?' At least that sounded a little less stupid. I felt her eyes upon me and tried not to pant too heavily under the weight of the blue suitcase.

'The ivory tower has its attractions.'

The real world, in the shape of Platform 4, was coming to an end: ahead lay the steps of the Underground, where a British Rail porter's writ did not run; if they ever ran. My relief at getting rid of the suitcase was tempered with regret that I could not prolong my stay in the company of this smiling creature. She looked at me as I stopped and laid the suitcase down at the head of the stone stairway.

'End of the line,' I said.

'Would you mind terribly?' she said, looking from me to her suitcase, to the stairs, to me again. Her smile was pleading for help. 'I need to get the tube to Kensington, I'm . . . I'm staying with friends tonight.' A sudden surge of people upwards from the Underground pushed her against me: her hair smelt of apples. 'I'd be most grateful.'

'Grateful enough,' I gulped. 'To have a drink with me? I mean, a drink or a coffee?'

Beyond the crowd spilling around us I could see old Stowellie watching me, his long face puckered in its habitual frown. The hazel eyes behind the dark-rimmed glasses were also appraising me.

'Are you a regular porter? I mean, you don't sound like . . .'

'I'm a porter, sure,' I heard myself say. 'But I'm really a writer.' The four foolscap pads stacked on the table at the Eden lent some kind of validity to the words.

'A writer?'

'I've just finished my first book.'

'A novel, I suppose?' The smile was ironic.

'No,' I blurted. 'A memoir of a childhood in Ireland.'

'A personal history?'

'I have a First,' I knew I'd cringe later on at my own words but I didn't care then. 'I mean, I got a First in History.'

The plucked eyebrows arched above the dark glasses. 'So you're just here until your first book launches you into a long and successful literary career.'

'Absolutely.' I could see Stowell making his way towards me, probably to reprimand me for standing gossiping with a female, and a passenger to boot, in full view of the disapproving public. 'Look,' I said, picking up the case again. 'I'll be glad to get your stuff down to the Underground but I really would like to see you again.'

'My mother wouldn't approve,' she said, starting down the stairs with me. 'But I could always tell her that you're a literary giant doing some hands-on research at Paddington Station.'

'Does she have to know?' Stowell's ankles and feet disappeared from view as we descended below street level. 'Your mother, I mean.'

'We'll let our shared drink be our secret.'

I stopped on the stairs, turning to look at her. '*You mean it?* You'll have a drink with me?'

'Yes, but not now, my friends are expecting me. Let's do it tomorrow, at lunchtime, before I head off home to mother in the wastelands of Guildford.'

It was strange, the way the rancid air in the Underground suddenly blew sweet and cool upon my face. I threw the Jamaican Underground ticket collector a jaunty salute and he flung the gate open for us with a flourish.

'Man, you gotta load on there!' He beamed, his eyes unashamedly working up and down my new drinking companion. Dream on, man, I thought, I'm the one she's having a drink with.

As we made our way out onto the platform I could hear the rumble of an approaching train. 'Where?' I asked her, edging my way towards the front of the platform. 'Where d'you want to meet tomorrow?'

'Ring me but leave it until after 11.00 as we'll be up late tonight.'

The beam of the approaching train was visible now in the mouth of the tunnel. 'The number . . . What's your number?'

The waiting passengers pressed around us.

'2 . . . 7 . . . 4 –'

'Wait!' I interrupted. I was flapping my hands at the pockets of my BR uniform. 'I don't have a pen.'

The train was clanking to a halt. From the open doors hurrying travellers spilled past us towards the mainline station.

'Some writer you are! Here.' She was handing me a black biro: people pushed past us into the open doorway.

'Shoot,' I said, and as she rattled off the number I scribbled it on the back of my hand.

'Mind the doors,' I heard the metallic voice announce, as I

pushed her ahead of me into the carriage and shoved the huge case in after her.

The doors were closing when I suddenly realized. 'Your name,' I called. 'What's your name?'

'Elizabeth,' she called back.

The doors fully shut and I was left standing in the gloom, looking into the lighted carriage at her smiling face, and I remembered I hadn't even told her my name, and then the train was pulling away, and I watched it gather speed until it swallowed by the dark tunnel. I looked at the scribbled telephone number on the back of my hand and I began to wonder if she hadn't just been kidding me along, that I'd dial the number and find it didn't exist or that it was the number of some take-away out in the unvisited reaches of the East End.

Elizabeth answered the phone herself when I rang next morning at exactly 11.01.

'It's Daniel,' I said. 'From Paddington Station.'

'Daniel! I wondered about your name. We tried out a few names for you here last night but none of us came up with Daniel.'

The piss-scented smell of the phone booth on the Harrow Road was suddenly dispelled by the notion of a powdery, perfumed aroma of girls in a flat in Kensington; it was a heady feeling, looking past the two fat black women, gossiping at the greengrocer's stall, into an airy room where unknown girls speculated about my name. And yet it was too risky to ask what names they had flung back and forth among the imagined wine glasses. Instead I asked, gingerly, where I could meet her. I wrote down the name of the pub she suggested, together with directions from Earl's Court tube station, but it wasn't really necessary: I hung on her words, astonished by my own good fortune, even more astonished by my own daring in asking her to come out with me. And something else: the gallery of taped cards in the smelly booth, advertising everything from French lessons to

English spanking, seemed to crowd oppressively upon me with leering intimations of intimacy, an odorous residue of the kind of warmth I had not felt since leaving Galway. I hurried from the phone booth as though from an enemy.

I got to the Cap & Bells at 12.50, ten minutes before the arranged time. The first taste of the pint of ale almost made me tipsy: I hadn't slept since coming off my shift at 7.00 and my stomach had refused its usual breakfast-sandwich. When she walked into the pub I felt I was drunk. She was wearing the same afghan coat but the mauve turtleneck had given way to a lemon-coloured, rollneck sweater and the short skirt was gone in favour of blue denims that made her legs seem impossibly long. And time was impossibly short. She had a train to catch at 3.00 pm, she said, and I kept looking at the fading clock up among the bottles and the mirrors, fearing that at any moment she would stand up from the small round table and say it was time for her to go.

I desperately wanted to impress her and I had no idea of how to go about it: Jean, after all, was the only girl I had ever been out with. I started to talk about college life in Galway but soon discovered that Elizabeth was unimpressed by my posturing. She'd taken a First herself at Cambridge and was now halfway through a doctorate at Oxford. She at least had followed through on her ambition, I thought in awe, whereas I had run away.

'On what?' I asked.

'Oh, just some old nineteenth-century twit with daft notions about the place of the female in society.' She waved her hand dismissively. 'Tell me about your book, Daniel. At Cambridge I knew a lot of people who were all going to change the face of English literature with their first book but you're the first writer I've ever met in a railway porter's uniform.'

I blushed.

'You looked very dishy in it too,' she added, laughing. 'Even if you did seem reluctant to help a damsel in distress. Now tell me about this memoir of yours, it sounds most interesting.'

When I started telling her about those early days in

Paternoster, I forgot to try impressing her; it was at that point somehow, in my artless way, I began to impress her, or at least to hold her interest long enough to stay for a second glass of lager-and-lime. The big hand went on jerking its way around the fading face of the bar clock but Elizabeth stayed where she was, sitting opposite me beside the window with the pulled-back velvet curtain, smiling her pink-lipped smiles and asking her interested questions. Only a bunch of suits and a lone drinker remained in the Cap & Bells when we stood up to leave at 3.00.

'You've missed your train,' I said, trying not to imagine her naked.

'Never mind.' The long fingers waved, flashing a couple of silver-snake rings. 'The next one will do.'

Perhaps it was the lack of sleep and the alcohol that did it but, when we stepped out of the pub into the afternoon, Earl's Court seemed to shine with a kind of mystical splendour. I felt her hand take mine and my head and heart grew lighter: cars and shops and buildings shone brilliantly under the dark December sky but only I could sense that brilliance. She said something I didn't catch but I smiled anyway and her fingers tightened around mine: I remembered another time, walking home with my father from the Sportsground, when another sky had showered those other streets with a silvery light.

'Will I have to tip you for this?' We were standing in a small sitting room made even smaller by the huge, dark-brown couch on top of which Elizabeth was now trying to wrestle her big suitcase shut. 'I mean,' she went on. 'For carrying my bags into Waterloo Station? Do you have feudal rights in other stations apart from Paddington?'

'Just the same as before,' I said. 'Just have a drink with me the next time you're in town.'

'I think we can do better than that, Daniel.'

She'd stepped out of her shoes when we'd come into the flat and despite her long legs still had to stand on tiptoe to kiss me. The pink mouth was soft as silk; her tongue charged against mine with electric contact. She didn't resist when I drew her towards me; her breasts pushed firmly against my chest. I felt her arms tighten around me and I brought down my hands to cup her buttocks in my palms. Soft, murmuring noises swam from her mouth into my own as I drew her tighter against me; the swelling in my groin obvious against her pelvis.

'No,' she said suddenly, her hand flat on my chest. 'No,' she said again, leaning backwards in my embrace.

I let her go; I let her withdraw. 'Sorry,' I said, gasping for breath.

'Nothing to be sorry about, Daniel. It's just that there's a time and place, and this is not the time, whatever about the place.'

The "place" was Phyllis and Marlena's flat. They had "come down" from Cambridge with Elizabeth the year before and had gone to work in advertising and publishing. Every available space was crammed with magazines, newspapers and women's clothing.

'It's an okay place,' I said, thinking of my own Spartan quarters in the Eden Hotel.

'It's brilliant,' Elizabeth said. 'Especially as it gives me a bolthole to run to over Christmas. I just couldn't stand Surrey from now until next term.'

It was a small step from there to making arrangements to meet up when she came to town again. I dutifully wrote down her home number, adding the best times to call her; I wanted to ask her if there was a boy-friend in Oxford, or Cambridge, or Guilford, or anywhere but thought silence was the better option; it seemed to me that Elizabeth wasn't the sort of girl who'd welcome such questioning. And yet who was I to know what any girl might want? For the moment I was happy to haul the blue suitcase as far as Waterloo; I was even happier just to be panting alongside this fabulous creature in jeans and a rollneck sweater.

Afterwards I would wonder what she saw in me that December day: a gauche, even bashful, young Irishman who was masquerading as a writer. All I could think of, was that it must have been my innocence and my willingness to please; like Mutt, like Prince. Elizabeth was the kind of woman who liked to take charge and at that time I was only too willing to be taken charge of. I had been alone for two years by then in a life I had created for myself: a penitent life that was almost monk-like in its austerity and regularity but where I rang my own bells, created my own timetable. I didn't notice that Elizabeth liked to boss me about or, if I did, perhaps I just liked being bossed about – for a while anyway.

We met three times during her Christmas break, always at the flat in West Kensington. On the third occasion, a Saturday morning when neither Phyllis nor Marlena had returned from a Friday night party, we made love. Spent in her arms, her breasts crushed against me in the narrow bed, I sensed a kind of peace I had not felt since that day in the Spinney when Jean had told me she wanted to be on her own. When I leaned over to kiss her, her fingers found me and in their cradling I sought and found again the release I craved.

By then I knew that Marlena was the redhead in the flat, the one who worked in the publishing industry, for a literary agent. By then, too, someone Marlena knew was typing my Paternoster saga up. I thought little of it: only in late February when Elizabeth, by then back in Oxford, told me on the phone that Marlena thought the now-typed-up story "had possibilities", did I allow myself to harbor hopes.

I let Elizabeth take charge. I was content to carry on with my porterly duties at Paddington, phoning her most nights from a phone that was safely hidden from Stowell's supervisor's eyes. Most Sundays I travelled out to Oxford as soon as I came off my shift, my porter's gear wrapped up in the same old holdall I'd taken with me from Galway. By 8.30, using the key she had given me, I had let myself into Elizabeth's house, into her bed, into her arms. I had given up wondering about competitors: Elizabeth's life seemed centered on her nineteenth-century male chauvinist author and more importantly, on my own willing body.

My mind too was willing: the world portrayed in the *Connacht Tribune* was beginning to seem almost like a planet of aliens. On one of these Sunday mornings, handing her the cup of instant coffee I'd just made, I was struck by the strangely self-satisfied look on Elizabeth's face. The electric fire in the room was fully on: she was sitting up in the bed bare-breasted, almost smirking to herself.

'What?' I said. 'You look like that cat that knows where the rest of the cream is stored.'

'I do too.' She made a grab for me under my shirttails but I drew back from her.

'I know you,' I said. 'You've got something on your mind.'

Her breasts quivered as she reached for her glasses on the small bedside locker. She studied me, knowingly, after she'd put them on. 'I told you Marlena's boss liked your book.'

'Yes.' That had been weeks earlier but I had refrained from asking more. 'What about it?'

'It seems you could make some serious money out of it.'

I sat on the edge of the bed, looking at her with wonder. 'It doesn't make sense,' I said. 'Stuff like that, about a boy in a poor street . . . Why should that make money?'

'That's it exactly! Marlena says it's the lure of innocence. Look at the world we are inheriting. The miners are threatening another strike; Heath has lost touch with the people; America's got rid of Nixon; innocence has been murdered. End of Marlena's exegesis, end of reasons why a book of innocence might make money.' She smiled at me. 'I didn't want to tell you this until it was certain but there's a substantial offer on the table from one publisher and Marlena thinks they can rattle a few more coconuts out of the trees before the deal is done.'

'Before the deal is done?'

'You're going to be published, Daniel Best, and you're going to have money. Maybe you're even going to be famous. What d'you have to say to that?'

'I don't care about the money,' I said. 'I just care about you.'

'I have expensive tastes,' Elizabeth laughed. 'It might be a good thing to care about the money as well.'

'It wouldn't be happening if I hadn't met you.'

'Aren't you even curious about who's going to publish your book?'

'Not really,' I sipped at my coffee. 'It was just something I wrote, and now it's finished and the money won't go astray, but that's about it.'

'No,' She shook her head. 'That's not about it! You have the knack, my Irish lover, and you have to keep on writing.'

'Could I get back into bed first?' I pushed my hand down between her legs. 'Please?'

'Only if you promise to keep on writing.'

'I promise,' I said, pulling the blankets back. 'I promise.'

And I shouldn't have: promises, after all, are made to be broken but I was too young then to know the truth of that old saying.

Chapter 20

It is 7.00am on Tuesday, 1 December 1998. From the Spinney I watch the outlines of my hometown edge into morning focus. Once more the earth has kept its promise: once more it has gone on turning on its axis and daylight breaks again over the streets and buildings of Galway. In this morning darkness a stranger could not tell one shape from another but mine is no stranger's eye: this town-turned-city is as familiar to me as a body you have slept with, desired and despaired of, for the length of a lifetime.

From up here the bay is hardly visible but I know the waters are there, grey in the grey morning; beyond the bay the hills of Clare are solid and unseen. Below me I can see the ghostly rigging of visiting boats in the docks; slowly the forms of cathedral dome and college quad swim into my vision. Over on my left the barracks-like structure of Roche's Stores is oddly pink in the cold, misty morning, like some childish addition to a Renaissance etching. There is nothing childish about the two massive cranes that dominate the emerging skyline: like dinosaurs they tower over the streets, one over the docks, the other closer to hand, next to Bishop O'Donnell Road. To my sleepless eyes the word

CROTTY on these huge, green metal structures is like a wound in the morning.

Or a scar on the face of your beloved.

Perhaps I'm the dinosaur, sitting here in the car with the engine running, waiting for the world to pass me by. It already has. Driving through the sleeping streets to get here, I felt invisible. No curtain twitched to mark my progress. No dog barked. A couple of cars passed me, headlights dipped, and I had a glimpse of overcoated drivers bound perhaps for early meetings in Dublin or perhaps just intent on the pursuit of the early worm. I am the early bird that same worm has no need to fear. Just as the cityscape below me sharpens into focus, so do the omissions of my life push their way through my own mental fog, clamouring for attention.

I still have not written to Bee. I am afraid to write to her. I am afraid to tell her that I have set my face against treatment: I am afraid to spell out my own fear of dying like an inhuman wreck, withered as much by the treatment as by the lumps in my armpit. The fear consumes me in another way: I can smell the bleakness that awaits her when I am gone, like the cold taste of mist gathering in your mouth and nostrils. And like the touch of acid rain, eating the flesh of your heart when the dogs are gone, the kennels destroyed. In this morning mist I hate myself: I would do anything for Bee except the one thing that she desires. I would bequeath her love but her legacy, like my own, will be the enduring embrace of loss.

The mist is giving way to rain: stair-rods of rain spearing the roof of the car, cascading on the windscreen. I switch on the wipers and then turn them off again. Somehow it seems right that I should have the city hidden from me; even the sky is obscured. I am alone in my personal time-capsule and as always I travel into the past, where loss begins and never ends.

I had lost Elizabeth before we were even married. The event itself, me in wide lapels and she in a calf-length cream-coloured suit, took place in the summer of 1975 at Guildford Registry Office. My mother sensibly declined to travel; only Phyllis and

Marlena joined Elizabeth's divorced mother for the happy event. I recited the meaningless words after the bespectacled registrar and tried not to think about Jean as I slipped the ring on to my new bride's finger.

I didn't succeed. She was always there at the edge of my heart, even in those dozy moments after lovemaking when your body seems liquefied with happy exhaustion and you feel that you have found, however briefly, a place to be safe. Even there I was not safe from my own wanting: sometimes I'd shut my eyes and I'd feel Jean's pale body against my own, trembling under the unseeing gaze of the teddy bears on the window sill.

Perhaps I should have told Elizabeth more about us. Even when my tongue was loosened after wine or beer, I guarded the entrance to that part of my past. She didn't press for information about old girl friends; she took my word for it that, apart from one sort-of long-term interest, I'd always been more interested in books than in girls. The acceptance of *The Prince of Morning*, I suppose, made it easier for me to sell the revisionist version of my sudden ditching of my studies and my departure for London. History had suddenly palled, I told her; writing was the thing and, as for Joyce before me, emigration was essential. And where else would an aspiring Irish writer go but to London? I almost believed the yarn myself; why should she doubt it?

And so I made my promises to love and to honour and to cherish: and the words meant little to me. By the time of our marriage, *Prince* was in the shops and, courtesy of the substantial publisher's advance, Elizabeth and I were the owners of a mortgage-free flat at the Kilburn end of St John's Wood. And that too meant nothing to me: when I look back on it now, from my perch on the Spinney, it all seems like a game, a game of phone-calls and sex, of dinners and sex, of Paddington Station and sex, of *The Prince of Morning* and sex, of buying the flat and sex. And of marrying and even more frequent sex.

And then of less frequent sex.

Elizabeth went on taking charge of it all; I went on letting her take charge of it all.

Or almost so.

Jean was still hidden in my heart; so also was the fear, no, the certainty, that the second book Elizabeth expected simply was not in my giving. I clung to my porter's position as to a life-raft; only at the end, a week before our marriage, did I finally lay aside the trappings of my office. When I took off my navy-blue uniform for the last time, I felt in myself no sense of liberation from drudgery; I felt instead only the loss of a way of life that had been, in its dull way, friendly and comforting.

While Elizabeth set about writing up her doctoral thesis, I roamed the streets of west London, supposedly preparing myself for the task of writing my sequel to *Prince*. I knew that the real pressure would come when she had completed her own task, when she had more time to take more charge of my own efforts. She had no interest whatever in Ireland or Galway but her commitment to my written account of that world was total; so was her belief in me. She loved me, I think; so, in my own way, did I love her.

The falling rain drums not only on the roof of my old car but also on the doors of my heart. We might have made it, she and I, if I had been honest with her and with myself. And it would have been better if I had never written that wretched book.

Sophistry, I tell myself: if there had been no *The Prince of Morning*, there would have been no relationship with Elizabeth. From the moment of our first meeting on Platform 4, I had played my fraudulent card; I could not blame her for expecting that I would lay down the rest of a trump suit.

I couldn't; in my heart I knew that. In my heart I knew also that there would be trouble between us when she discovered that I had neither the desire nor the ability to produce the expected sequel.

'When are you going to start writing?' she asked me one morning, a morning like this, with the rain belting against the window of the kitchen.

'I'm not ready yet.'

'You've been saying that for over a year.'

'I'm still at the planning stages.'

'Daniel!'

'What does it matter, Elizabeth? The money is still coming in and now that you've got a job . . .'

'I married a writer, not an unemployed layabout!' She stood up, angrily pushing back her chair. 'Some of us have work to go to.'

I can still recall the relief I felt that morning when she left for the North London College of Further Education: I almost envied her the zest with which she handled a low-level lecturing job which wasn't at all what she wanted after taking her doctorate. I missed my old job but I hadn't the heart to tell her I wanted to pull on my old uniform again. Translation: I was afraid to tell her. Somewhere inside me I was afraid of losing another part of my life, however unsure I might be of my love for her.

Gabriel got me out of that spot of bother. I thought little of it when Marlena's agency forwarded a letter from some unknown magazine publisher asking to meet me but I replied to say I'd be glad to meet him. I'd done a lot of interviews about the book; the only difference about this one was that it came more than a year after the book had been published.

Gabriel didn't want an interview: instead he wanted a regular column for his embryonic weekly magazine.

'Why me?' I asked him. 'Nobody ever heard of me in America.'

'They will, Daniel, believe me they will.' He sucked noisily at his pint of Guinness. 'When *The Prince of Morning* comes out in the States next spring, believe me they'll notice you and remember you.'

When they threw us out of the pub, we went back to Gabriel's hotel in Bayswater. By the time I left the hotel, pissed on bottled beer at 3.00am, I had agreed to his request to write a column on anything that took my fancy.

'Just give it that same kind of cockeyed innocent feel you've managed to get into your book,' he said, as I left.

When I poured myself out of the minicab in St John's Wood, I felt, for the first time in years, a kind of happiness and I knew it wasn't just induced by the booze. I had expected Elizabeth to be pleased, even impressed, by my new status as an American magazine columnist.

'Fish-and-chips wrapping material!' Her tone was glacial. 'Or hamburger and fries, whatever they go for over there.'

When I reached for her that night, she pushed my hand away: it was the beginning of the long descent, through drinking and sullen arguments, often spread out over days, that would eventually lead to the disintegration of our marriage. Or perhaps not: perhaps the disintegration began before ever we exchanged our registry office vows. Not even the birth of Bee could save us.

'When are you going to get down to your book?' Bee was about five then; the question hadn't been asked in a long time.

'Does it matter?' I asked. Bee was half-listening: I caught her glancing over at us from the couch, where she was reading a new Ladybird. 'We make enough, don't we? We've got the royalties and Gabriel pays well –'

'And there's my money,' she interrupted.

'And there's your money, yes.'

'But that's not the point, Daniel.'

'What is the point, Elizabeth?'

'You promised me,' she said. 'I asked you and you promised.'

'What did you promise Mummy, Daddy?' Bee was looking straight at us, her face solemn with adult curiosity.

'To love you always, sweetheart,' I said, trying to keep my voice level.

'Aren't you going to keep your promise, Daddy?'

Her face was wreathed in a beatific smile: she could never imagine that her father might break his promise.

The rain clouds have vanished as suddenly as they appeared. The sun is shining now, lighting up my broken promises in the town that suddenly sparkles like silver below me. Stephen phoned me yesterday; maybe that's why sleeplessness brought me to the Spinney at 7.00 this morning. He wept on the phone.

'I told you everything a week ago and you've done nothing.'

In his breaking voice I could hear the despair that was his constant companion. 'You promised you'd help me, Mr Best.'

'I will,' I had told him and had put the phone down.

Stephen is right. In a week I have done nothing, not for him, or for Bee, or for Kelly Carpenter. I have paid Kelly's rent but what does that cost me? My mother's nest-egg had been left untouched, eight years after her death; the accumulating remains of her years in the Crotty household. It will belong to Bee in the near future; I know she would not begrudge the little that is spent on Kelly. It is the time I am unable to give, the energy.

Not that I even use it wisely for myself. Jeff has written me a formal letter, pointing out that, as I have refused to accept the treatment he recommends, he would like to know if I am attending another physician. The letter arrived a couple of days ago: when I looked at his sprawling signature, all I could think of was that the hand that had held the pen had touched the other girl in the apartment in College Court and would have fumbled with Kelly's things too, were it not for Leonard's proprietary interest.

I taste my own sourness, sitting here above the shining city. I am repelled by it: I would disown this lump-ridden body if I could. Just a few weeks gone since that day in Jeff's surgery, when I first heard of my own fate – and of Kelly Carpenter's – yet in that time I have developed the feel of an ending in myself. I wonder if Bee would notice the difference in me. Only three weeks have passed since she was here with me, yet now I should be afraid to let her look into my eyes. Your own fear is not a thing you want your daughter to look upon.

Ten minutes past nine, the dashboard clock tells me. The two hours I have spent here have shown me no more than what I already knew – a terrain of unkempt and unkept pledges where the heart is afraid to venture.

It is time for me to venture back down the hill to Paternoster. Although the sun still shines, I am chilled, as though the night had wormed its frozen way into my bones. I am reversing the old

Merc, angling my way towards the exit from the Spinney, when I hear the *put-put-putting* of a labouring engine in the lane behind me. Even before I turn around to look, I know whose car it is, come to keep its regretful morning appointment here above the town he has betrayed.

I stop reversing as the old Fiat estate car pulls up alongside me. When our eyes meet, I see the recognition dawn in Stephen Conroy's face; shock at first in the thin face, and then a flush of anger suffusing the pale features. When he steps out of the car it is my turn to be shocked: he looks not just disheveled but also unwashed with a few day's unshaven beard darkening his face.

I lower the window, preparing myself for his wrath, yet in front of my eyes he is diminished: his anger seems to evaporate in the watery sunshine and I am left staring at the husk of a man who has come to the end of his tether. I have no wish to see him like this, naked and pathetic, but there is nowhere for me to hide.

'Mr Best?'

The hesitancy in his voice offends me; for his formality I feel only the stirrings of contempt. He should come at me with both barrels blazing and lay about me with anger. I say nothing.

'You promised to help me.'

Still I am silent.

'What am I going to do, Mr Best?'

From the corner of my eye I can see the giant crane moving above the docks, its green arm labouring across the sky. In a little while another Crotty excrescence of luxurious apartments will have been added to the city skyline. I realise that Stephen is sobbing. In the same old rain Mac his thin body twitches like a diviner's leg.

'My wife, my girls . . .' His sobbing scars the morning. 'You told me you'd help me.' His haunted expression pierces my own numbed defenses. Perhaps what I am feeling is no more than the savage yearning for revenge against the silver-spooned bastard who got between Jean and myself all those years ago.

'I will, Stephen,' I tell him. 'This time I really will.'

This time I really meant it but I swiftly close up the window of the car and the mud churns under my wheels as I fling the old Merc towards the lane. Stephen's racking sobs go with me, like the crying of curs left abandoned in the rain.

Chapter 21

I drove straight to Merchant's Road. The rain was easing off by the time I swung into St Benen's Court: the windows of the office building that surrounded the courtyard sparkled in the watery sunshine. Every wall bore the same notice:

PRIVATE PARKING FOR CROTTY DEVELOPMENTS: CARS PARKED ILLEGALLY WILL BE CLAMPED.

Some of the spaces had registration plates pinned to the walls; for a moment I wondered if the spot I had pulled into, marked for a '98 registration, might be Leonard's own.

I wasn't getting off so lightly. Two spaces along, facing a space occupied by a black 1998 Lexus was a plate marked simply: CHAIRMAN. Leonard was inside, no doubt about it. I felt the anger kindle in me again, and I let it burn: perhaps rage could do for me now what alcohol had done all those years ago in the Crotty's front garden. Or perhaps not: what had to be done and said now must be done in the light of day, unhidden by any rain-sodden darkness.

The windows that looked out on St Benen's Court were of darkened, smoky glass but I felt watching eyes upon me as I got out of the car. Leonard himself might be watching me: I half-hoped he was. Or perhaps I'd be met inside the front door by an irate secretary pointing out that I had invaded somebody's parking space.

I wasn't. The area inside the double-glass doors was deserted but the mahogany board on the marble wall between the staircase and the elevator left you in no doubt that here you were at the heart of the Crotty empire. The names of a plethora of Crotty companies were fanfared in elegant gold lettering on the polished wood: Crotty Enterprises, Crotty Developments, Crotty Urban Renewals, Crotty Homes . . . Prospector Enterprises. Just for a moment I felt daunted by this array of Crottiness but then my anger, and perhaps my resentment too, kicked in again and I jabbed resolutely at the lift button. "Reception – Fourth Floor" another sign in the deserted lobby had read, I was reluctant to commit my ailing legs to so many flights of stairs.

The elevator was one of those stainless steel capsules that you half-expect to deposit you at the top of a gantry in Cape Canaveral. Even the voice that told you that you were on the Fourth Floor sounded digitalised, as though you were en route to the stars, the stars of my father.

The elevator opened into a spacious, carpeted reception area. The blonde girl at the reception desk smiled at me as I stepped gingerly out of the lift. She was no more than eighteen, I thought, but her professional smile and "good morning" held all the assurance of someone who knew and liked her place in the world's scheme of things.

Who did I wish to see, she wanted to know?

'Len,' I smiled. I had decided to play the old pals game.

And could she tell Mr Crotty who was calling?

'Daniel,' I told her, glancing around the area.

That would be Mr Daniel . . .?

'Best,' I said, struck by the silence of the area. 'Tell Len that Daniel Best has come calling.'

I thought I saw a flicker of recognition in the made-up blue eyes when I spoke my name; on the other hand, she perhaps just picked up on the hostility that I couldn't quite keep out of my voice.

And then she was on the phone and I realized that it was not Leonard but some secretary she was speaking to and she said 'yes' a few times and I caught her glancing at me – yes, she had come across my ubiquitous Prince, I was sure of it now – and her smile was apologetic when she replaced the phone.

'I'm sorry, Mr Best, but Mr Crotty is tied up right now. Could I make an appointment for you?'

'Of course.' I'd anticipated this through the fog of my anger. 'You do that.'

Once more we smiled at each other. Once more she picked up the phone; once more I listened as she spoke to Leonard's secretary and, when she was done, wrote out the date and time of my appointment with the emperor of Crotty Enterprises. It was for the following week.

'Nice offices,' I said, pocketing the card.

'It's lovely, isn't it and the view is spectacular,' she laughed self-consciously. 'I mean, if I only had time to look at it.' Her jewelled fingers gestured towards the city skyline beyond the windows.

'I bet Leonard's office has a great view,' I said.

'The best,' she giggled, pointing upwards. 'The penthouse! The whole top floor, with windows all round.'

'I hadn't realised there was a higher floor than this one?' I tried to look puzzled.

'Oh yes but access is only from this floor by the private lift or the stairway.'

I was opening the door she was pointing at before she realised what I was doing.

'Mr Best . . . Mr Best –' She called after me but I let the door swing shut. A shallow staircase of wide steps led up to the penthouse level. Here the air seemed brighter, as though we really had climbed up among the heavens. The blonde secretary had been right: there were windows on all four walls offering a 360-degree panoramic view of the city. Every available inch of space between the windows was hung with framed colour photographs of Leonard Crotty in various locations, always in the company of instantly recognisable politicians and businessmen. I disliked everything about the place on sight.

Leonard himself was standing at an outsize drawing board to one side of an equally outsize desk. He was in the company of two younger men, both of whom were pointing out something to him, on the plans laid out on the drawing board. All three of them turned towards me when they heard my steps on the stair – and perhaps also my laboured breathing.

'Well, I'm honoured.' The tone of Leonard's voice made it clear that he felt anything but honoured. 'The scribe of Paternoster Lane in person.'

I said nothing, standing at the top of the stairs, trying to catch my breath. I had not anticipated finding him in company.

'Not like you to be stuck for words, Daniel.' Leonard's smile was icy. 'Gentlemen,' he went on, not bothering even to look at the others. 'May I present to you, Mr Daniel Best, internationally known author and columnist, the *prince of morning* himself.'

The two men smiled nervously but neither spoke. I couldn't blame them for their nervousness: the raw edginess in the room was palpable. I nodded in reply to their hellos but I barely took my eyes off Leonard. Close to, I could see that he was in better shape than I had expected; with a deep tan and wavy, still-ungreyed hair it was easy to see what had drawn Kelly Carpenter towards him.

'So, what can we do for you, Dan? I'd ask you to sit down but . . .' The gold cuff-link flashed as Len gestured towards the drawing board. 'But we're sort of up to our necks right now.'

'You can say that again.'

'Sorry?' His blue eyes narrowed.

'I want to talk to you about the Spinney.'

'The Spinney?'

'That's what I said.' I longed to get off my feet but pride and anger wouldn't allow me to drop down into the chair I was leaning on.

'Ah! You're after an early booking, old son.' Leonard's smile took in his two acolytes but the blue eyes were unsmiling. 'Not that I can blame you, we could sell that development ten times over, couldn't we, gentlemen?'

Yes, they smiled uneasily, one either side of him, Galway's version of Rosencrantz and Guildenstern, yes, they surely could.

'And College Court,' I went on, 'I want to talk to you about a particular apartment in College Court, the one that Kelly Carpenter has been staying in until recently.'

It was as if the sun had disappeared. Leonard's face darkened; for a moment I thought he would step towards me and strike me. When at last he spoke, his voice was harsh and almost strangulated.

'Gentlemen,' he said, without taking his eyes off me. 'Would you excuse us, please.' They left hurriedly through a door at the other end of the room. 'What the fuck d'you think you're playing at, Daniel? Bursting in here unannounced, making accusations. Just who the fuck d'you think you are?'

Leonard wasn't quite as tall as me but he seemed to tower over me in his rage. I had never feared him and I wasn't going to now, even though the strength had left me and my legs no longer went as fast as I wanted them to.

'Well? What the fuck d'you think you're playing at?'

'Maybe I'm the avenging angel, Leonard, come to seek justice for the little people that you think you can walk all over.' I sat down, unable to go on standing any longer but not caring if he knew that. I was enjoying myself at his expense. 'Sometimes the little guys need help against the big bullies like you and . . .' I pointed at the array of photographs. 'And all these other bullies, who are in your gang, your mafia.'

'Christ on a skateboard.' Leonard seemed genuinely puzzled. 'You really do think you're Robin-fucking-Hood, don't you?'

'I think I'm Kelly Carpenter's friend and I want to see her treated right.'

'Who's Kelly Carpenter? Have I met her?'

'Frequently. She's the college student you set up in College Court for your own pleasure and who is now pregnant with your child.'

Leonard looked at me for a long time, trying to understand my motives. 'She's a floozy, that's what she is. She's also a fucking idiot who didn't know when she was well off. She could also be a fucking gold-digger who deliberately stopped taking her fucking pills so she could take a pot-shot at me.' He grinned at me. 'Have you thought of that, Mr *fucking* Robin Hood?'

'No,' I said. 'But maybe I'll call one evening and discuss it with your wife.'

'You come near my house, Best, and I'll beat the living shite out of you. That's a promise.'

'Just like you did all those years ago up at the Spinney.'

He flushed.

'That was then,' Len said. 'And this is now. Look at you; you fuck, out on your feet. It won't be long anyway until they're carrying you out in a fucking box.' He stopped, folded and unfolded his arms, leaning against his desk. 'I didn't mean that,' he said. 'I mean . . .'

'Pillow talk in College Court, eh, Leonard. Jeff always had a big mouth.'

In different circumstances I might have been touched by his embarrassment. As it was, the pity in his expression merely enraged me: it's the way you feel when you look into another's face and read in its lines the knowledge of your own passing.

'Is she okay?'

'Kelly? Who knows?' I shrugged. 'Her future is on the line.'

'I hear you've set her up in a flat.'

Again I shrugged.

'It's a small town, Danny.'

'It's a changing town and not for the better.'

'It's progress, Danny.'

'It's greed, Len, just fucking greed.' I could hear Bee's words in my heart.

'You always were a dreamer, Danny.'

'Is that what Stephen Conroy is?' I said calmly. I saw him flinch: this was news to him, that I should know so much. 'Is he a dreamer too, dreaming of a job he used to have and a salary he used to have to look after his family?'

224

'You've been digging, haven't you, Danny?' Leonard Crotty settled himself on top of the big desk and his eyes studied me like some rare specimen or a virgin site, or a virgin for that matter. 'What's this all about, Daniel?' The blue eyes were shrewd, narrowed. 'Has life disappointed you? So you're searching for some last lost cause to make your life seem worthwhile. Is that it?'

I felt the sweat damp in my armpits and I knew it was not caused by the morning's exertions. It was the sweat of fear; fear of that other road I had no wish to walk.

'Maybe the old demon guilt has caught up with you at last, Danny, is that it?' He saw the fear in my face and he laughed dryly, homing in on his prey. 'Yes, guilt, Danny. You fucked-off without a by-your-leave all those years ago and left your mother to fend for herself –'

'Leave my mother out of this,' I spat out.

'Why should I? I liked her . . . Perhaps even more than you, you fuck. All those years she was in our house I got nothing but kindness from her and I liked her. Damn it, Danny, you wouldn't let me visit her at the end.'

His words brought that rainy evening back to me: the door of Paternoster open and the rain sleeting down and the look of astonishment on Leonard's face when I'd told him I'd prefer him not to visit my mother again. He'd given me a deep, searching look before shrugging his shoulders and stalking out into the rain. He'd stayed away after that but he'd been there in church, a few months later, at my mother's funeral mass.

'I'm not here to talk about my mother,' I said.

'No, you're here to squeeze money out of me for a couple of strays who've crossed your path. Now tell me, old friend Daniel,' he said, pushing a photograph to one side on the desk. 'Why the fuck should I do anything for you?'

'Because if you don't,' I told him. 'You might be on the end of some unpleasant publicity.'

'There are laws of libel in this country.'

'Fair comment is allowed and so is the impartial presentation of facts.'

'You have no facts, just a tale of a stupid girl who got pregnant and an idiot clerk who made a mistake.'

'D'you want to take that chance? Wait and see if that's how your family and friends will see it?'

I watched Leonard weighing his options. His gaze swung towards the docks, a block away: in the pale December light you could see the massive crane moving ponderously above the rooftops, writing his name across the sky. He turned back towards me, idly picking up the brass-framed photo on his desk and turning it over in his hands. Abruptly he laughed.

'Why not?' he said. 'We all have to pay for our sins and our pleasures. Why shouldn't I pay for mine? So you win, Danny, I'll take care of your pair of lame ducks.'

'What does that mean? I need to know.'

'You need to know fuck-all, Danny, except that I've given you my word. You're not fucking God. I'll look after Kelly's little bastard properly and I'll find some fucking, filing job for Conroy to do . . . Something far away from me so that I don't have to be too aware of the little shite's existence.'

'How do I know you'll keep your word?'

'Because I've given it to you.' He put the photograph down on the desk and got to his feet. 'Now would you kindly fuck off, Daniel, no offence, and let me get on with my work.'

I shook my head. From somewhere in the corners of my mind came the recollection of my mother on that first day at the big house, tenaciously chanting her mantra until she got what she thought was her due. 'There's something else,' I said.

Len seemed still occupied with the colour photograph on his desk. I could see him in the centre, large and pale in a short-sleeved shirt with, next to him, a woman in a white dress: the other faces under the cloudless blue sky were black, smiling brilliantly at the lens.

'Don't push your luck, old son.'

I had my own mantra to chant.

'The Spinney,' I said.

'What about the Spinney?'

'I want your word that you won't build on it and that . . . that you'll hand it over to the city.'

'Are you out of your fucking mind? You come waltzing in here with ridiculous demands!'

'You got your planning permission through blackmail. I want you to give it up.'

'I've had enough of this shite,' Leonard said. 'Now get out of my office.'

'There's nothing agreed,' I said. 'Until everything is agreed. If you won't do this, I'm going to expose you, no matter what you do for Stephen Conroy or Kelly Carpenter.'

'Then you'd better get a move on 'cos you look like you're not going to be around for too long.'

'I can't do anything about that but maybe my words will live longer than me.'

'How noble . . . How fucking noble.' Len's mouth grimaced in contempt. 'Have you any idea what an outfit like mine means to this town? D'you think there's nothing more to this company than just a bunch of pictures of me shaking hands with a bunch of heads from here, there and everywhere? Is that what you think? Let me put you straight, Danny Boy. Last time I looked, and that was last Friday's payday, I was the employer of almost six hundred men and women in this country alone and that's just direct employment. There are another few thousand people with sub-contractors who work almost exclusively for us in this country alone. Overseas we have ongoing projects in nine different countries, all of them bringing revenue into this country. This isn't some cowboy outfit, Danny, it's a major player and sometimes it's not easy running it . . . Not that I'd expect you to appreciate that, with your fondness for chasing after windmills. But you'd better appreciate this. The pieces of this organisation hang together precariously; sometimes cash flow from one project keeps another going. The Spinney is important to us and we're going ahead with it whether you like it or not.'

Despite myself I was stirred by the passion of Leonard's outburst. The gallery of smiling, hard-hatted, foundation-laying, topping-out photographs told their own story: Leonard Crotty moved in a universe of power and in a way, his progress was the story of the rise and rise of the Celtic Tiger. Perhaps he was right: I was tired and should leave well enough alone.

And yet something wasn't right. Something about the photograph on Leonard's desk was troubling me, like an elusive melody imperfectly remembered. I stood up and walked slowly to the desk. There was a curious smile on his lips as I reached for the photograph; the smell of his aftershave, close by, seemed to snare us together in an old intimacy. I felt his eyes upon me as I studied the photograph.

It was her. Looking strangely formal in the white cotton dress, stiffer somehow than I recalled, but it was her. The hair lighter, bleached by the African sun, but still the hair that I had caressed and kissed all those years ago. Her smile was frozen but it was the smile I remembered, the lips parted, ready for kissing. She looked as if she belonged there, under those endless skies, in the company of all those black faces posing in front of a low-rise, white-painted block. So did Leonard, shaking hands with her. At the edge of the photograph was a notice board that said in capital letters:

MALULA HOSPITAL EXTENSION
MAIN CONTRACTORS:
CROTTY INTERNATIONAL DEVELOPMENTS.

'You were a bastard to her.' Leonard's words interrupted my reverie. 'She needed you after the accident but you never even wrote. How could you just leave her like that . . . I mean, a woman like Jean, how could you do that to her?'

He went on, heedless of my silence: 'I know she wrote to you that time your mother died, but you never even answered her. How could you do that when you knew she was always mad about you?'

I still had the letter, could recite by heart the address and PO Box number of the Malula Hospital in the photograph in my hand. Elizabeth had also written around that time, to say that as we'd been separated so long there was no point in having a contested divorce and that, she was sorry about my mother and that, her solicitors would be in contact with me in the near future.

'She keeps in touch,' Leonard was saying. 'She always asks about you, although for the life of me I can't see why she bothers.'

I'd given up the heavy drinking by the time Jean's letter arrived but I was still paralysed by the death of my mother, my impending divorce, and my own uselessness.

'She's due home about now,' I heard Len saying. 'Her mother's not well. Jean is coming home to look after her.'

And he'd be seeing her: I hated him for that as much as I hated him for the truth of his accusations.

'Maybe,' I said, putting the photograph down. 'You could arrange to build another hospital extension and make some more money out of her.'

The tan faded, his face grew white with rage.

'You're a shite, Daniel, you know that? A first class, superior kind of shite. You're so sick you're not even worth striking.' He fixed the photograph on his desk— I could see his hands were trembling – and then he turned back to me. 'It's none of your business but, just to keep the record straight, this company never took a penny for building that extension. We supplied the materials and the labour; I called in favours to fit the place out. But no money changed hands.' He shook his head. 'I did it because I like Jean and because I admire what she does but I don't suppose you'd understand simple stuff like that, simple loyalty.'

'I understand about Kelly Carpenter.'

'Fuck off, Danny. She's a floozy, I told you.'

'She's a human being.'

'Yeah sure! You'd know all about that, with your record. Now why don't you just fuck off out of my office and crawl away into some corner to die: you're not even man enough to go for treatment.'

So Jeff had told him everything: I wasn't surprised and it no longer mattered. 'At least,' I said, not caring that it sounded childish. 'I'm not the same kind of man as you and your father.'

'No,' Leonard laughed. 'You're just like your own oul' fella, afraid to carry on and face the music.'

Something turned in the penthouse air, something dark, slithering towards the light.

'What does that mean?' My voice was a whisper.

'Get off the fucking stage, Daniel,' Leonard spoke harshly. 'The whole fucking town knows what it means . . . Just like you do.'

'What are you talking about?' I could feel the dark slitheriness oozing upwards along my flesh. 'What do you mean?'

'Just get out of my office, Danny, and don't bother to come back.'

'I don't know what you're talking about.'

'Then you must be the only person in Galway who doesn't.' He picked up the phone. 'I'm going to phone the guards to have you removed from my office, Danny. It would be better if you didn't make me do that.'

'Tell me what you meant,' I pleaded.

'Fuck off, Daniel.'

Chapter 22

'Get in the car, Paudge.'

'What's up, Danny boy?'

I could see the puzzlement, even fear, in Paudge's small, rodent-like features. He was crouched on the edge of the pavement; his woolen- capped head stuck in the open window of my car.

'Just get in.'

'What for? What d'you want with me, Danny?' The fear was deepening now, the pale eyes darting from side to side as though searching for an escape route.

'Just get in the car, Paudge.'

'But why –'

'Don't make me fucking drag you in here, Paudge.'

The skinny Adam's apple bobbed in the scrawny throat, the eyes went on with their restless searching, but he straightened and pulled the passenger door open and sat in beside me.

'You don't look so good, Danny.' I could hear the nervousness in Paudge's voice, the edge of fear that is forever expecting accusation or punishment. 'What's up with you?'

'You and I are just going to have a little chat.' I had to will my hands into steadiness as I eased the car away from the kerb.

'But where are we going?' Panic in the reedy voice now. 'I have to stay here on the street.'

'We're not going far, Paudge.' Just far enough for me to get my thoughts together. I'd driven in a kind of daze from Leonard's office to Paternoster; it had been an act of impulse, seeing Paudge at his regular sentinel post, to pull up and harangue him into the car.

'But can't we talk here, Danny? I don't like to be far away from the oul' street, it doesn't suit me away from the place.'

Paudge's words only made me drive faster. The further we got from his daily stomping ground, the greater the chance that I could find out from him the name of the shadow that Leonard's dark words had dropped upon me. Or maybe I already knew its name and was merely afraid to look in its face.

Two or three times more Paudge protested but, in the face of my stony silence, he fell quiet. The promenade was quiet in the December morning; I felt Paudge's silence settle into acceptance of his unexpected excursion. We drove past Salthill, then on through Barna.

'Jaysus, Danny, I never knew the country was like this.' There was a wheezy, forced astonishment in Paudge's voice as we sped past the endless sequence of bungalows and B&B's. 'All them fuckin' rocks and stone walls'd give you a pain in your head,' he ventured.

I pulled over near Spiddal. Paudge looked at the sea crashing on our left before he spoke. 'Jaysus, Danny,' he said. 'Where are we? We must be fuckin' miles from our own street?'

I shook my head. The trembling had left my hands and I was clear about what I feared to know. 'Drop the act, Paudge. Fellows like us, are never far from Paternoster, no matter where we are.'

'What's that supposed to mean?'

'It means, Paudge, that nothing happens in the Lane that you don't know about.' Behind his ferrety-face the sea was grey and angry. 'Nobody breathes or whistles or breaks wind on the street, Paudge, but you know who did it. Right?'

I was glad that he looked frightened.

'How old are you, Paudge:'

'Sure you know damn well I'm twelve years older than yourself, Danny.' He licked his lips. 'I'm 60 this month.'

'You're the unsung historian of Paternoster, Paudge,' I went on. 'The watcher on the corner, the chronicler of curtains lifted and doors ajar.'

'Jaysus, Danny, would you talk like an ordinary fuckin' Christian and not be goin' on like that.' The pointy Adam's apple rose and fell in its grizzly folds. 'You're making me nervous, out here in the middle of fuckin' nowhere.'

'Tell me about my father,' I said.

'About your Dad?'

'Yes.'

'Sure what the fuck would I know about your father?' Behind him the sea was darkening to primeval sludge, creeping towards the car. 'Don't you know all about him yourself?'

'Tell me about the time he died.'

'Fuck this, Danny. I don't know what the fuck you're talking about.'

'I might break every bone in your body, Paudge, or I might just drop you somewhere in the back of beyond . . . But you're going to tell me anyway.' Even the shingle was slithering towards us now, black scales in the pounding surf, thrusting their heart of darkness against my own. 'Tell me about that race that our Prince won and the way my father never came home after it.'

'Danny –'

I swung at him then, grabbing him by the neck of his shirt and squeezing until his Adam's apple scraped against my knuckles. I saw the fear in his eyes as I shook his head like an old rattlebag, backwards and forwards.

'Danny!' He was gasping for breath when I let him go. 'Why d'you want to know this?'

'Because I'm the only one in the town who doesn't know.' Or didn't want to know.

'Your father was a good man, Danny.'

I made as if to grab at his neck again but my own strength was failing. 'Fuck you, Paudge . . . Just tell me.'

He gave in then and began to talk. Sometimes I had to prompt him with a question but I didn't have to ask much. In my heart I knew the story. I think I had always known it: I had merely clothed it with the darkness that was now moving towards me along the shingle.

In its own way the story that spilled and dribbled from Paudge's thin lips was a trite enough tale: a commonplace yarn of greyhound-racing and gambling in the Ireland of my childhood, bets placed locally and in Dublin at the generous odds on offer about a dog that was known to have no chance and the harvest of winnings collected on the track after the impostor's victory and at the Dublin bookies on the Saturday morning. Simple and safe, with the real Prince stowed safely at a friendly farm somewhere in the county.

But not foolproof.

'Someone squealed,' Paudge said, licking dry lips. 'And it all came out in the wash the next day, and the guards were back at Crotty's talking to your father.'

Paudge's face blurred before my eyes: I remembered that Saturday lunch-hour, how my mother had kept the stew hot for my father, how I had watched the street, waiting for him to thrill me with the tale of our Prince's glorious, shining, noble effort.

'Was Crotty in on it?'

'Who else? Not that anybody could pin anything on the likes of him, Danny, you know the way the fuckin' world is. The way I heard it, it was that fucker set it up and it was him made the money out of it.'

'But why . . .' I was wrestling with the darkness now. 'Why were the guards only after my father?'

I saw the pity in the rheumy eyes.

'Sure didn't he own the oul' dog, Danny, and wasn't he the trainer if you could call it that?'

There was no point in holding back now: I had to know.

'And afterwards,' I said. 'My father never came home. What really happened to him?'

'Danny, you don't want to hear –'

'Tell me!' I spat it at him. 'I want to hear it.'

And so I heard it, sitting there beside the angry sea, from a wizened neighbour who had known all my life what had happened to my father. And as I listened, I knew too that I had always known the truth and that it had shaped my life in more ways than I cared to admit. Even the book, which gave me my living – especially that book –, was a fiction that I had perpetrated to conceal the truth more completely.

'Danny?' Paudge's voice seemed to come from the darkness that was drowning me.

'What?'

'Will you drive me back now, Danny. Please.' Fear and pity were written on the thin features. 'I hate the fucking countryside.'

I started the engine then and swung the car around and we made our way towards town in total silence. The Lane was silent when we got back. It was still only lunch-hour: only a few hours had passed since I had pushed my way into Leonard's office yet in that brief span darkness had settled upon my world. I looked at the street with eyes that had been closed but now were opened and I knew that it would never again look the same to me: yesterday had become a lie that would darken whatever days were left to me.

'Danny?' I felt Paudge's tentative hand on my arm. 'I'm sorry, I wish you hadn't make me tell you that stuff.' He swung the door open and stepped out. He called my name again and, when I turned, he was leaning into the car again. 'Your father was a good man,' he said. 'Don't forget that . . . He was a good man.'

The door slammed shut and I was left alone with my thoughts.

Did I sleep, sitting there in the car, or was it a waking dream? It's a dream that lingers still: it should be a nightmare, spun from the stammered tale of Paudge's pitying words, but in fact it does not terrify me. Anger yes, Dad for what you did to yourself and to us, but mostly pity for the loneliness of your going. And in my own pity I find a kind of gentleness that clothes my own wounded heart. Your face breaks into a grin under your helmet of curls and I am once again a boy.

I do not see you on that morning after Prince's triumph, when you step into my room before you go to work at Crotty's. But in my vision you are alive, bending over me in the bed, a boy wrapped in the blanket of your love. From the vantage point of my years I sense your confusion and your shame, your regret but your hope too for the good things, the tiny comforts, that the plundered gains would bring to our house on Paternoster.

And I sense your fear when the guards arrive at Crotty's yard; you, who prided yourself on your right to look, smiling at any man, are racked by shame. Maybe you speak to old Crotty; does he counsel you to take your medicine? Does he assure you that prison will pass but the benefits of your pitiful loot will linger longer? Such calculations weigh not at all with you; you were always your own man but now you are someone else's creature.

Where do you go while we wait through the lunch hour for your step in the hall? Do you walk by the docks, out by Lough Atalia and down by the Sportsground where you had eaten the ashes of deceit and pocketed the fool's gold of Crotty's greed?

That long day drags itself towards your darkness. Whether you walk or hide or sup your pint in some unfamiliar pub, I know not, but I know your heart; as night falls you weigh your own pain against the shame that must visit us in Paternoster and now, all these years later, my own heart breaks with yours as your decision is made.

And I watch you now with eyes that are all cried out, as the light fades and darkness settles over the bay and the docks and the careless town. You let yourself back into Crotty's yard and you force the door of the high-ceilinged warehouse and you feel your way among the familiar aisles of lumber until you reach the ladder. And you climb slowly, the hempen rope coiled around your shoulder, until you reach the highest beam in that dark and vaulted space. With the hands that always held me safe you knot the rope around the beam and you place the noose around your neck and you let go with courage; you are thinking of Mammy, and of me, as you step out into space and for a moment you tread the uncaring air and then the darkness gathers you into itself and you swing there through the long and silent night at the end of old Crotty's rope.

I pity you and I forgive you, Dad, but still my heart bellows its own agony: why, Dad, why did you have to leave us?

Chapter 23

Are the sins of the fathers visited upon the children? Or do sons willingly repeat their fathers' crimes?

My own words stared back at me from the screen. Someone was going to pay: for my father's pain, for my own. In the small front room of Paternoster, the rage and grief of all the years seemed to glare at me from the turquoise monitor of the computer and, I sent that pain back, screaming more loudly, through the innocent keyboard. Someone would pay for the murder of innocence in our town, in my life and, I knew who that someone was:

This tale of corruption from the Emerald Isle spans half a century and two generations of an allegedly respectable Irish merchant family. It's a story rich in the elements of an epic movie – fraud and dishonour and death; at a simpler level it's a tale of an ordinary man, an unscrupulous employer and a greyhound that couldn't run very fast. The only thing it doesn't have, in Hollywood terms, is a happy ending.

But let's begin at the beginning, almost 50 years ago, in a sleepy town in the west of Ireland, with that less-than-fleet-footed greyhound. His name was Corrib Prince.

The day had grown dark by the time I had come to in the car and hauled myself into the house. Now it was well after midnight. I hadn't bothered to close the curtains; from time to time voices made loud with drink and high spirits would come rolling in from the street and I'd catch a glimpse of young people hurrying past my window as though they had promises to keep. I'd turn back to my keyboard: I'd had my own miles to travel before I slept.

After the way in which Leonard and I had parted, I no longer knew if he intended to look after Kelly Carpenter and Stephen Conroy. Neither did I care. All that really mattered to me now, was that Leonard and his clan should suffer for their sins. I would hurt them the only way I could, with my words. And I would make them suffer in the way that my father had suffered; I would hang Leonard on the gibbet of shame and I would let him swing there for the world to see and to sneer at.

All through the night I tapped away at the keyboard, shaping the pain, polishing the anger. The voices and the footfalls from the street mingled with the phantoms in my head and as the night wore on the noises from Paternoster began to die until finally, I was left only with the company of my ghosts. But they were more real to me than the unknown faces and figures on the pavement outside my window: I knew the touch and the feel of them; their voices spoke directly to my heart. I could never quiet their pain, I knew that, but perhaps my poured-out anger would afford them some satisfaction. That, and the visitation of fear and shame on those who had hurt us.

It was after 6.00am when I keyed in the last word. It was a long piece, almost 3,000 words, much longer than my usual column. I knew that I would have to persuade Gabriel to run the article. He'd quibble at the length but his real concern, I knew, would be the risk of libel and damages. I'd be able to set his mind at rest: old man Crotty was dead and we could say what we liked about the bastard; as for Leonard, I had the facts and figures, the dates and the names, to lend substance to my allegations.

The light from the streetlamps on the Lane was paler now,

casting a yellowish glow into the room as the darkness paled towards daybreak. In the paleness of the light even my words on the monitor looked fainter, as though they were already fading. We were all fading, I thought grimly, every minute of our lives. Anger and grief had sustained me through the long night but now I felt drained. In spite of myself, I found myself reaching for the undeniable presence of the cancer in my armpit. The disease would win but not just yet: I would go on for as long as it took to see my words in print.

Exhaustion overtook me; I fell asleep in the chair, with the voices of my phantoms whispering to my heart.

The doorbell wakened me. I moved; the computer disturbed, flickered into life. In the blue light of the monitor I blinked, stretching towards consciousness. I saw my own words on the screen and the night came back to me. My back hurt when I stood up; I wondered if I was imagining the lumpiness near the right side of my chest.

The bell rang again. An Alberta matriarch, I thought, or maybe some earnest kid from Cumbria, *Prince* at the ready for my scrawled signature. When I switched off the light in the room, the morning was dark with December dreariness. The clock in the corner of the screen showed just after 10.30. I stretched, yawning, unwilling to confront the battlefields of the night and the previous day. A shave and a shower would be welcome; better still, get back to bed although I knew that sleep would elude me. Once more the doorbell rang. Whoever it was would have to put up with my scruffiness. In my stockinged feet I shuffled along the narrow hall.

When I opened the door and saw her standing there on the footpath, I thought at first that I was sleepwalking with the phantoms of the night. The blue anorak, zipped up to her neck against the cold and the rain, seemed too big for her; she was bare- headed and her hair, damped flat by the rain, was bleached lighter than I recalled. Neither of us spoke, and then she blinked away the drops of rain falling on her face, and she smiled, and amid the lines weathered upon her face by the years and by the sun I saw it: the faint scar, jagged and pink-edged, running down from her left eye.

'Aren't you going to ask me in out of the rain, Daniel?' she said, her eyes crinkled in a grin.

'Oh, Christ, forgive me,' I said, and I stood aside to let Jean pass by me into the house.

Chapter 24

In the kitchen I busied myself with courtesies. I took her coat and draped it over the back of a chair. I found a fresh towel for her to dry her hair. I turned up the thermostat and seated her close to the radiator. I was about to plug in an electric fire but she stopped me. Tea, I said, we should have tea. I felt her eyes upon me as I held the kettle under the tap and then plugged it in. Cups, I said, we needed cups. I threw her a glance while I put cups and sugar and milk on the table and saw the small smile upon her lips.

'Shall I make some toast? You must be famished.'

'Daniel.' It was so strange to hear my name spoken again in this kitchen by the voice that I had dreamed of. 'Don't make a fuss, there's no need. Let's just have a cuppa.'

'Are you sure? It's no trouble to make you something to eat.'

'I came to see you, Daniel.'

I was relieved to have to turn away to ready the teapot. There was an awkward silence as the kettle seemed to take forever to boil, but when the tea was finally made, I had to turn and face her.

Jean poured. Over the cups I looked at her. She was wearing a blue sweater over a white blouse; the denim jeans and trainers surprised me.

'You don't look like a nun, Jean.' Her name sounded strange spoken aloud.

'What's a nun supposed to look like?'

I thought of the nuns of my youth, their bodies hidden in long, dark folds, their faces shining and innocent in white wimples and mysterious veils. 'Not like you,' I said.

'Maybe I'm not a proper nun?' She smiled at me.

'Are you? I mean, are you a proper nun?'

'I'm a doctor,' Jean said.

'Is that why you're here? Because you're a doctor?'

'I know what you're talking about, Daniel, I can't deny that. I got a phone call last night but that's not why I'm here.' She put her cup down, gently, on the table and her great dark eyes locked onto mine. 'I'm here because I'm your friend.'

No words came to me.

Her eyes held me, hypnotic, spanning the years to that other time when we had sat in this kitchen, ever mindful of my mother's watchful presence. 'I'd like to think that you're my friend too, Daniel.'

'I'm some friend alright,' I reached out across the table as if to touch her face but drew my hand back again. 'To leave you like that! I'm . . . I'm so sorry.'

'It was a long time ago.'

'It only seems like yesterday to me.'

'Yes, I know.'

Silence gripped us. I felt that in the space between us she could see what I could: choices not chosen, turnings not taken. Lives that had not been lived.

'You have a daughter.'

'Beatrice.' My daughter who was still waiting for a letter from me, I thought. 'My busy Bee,' I smiled. 'She's sixteen and she's beautiful.'

'And her mother? Is she beautiful too?'

'Yes.' I looked at her then and held her glance. 'We split up a long time ago.'

'And does that seem like yesterday too?'

'The loving was over a long time before we parted.'

'Maybe I shouldn't have asked but becoming a nun doesn't stop you from being bitchy.'

'You were never bitchy, Jean. Never.'

'You might not say that in a few months time.' She saw the look of puzzlement on my face. 'Mum's in the advanced stages of Alzheimer's. I've come back to help Kate take care of her. Kate's got the patience of a saint but me, I don't know if I'm going to be much of a help to her. Even this morning, before coming here, I snapped at her before I left the house,' Jean shrugged. 'Me, the anointed nun, off to Mass every morning but not able to keep a civil tongue in my mouth with my own mother and my own sister.'

'Maybe you're tired.' Up close I could see how tightly the skin seemed drawn across her face, how deep the fine lines etched that tanned skin and how they somehow disguised the scar.

'Look who's talking. You look as if you haven't slept for days, Daniel.'

'I just need a shave. If I'd known you were coming,' I shrugged.

'Would you prefer if I hadn't come?'

'God, no, of course not. But . . . but who phoned you?'

'Len. He just said you weren't very well and that you could do with cheering up.'

'Anybody'd need cheering up after spending time with him.'

'The pair of you are like children,' Jean shook her head. 'Aren't you ever going to let go of this silly feud?'

'Is that what Leonard called it, a silly feud? Try telling that to Stephen Conroy who has a sick wife and three daughters but thanks to Leonard has no job to let him take care of his family.' I couldn't hide the bitterness in my voice but I didn't care. 'Or tell it to Kelly Carpenter who's just a kid who might have had a life but now thanks to our friend Leonard is going to have a baby to make that life impossible. Or tell it . . .' I swallowed, gulping back tears. 'Tell it to my father, he had a life too, until Leonard's fucking oul' fella helped him get rid of it . . .' I broke off, unable to go on.

'What are you talking about, Daniel? I mean, about your father?'

'You mean you don't know?' I snuffled back tears. 'Leonard flung it in my face yesterday that everybody in town knew it except myself.'

'I don't know what you're talking about, Daniel.' Her voice was gentle. 'Len phoned last night like he usually does . . . We've always kept in touch and I asked about you and he said that you weren't you, that's all. Honest.' Her hand reached out across the table and I felt her fingers rest on top of mine. 'We've known each other a long time, Daniel . . . That's why I'm here. You look like you need some help. You're overwrought. Maybe that's why you're making these accusations, implying them anyway, about your father and Len's.'

'You really don't know?' Her hand was cool on mine, firmer but softer too than I had remembered in all those years. 'You don't know what I'm talking about?'

Jean shook her head.

'Tell me, if it helps,' she said.

I started to tell her, haltingly at first, and then I felt walls tumbling around my heart. Perhaps it was the unexpected nearness of her in the kitchen in Paternoster; perhaps it was the remembered tenderness of that first night, so long, long ago when we had walked together along the darkened streets of our town and I had first spilled out to her my memories of a laughing father who had been taken away from me so abruptly. Now, once more, with a different story, I spilled it all out again to Jean but this time my grief was sharp with anger and my tears were bitter on my face.

'Why did he do it?' I whispered at last. 'Why? Didn't he know we'd love him anyway, no matter what had happened?'

Her fingers tightened around mine.

'You have to believe,' Jean said. 'That he acted out of love.'

'Or maybe he was just cornered.' The bile erupted in me. 'Crotty was in it with him, and God knows who else, but nobody paid for it except my father. Nobody until now.' I released my hand; wiped my wet eyes with my fingers. 'Someone else is going to pay now, even if it's the last thing I do.'

I waited for her question, but none came.

'I've written it all down,' I pushed on, my anger gathering momentum. 'Every last word of it, from what they did to my father right up to today, with Crotty's fiddling at City Hall and his whorehouse in College Court.'

Again I waited; again she remained silent.

'It's going to make quite a splash,' I went on. 'For the first time my ridiculous column in *NewsTruth* is going to achieve a practical end and, for once, Leonard Crotty is going to end up where him and his family deserve: right up to their necks in the brown stuff.'

I wanted her to plead with me, argue with me, but she only went on looking at me with her wide eyes.

'Have you nothing to say to me?' I asked at last.

'What d'you want me to say, Daniel? That perhaps you're mistaken? That you seem hell-bent on destruction, regardless of the consequences for yourself or anybody else?'

'Destruction is exactly what I want for that other shower and as for myself . . .' I shrugged. 'I think you knew before you came here that the consequences for myself don't matter any more.'

'I can't accept that, Daniel, not after the life I've lived.'

'I've made my decision.'

'And your beautiful, sixteen year-old daughter? What about her, Daniel? Are you going to give up on her, just like . . .'

She didn't finish. She didn't need to: my face told her that I knew what she was going to say anyway.

'Forgive me. I'm only talking to you like this because you and I were once special to each other.'

'You're still special to me,' I said. 'Nun or no nun, you always have been.'

'If that's true,' Jean said. 'Will you do something for me as a favour?'

'Yes, you only have to ask.'

'Will you let me read this article you've written. It obviously hasn't been published yet.'

'Okay, but it won't do any good.'

'Let me try anyway,' she smiled. 'Working in Africa for 25 years has made me something of an expert in handling hopeless cases.'

'D'you mean me or Leonard Crotty?'

'Maybe I mean both of you.' I felt a pang as she stood up from the table. 'I'll have to get back. I promised Kate I'd be back in time to let her home for lunch. She still has a couple of my nieces at secondary school coming home every day.'

'And will I see you again?'

'I hope so.' She took my hand in hers. 'I wanted so much to see you, Daniel, before this. We don't get home much but I have been back a couple of times since your mother died and I thought about calling on you but . . .' She smiled up at me, shaking her head.

'But I didn't answer when you wrote and Leonard probably told you that I wasn't very welcoming.'

'Something like that.'

'Maybe I should've gotten sick sooner,' I said.

'Don't say that! It's like blasphemy.'

'Ah, you're sounding like a nun now.'

'I'm sounding like a doctor,' Jean said. 'Whose business is the living.'

I turned away from her and went into the other room to collect the pages I had printed out earlier that morning. When I came back she had her coat on; she folded the pages carefully and put them into her side-pocket.

'When will I see you again?'

'I'll try to come tomorrow, it depends on Kate . . . and on my mother, of course.'

'I'm glad you came.'

'So am I.' Once more she took my hand. 'Nuns have changed, you know, it's okay to give them a hug now.

I put my arms around her then and I held her thin body close to me and for those moments the world stopped turning and my heart forgot to fret, as she leaned against me and I breathed in the fresh smell of her hair and my lips brushed the jagged scar that my own hands had marked her with. We didn't speak when she drew away from me. We walked together to the door and her fingers squeezed mine before she stepped outside.

My eyes followed her, slight and nondescript in the gently falling rain, until she reached the corner where Paudge, for once, was absent, and then she turned and waved at me and I waved back. I stood there in the open doorway for a long time, my fingers still tingling from the touch of her, my heart shaking with the wonder of her presence in Paternoster Lane.

Chapter 25

After Jean had left, the tiredness engulfed me. I lay on the couch in the front room but managed only to doze fitfully throughout the day. Twice the phone rang but I felt unable to reach out and pick it up. I just lay there listening to the messages: Kelly's voice was brisk and cheerful, still singing the praises of her new flat and demanding to know why I hadn't visited her for three days. The sound of her energetic good humour exhausted me almost as much as Stephen's mournful, pleading voice, begging for information 'about what's going on'.

Late in the afternoon Gabriel's e-mail came through: he'd received my "interesting piece", was "assessing it with due diligence", and "would be in touch". In other words, the lawyers had been summoned.

Of the three, it was the only message, which made me want to get off the couch and reply yet, when I tried to rise, my body seemed manacled to the couch. Even my eyes grew heavy; I felt sleep overwhelm me again.

When I awoke, it was dark, and I was covered in sweat although I was shivering. I was seized by a sudden spasm of coughing that seemed to last for minutes; the dark-brown stains of blood on the soiled tissues that I took from my mouth terrified and hypnotised me. I managed to get up and hauled myself up the stairs. I took a sleeping pill and then thought, what the hell, so I took another. My sleep was dreamless.

In the morning my whole body ached. I showered and shaved slowly. Dressing, too, was a slow business, undertaken in small stages, punctuated by bouts of coughing, but I was dressed and ready for Jean when the doorbell rang around 10.30.

She smiled when I opened the door to her. I felt my knees buckle, my hands clawed at the air and then I felt Jean's body against mine, supporting me along the hallway towards the kitchen. She helped me to an armchair and I slumped there while the kitchen somersaulted around me. I felt her cool hand on my brow, then her fingers closed around my wrist.

'You have a fever, Daniel.' Her voice seemed to come from a long way off. 'I'll have to get you to the hospital.'

I struggled for words but she hushed me.

'The keys,' she said. 'Where were the keys of my car?'

I pointed them out to her and then I found my voice. 'Don't let them start any chemo,' I whispered. 'Promise me that.'

'Don't worry,' she squeezed my hand. 'You're not on the way out, I promise you.'

'I know,' I croaked. Her face was swimming in and out of my vision. 'I know,' I said again. 'I've still got things to do.'

'You're a hard man, Daniel Best.' There was a brittle edge to her laugh. 'Now let's get you into the car.'

I could smell the sweet freshness of her, like cut grass and apples, as she looped my arm across her shoulder and we made our stumbling, coughing way along the hall.

They kept me in hospital for five days. I slept a lot; whenever I opened my eyes, Jean was there, sitting alone in the small room. I dreamed sometimes that she was holding my hand; once, when

I stirred and opened my eyes, I realized that I had not been dreaming; I felt her fingers tighten around mine before I slipped again into exhausted sleep.

She was dozing in the armchair beside the bed when I woke on the second evening. I turned my head slowly to look at her, conscious of the tubes running from my left hand and from my chest to the plastic bags strung up beside my bed. In repose the lines had disappeared from around her eyes and the corners of her mouth; I could see the darker roots of her sun-bleached hair.

She stirred, as though she felt my gaze upon her, and blinked her eyes open.

'You're awake,' she smiled.

'You're the one who should be sleeping,' I said. 'You look knackered.'

'Last night was a busy night.' She grimaced. 'My mother couldn't settle . . . She kept talking to Dad, telling him the grass needed cutting before we could go away to Dublin on holiday. Poor Dad, he's been gone for ten years and still he's being told to cut the lawn.'

'You won't be able to keep going like that, burning both ends of the candle.'

'We do what we have to do.' She leaned closer to the bed. 'You know what you're going to have to do, Daniel.'

'Yes, I do,' I said. 'But I think we're talking about two different things.'

'You're going to have to take your treatment.'

'What I'm thinking,' I said. 'Is that other people are going to have to take their medicine.'

Jean shook her head. 'You're as mulish as ever, Daniel Best, you know that?'

'Probably,' I took her hand in mine. 'But I'm also constant in my affections.'

'And I'm still a nun,' Jean said, but she didn't take her hand away.

Through the windows I could see the lights shining in the hospital grounds.

'Is it the same night? Or have I slept through a whole night and day?'

She laughed. 'It's still the same night . . . You've been sleeping.'

'It's late.' From beyond the closed door of my room I could feel the fretful silence of the night settling around the hospital. 'You should be at home with your mother.'

'I went home while you were sleeping. One of Kate's girls offered to stay the night so I thought I'd come back for a while and sit with you.'

'I'm glad you're here but you don't have to stay.'

'I'm used to hospitals. It's what I do, remember?'

'I remember,' I said slowly. 'That you spent some time in this hospital because of what I did.'

'Neither of us is likely to forget that,' Jean said. 'But we have to forgive each other and forgive ourselves too.'

'But . . .' I was puzzled. 'What should I have to forgive you for?'

She turned her head from me then but in the darkened window I saw the reflection of her face, pale and pained. 'For what I did to you,' she said simply. 'I took away from you the future you longed to have . . . The future you were entitled to.'

'There was no future without you.'

'That's what I mean.' She went on staring, unseeing, through the dark window. 'All I wanted back then was just a little space. It was like I had a little growing up to do and I wanted to be allowed to do that. I just couldn't explain it at the time, not even to myself.'

From the dark glass of the windows our faces looked back at us, like images from that other time.

'But why a nun? Of all things, why did you go off and do that?'

'I felt I had done wrong, hurting you and confusing Leonard. It was a way of punishing myself and doing something worthwhile at the same time.'

'And now, Jean,' I could hardly hear my own whisper, 'd'you think it was the right thing to do?'

'Did you always do the right thing, Daniel? *Did you?*' For a few moments the room crackled with her anger. I heard her slow intake of breath and then she reached for my hand. 'I'm sorry, I didn't mean to let fly like that.' She let my hand fall on the coverlet and she stroked it gently with her finger. 'We do what we do and we live with the consequences. What I did has made a difference to a lot of lives. Ever since I set foot in Nigeria I've felt that I was making a real contribution. Nothing can change that.'

Something wistful in her tone hovered in the room.

'But why should anything change it?'

'It's a long story.'

'I'm not going anywhere.'

'I've made a difference out there as a doctor.' Jean looked at herself in the window, the cropped hair, and the simple, white blouse. 'I'm not sure any more about the rest of it.'

'You mean about being a nun?'

'Things aren't as simple as they used to be. When I went to Malula first my Order had another doctor there and a couple of nurses. The whole place was in chaos after the war in Biafra, every day we made a difference to somebody's life. Now there's nobody left but me. The thing is,' Jean went on. 'We're not needed any more. There are local doctors and nurses to do things now. Our time is gone.'

In the silence I felt I could touch her grief, her sense of loss.

'D'you think,' I said, taking her hand in mine. 'That *our* time is gone?'

Her smile was small and sad. 'You should go to sleep, Daniel,' she said. 'And I should go home.'

She gathered up her coat and scarf and once more took my hand. 'I'll come in to see you tomorrow,' Jean said and she stooped over me and I felt her lips brush my forehead. Long after she had left the room, her scent remained with me, bittersweet with the mingled memories of songs sung and left unsung.

On that third morning I was restless, eager to be gone from the hospital. I told the nurse I wanted my clothes but she merely raised an eyebrow.

'At 7.00 am ? The least you can do is wait until Dr Martin gets in here . . . she seems to spend all her waking hours with you.'

I had to think twice to realize that the nurse was referring to Jean.

'She's a friend,' I said. 'Not my doctor.'

'Isn't it strange then,' the nurse said archly. 'That her name is written down on your chart?' She gave a little rap with her knuckles on the chart hung from the bottom of my bed before sauntering out of the room.

When Jean arrived I asked her about it.

'Maybe I should have checked with you first,' she said. 'But Len had told me you'd already given Jeff his marching orders and . . .' she frowned. 'No matter what you accuse him of, he was still doing his best for you.' She sat on the edge of the bed and took my hand. 'Somebody had to be named as your GP to get you in here, even though you could probably have me up for malpractice, or misrepresentation, or something or other.' Her face was deadpan. 'Anyway, I told the doctors in here to respect your wishes and to treat you for nothing except your immediate problem, if I can call it that.'

'So I can get myself disentangled from this apparatus now,' I indicated the tubes and bottles. 'And get out of here?'

'You can but it's not a good idea. You should finish your treatment.'

I was silent.

'Don't you want to know what's the matter with you, Daniel?'

'Only if I must.'

'I'm not playing this game, Daniel.' The laughter was gone; I could hear the anger in her voice now. 'A lot of people are trying hard to get you well again.'

'I'm sorry,' I squeezed her hand. 'I am grateful.'

'So?'

'So tell me what's wrong with me . . . apart from the obvious.'

'You've got a blood infection,' Jean said. 'A treatable case of septicaemia – that's why you were coughing up blood, no matter how much you were trying to hide it. You're also anaemic. Your haemoglobin count is 6.4, when a healthy person's would be about 12.'

'Am I going to be okay? I mean, okay to go home again?'

'For the time being, yes. You had two units of blood the day you came in and this contraption is feeding you intravenous antibiotics.'

'So,' I persisted. 'I can go home?'

Jean picked up the chart. 'You're on a five-day intravenous antibiotic course, Daniel. Two days more and my guess is you'll be as fit as you're ever going to be.' She put the chart back on the bed-rail. 'What you really need is a serious course of chemotherapy to start taking care of the cancer. You know that, don't you? We're not playing games here, or talking make-believe. You really have come to the point of no return.'

My father had come to that point, his feet groping for purchase in the vaulted night of Crotty's warehouse; I shut my eyes against the image and gasped for breath.

'Are you alright?' I heard her ask me. 'You look strange all of a sudden.'

'I'm okay.' The brightness almost dazzled me when I opened my eyes. Through the window behind Jean I could see the slopes of the town, layer upon layer of chimney-topped houses rising to the bushy oasis of the Spinney, a splash of speckled colour amid the suburban landscape. The Spinney, too, had reached its point of no return.

'And you,' I said. 'Have you reached a point of no return, Jean?'

'You're quick, aren't you?'

'Is it so strange, after how it used to be between us? After the way we were?'

'I suppose not.' She got up and stood with folded arms looking out the window. I wondered if she could see the neat rows of houses under the Irish sky or if she were seeing in her mind the dry earth of northern Nigeria and the low flat-roofed buildings of the hospital under the blue savannahs of the African sky.

'Officially,' Jean said. 'I'm on extended leave to take care of my mother. Unofficially, and my Superior General knows this, I'm taking time out. Sometimes I can't see the point of being a nun any more; whatever good I do is done because I'm a doctor, not because I'm a purveyor of some brand of Christianity. I suppose I was full of it when I first went to Africa, I mean, full of the gospel message, but reality got in the way – the only gospel that counts is bringing good health and better education to people who never got a chance.'

'We're on the same side then,' I said quietly.

'Are we?' She turned to me then and her face seemed transfigured with sadness. 'Can you really say to me that we're on the same side when you lie here in a first-class hospital and expect me to understand your rejection of all that medical science can give you? I'm on the side of life, Daniel. Can you honestly tell me that you are?'

'I want to be,' I whispered. 'I really want to be.'

'Then for God's sake let me tell the staff here that you're ready to begin your treatment. You'll have to wait your turn but let me start putting things into place.'

My father was falling through the unforgiving air again and Bee was weeping in the empty, rain-drenched yard of Paternoster.

'You know what I have to do first,' I said. It was like a pact that I had sealed with myself: I could not begin to think of my own survival until I had hauled in that swinging body from the darkness and whispered in my father's ear that his passing was not unremembered, that pain had been paid with pain.

'I read your piece.' Jean had come to sit on the bed. 'Are you sure it's all true? All that about Len and Jeff and the Spinney? Are you certain, Daniel?'

'It's true. The tabloids will have a field day; love nests and corruption, blackmail and a student pregnancy.' I felt her hand stiffen in mine but I pressed on. 'With any luck even the British tabloids will want to get their snouts into this particular trough of filth.'

'And have you thought about what this would do to Len and Jeff and their families?'

'They should have thought of that themselves before they started interfering in other people's lives.'

The silence hung between us in the small, private room. From outside in the corridor came the sound of crockery clinking, the voices of domestic staff doling out cheerful greetings along with indifferent food. Jean stood up and drew on her coat.

'Let me speak to Len,' she said. 'It has to be possible to prevent all this . . . this mayhem coming into people's lives. Maybe I can get him to see sense. Maybe I can get both of you to see sense.'

'You're going to see him?'

'We're friends. Of course I'm going to see him.'

'Even after you know what he's done?'

'We've all done things we regret, Daniel.' Her voice was sad. 'But we're all of us much more than the sum of our mistakes, or of our regrets.'

The rebuke, gentle as it was, stayed with me through the long afternoon. The night was longer, without her. Life itself had been longer without her; now, suddenly, Jean was in my life again and life was not long at all. Only the night was long.

I was dozing when she arrived next afternoon. I sensed the door opening; when I opened my eyes, Jean was coming into the room. She wasn't alone.

'I don't want him here,' I said.

'D'you think I want to be here?' Leonard Crotty's voice was cold. 'I only came because Jean persuaded me to.'

'Stop it,' Jean said. '*Both of you.* I brought Len here, Daniel,' she turned to me. 'Because I want you to be sure of the truth of what he's offering, that it's not just something I dreamed up by myself.'

'So,' I said at last. 'What's this offer?'

Leonard looked from Jean to me then back again. Huge and comfortable in his dark grey suit, he seemed to fill the room; yet I sensed his discomfort too, as though he were missing the props of his business existence. 'I can't do this, Jean,' he said. 'I'm sorry, but I can't. You tell him what my offer is. But do it quickly, I want to get out of here.'

For a moment disappointment crossed her face: maybe, I thought, she had harboured some daft notion of having us shake hands and become buddies again.

'Very well,' she said. 'Len has made a generous offer of settlement and . . . and restitution.' Leonard winced at the word but Jean's expression did not soften. 'Len will take over the payments for the flat that you've found for Kelly Carpenter –'

'For how long?' I interrupted.

'Until she's finished college,' Jean said.

'All drawn up legally?'

'Yes.'

I nodded.

'Kelly will also be paid 100 pounds a week until the child is 21.'

'Index-linked?' Conscience-linked more like, I thought.

Jean looked at Leonard: his massive head nodded, like that other bullet-head inside the car in the Sportsground, a lifetime ago.

'And Stephen Conroy?' I asked.

'One of Len's companies will take him on, permanent and pensionable.'

'As what?' I snapped. 'He's not a labourer.'

'He's a clerk.' Leonard's voice was dripping with contempt. 'You have my word that we'll give him a position which reflects his talents and abilities.' His gaze swung round the room before settling again on me, propped up in the bed. 'We all eventually find our rightful place in life, don't we, Daniel?'

'Stephen's salary,' I swallowed my rage and my pride. 'What will you pay him?'

'The same as he was getting,' Leonard smiled. 'And of course we'll index-link that too. Satisfied?'

I felt Jean's eyes upon me, hopeful and worried at the same time.

'The Spinney,' I said. 'The Spinney stays the way it is.'

Leonard snorted. 'You tell him, Jean,' he said.

'The development at the Spinney has to go ahead,' Jean said. 'But Len's company will donate a six-acre site on the east side of the town to the Corporation and will stipulate its development as a leisure park, to a design approved by the Corporation, all paid for by –'

'No deal,' I cut in.

'But it's a generous offer, Daniel!' Jean pleaded. 'It's a bigger site than the Spinney!'

'The Spinney has to stay the way it is,' I repeated. 'You go ahead with your building there, Leonard, and all bets are off. You, your wife and your children can read all about the amazing Crotty adventures in every rag in the land. It's just too bad your oul' fella isn't around to enjoy the craic with the rest of the country.'

'Daniel, please –'

'Forget it, Jean.' Leonard's voice was low with fury. 'This little shit isn't interested in a deal; he's only interested in raking over ancient history. Let me tell you, pal,' he went on, stepping closer to the bed, 'you try to interfere with my business and I'll make you such a laughing stock that you'll be run out of town . . . that is, if you're still around to be run out of town.'

'Leonard, please –'

'You don't scare me, Leonard,' I interrupted Jean. 'Either you call a halt to your so-called development at the Spinney or I spill the beans. Every last one of them!'

'Who d'you think you are? Just who d'you fucking think you are?' His face was pale with rage as he loomed over the hospital bed. 'The Lone-fucking-Ranger? The Lord's personal avenging-fucking-angel? You're just a pathetic little scribbler with an inflated notion of his own importance. That was always your trouble, Danny boy, you always felt you were more important than the rest of us when the truth is that you were just . . . just . . . you're just fucking nothing.'

He drew himself upright then, his heavy breathing filling the room before turning to leave. Jean was pale and silent.

'I'm sorry, Jean,' Leonard said. 'I told you this wasn't such a good idea.' At the door he paused and I watched him look back at her. 'I'll call you later, okay?'

'Yes,' she whispered. 'Do that.'

Leonard didn't look at me again before he left the room.

For a long time we both went on staring at the open doorway after Leonard had left. I shifted in the bed and the metal spring creaked and groaned as though in pain. I stole a glance at Jean but her eyes were still fixed on the doorway; under the tanned and weathered skin her face seemed stretched in a white mask of pain.

'I don't know what to say.' Her voice was little more than a whisper. 'I'm not sure I know you any more, Daniel.'

I longed to reach my hand out to her; standing beside the bed, but the gulf between us seemed immense, spanning years and miles. 'You said it yourself,' I said at last. 'We do what we have to do and we take the consequences.'

'There are others involved too, Daniel.' I could hear the throb of anguish in her voice. 'If you publish that story a lot of innocent people are going to get hurt, people who've already been hurt by this whole sordid business. How do you think Stephen Conroy is going to feel about having his failings splashed across your magazine? Or his wife and daughters, for that matter? And what about that young girl, Kelly Carpenter? What do you think it will do to her life to be portrayed like this for the whole world to see? Or for her child, boy or girl, when the time comes to read their mother's story?' She turned away from me: I could sense the gulf widening between us but my own hurt and anger would not permit me to reach out to her.

'He can't be allowed to get away with what he's done,' I said. 'Can't you see that?'

'I think Len made a reasonable offer of restitution,' Jean said. 'But maybe what he said is true. Maybe you want more than that.'

'I want the Spinney to survive, Jean.'

'The Spinney is just a place, Daniel.'

'No!' I shook my head. 'It's more than just a place. It's like a symbol, a reminder of what we used to have. The whole town is being torn apart and being rebuilt in the image of Mammon, or Crotty, Jean. Can't you see that? Sometimes somebody has to make a stand and say this far and no further. Don't you understand?'

'So you'll sacrifice other people's lives to hang onto a symbol?'

'It's not up to me,' I said. 'It's up to Leonard.'

'What's happened to us all?' Her voice was so low that I could barely hear her. 'We were good friends when we were young; we knew who they were and where we stood with them. Now I'm not sure who anybody is, let alone myself.'

'Maybe that's life's only purpose: finding out whom we are.'

'I'm not so sure, that I like what I'm finding out.'

'Everything will be alright,' I said. 'Leonard will see sense.'

'And if he doesn't, can you live with the consequences?'

'Maybe I won't have to.'

I saw the anger well up in her face. 'You really have become a selfish bastard, Daniel. How can you say that? How can you trot out that fatalistic nonsense when so many people are working to keep you alive? Wanting to keep you alive? How can you?'

'I'm sorry,' I whispered. 'I didn't mean it, honest.'

And I didn't: for the first time since Jeff had spilled his news out to me, I knew that I wanted to go on living. Most of all, I wanted not to lose Jean again through my own willfulness.

'Daniel, I'm so tired of all the "sorry's",' she said. 'Won't you let me speak to Len again? I'm sure I can get him to forget what was said between you. You were both overwrought and I'm sure he'll honour his promises.'

'And the Spinney?'

'Let it go, Daniel.' Her eyes were wide, deep with pleading. 'In God's name, just let it go.'

'I can't,' I whispered. 'I just can't, Jean.' I saw her shoulders slump; saw the look of resignation in her face.

'I have to go,' she said.

'They're sending me home tomorrow. Will you come?' Our

eyes met. In hers I could read the doubts and the questioning; in my own heart I felt the stirrings of panic.

'I don't know, Daniel.' She shook her head.

'Please!'

'Let me think about it. I can't promise.'

She reached out and took my hand in hers and for a moment I was safe and the night air was unencumbered in Crotty's warehouse. Then she turned from me and she was gone and without her my world was empty.

Chapter 26

They let me out the next afternoon. I could feel no joy in being allowed home: all through the day I had been waiting for the sound of her step in the corridor and the sight of her smile in the doorway.

'Cat got your tongue, Mr Best?' the consultant asked when he stopped by with his gaggle of acolytes. He was a small, weedy man whom I had seen more than once promenading by the sea with his broad beamed, large-chested wife.

'Am I going home today?' I asked him.

'Since we're not permitted to do anything more for you,' he said primly. 'Yes.'

Getting dressed took more out of me than I might have expected but I took longer than I needed to. Finally, there was nothing more to delay me in that antiseptic room and I made my way downstairs, hoping all the while that I would bump into Jean on the way. At the front door I had to wait for a taxi; but it was Jean I watched for through the December rain.

The short taxi ride home through the rain seemed like a journey from one emptiness to another. That emptiness yawned wider and deeper when we turned in to the Lane and I saw the old Merc parked outside Number 1: I had told Jean to hang on

265

to it but even that offering, it seemed, was tarnished by my behaviour. I had to reach out and steady myself against the kitchen door when I got inside and saw the ring of keys coiled on the table: in my mind I could see her there, perhaps that morning or the night before, standing alone in my kitchen, touching the quilted tea-cosy on the worktop or thumbing the copies of *NewsTruth* on the chair, before placing the keys in the middle of the table and walking slowly out of the empty house.

I knew that it was my own intransigence that had driven her away. She had made it clear to me that she was still joined to her order of nuns but she had intimated too that that bond was in some way weakened; she had kissed my forehead; she had held my hand in hers. There had been reason to hope but now, watching the rain through the kitchen window, I knew that I had strangled that hope with my own mulishness.

Yet I knew in my heart that there was nothing else I could have done. As the long, dark afternoon crawled towards the deeper darkness of the night, the voices of the old terraced house spoke to me; my father winking at me behind my mother's back, his grin lighting up our kitchen like a lighthouse in a sea of night; Prince and Mutt jostling for his attention and mine in the small yard, smaller now, where the rain went on falling; Granda Flanagan's querulous, rasping voice and the rhythmic whirr of his wheelchair tyres as our apostolic procession marched through the narrow streets of our town towards the open road. Through the long, unlighted darkness of that afternoon I sat there, listening to those voices that would not be stilled. Set against the great and the good of our town, these were the voices of the puny and the insignificant: yet they too would soon be heard.

I could almost laugh at myself, at the melodrama of it, sitting there in my unlighted kitchen. But only almost. There was nothing laughable about my father's descent into the darkness; in my own clenched and sweating hands I could feel the rough coldness of the hempen rope that he had knotted around the highest rafter in the warehouse. The voice from that darkness was broken but was not silenced.

I had promised to be the voice of others, too, who were not ranked among the high and the mighty, yet, as Jean had pointed out to me, my words would bring only shame upon them. I could try to disguise Kelly and Stephen in my story but I knew well enough the ferreting ways of the tabloid press and no matter how I disguised them, sooner or later they would be outed and become the latest nine-minute wonder of Ireland's scandal-industry. The press pack would move on to fresher prey but, for Stephen and Kelly, those nine minutes under the searchlight would leave wounds from which they might never recover. Darkness was closing in on the winter day. By 5.30 the kitchen was clothed in gloom. I left the light off, as though I might discover comfort in the shadows. None came. The clock went on ticking. The voices went on whispering to me from the corners of the house. My heart went on asking questions and found only emptiness.

When the doorbell rang I hardly dared hope it was she: probably just some misguided school-kid trying to sell sponsorship lines in the rain. And yet when I opened the door, it was Jean, bareheaded, her face pale in the yellow glow of the streetlamp. She shook her head and the rain fell from her hair like pearls in the light and she dabbed at her eyes and I couldn't be sure if it was rain or tears she was wiping from her face. It didn't matter: she was on my doorstep and I had a sense of light and music spilling into the dark and silent house.

I drew her into the hallway and she smelled of rain and talcum powder when she stood close to me. 'I thought you weren't coming again.'

'I went to see Len, I couldn't bear it any . . .' Her voice trailed away. 'He's agreed to everything, Daniel.'

For a moment I thought I had misheard her. 'Everything! Even the Spinney?'

'You've got everything you asked for.' There was a kind of tired wonder in her voice. 'Kelly and Stephen get looked after and the Spinney is handed over to the city.'

'You're not kidding me?'

She shook her head.

'There's no catch?' I asked.

'Only that you give your word never to publish anything about any of this.'

'I don't have to sign anything?'

'Len says it's enough that you give your word to me.'

In her thin face I could see the lines furrowed deep by years of African sun and toil; yet I could see also the face of the girl I had loved and had never forgotten. We were both whispering, as though afraid to disturb the silence of the house. In that moment I thought of all the promises I had made: to Bee, to my Mam and Dad, to Elizabeth, to Dolly, to Stephen, to Kelly, to myself. I would contact Gabriel and retract the article.

'I give you my word,' I told her.

She took my hand in hers and drew it to her lips. 'You're still very ill, Daniel. You know you're going to have to start your treatment as soon as possible.'

'I know.'

'I could get you a Christmas tree, if you like.' Her smile was hesitant as she looked around the hallway. 'It would make the house a bit brighter for Christmas, for when your daughter comes. They're bound to let you out then.'

'The house is brighter, just because you're here.'

She laid a hand on my lips. 'We have to take things slowly, Daniel.'

'But you're going to stay?'

Her eyes, deep as forever, held my own. 'I hope so,' she said. 'I really do hope so.'

I held her close then, and in the nearness of her I found the joy that had been stolen from my life on that long-ago day when the skies spilled rain on our empty backyard and the dogs were gone forever: we went on standing there in the unlighted hallway, holding each other close, and I felt peace filling the house and I knew in my heart that we were not alone.

Epilogue

Six Years Later

The brass band was playing "Galway Bay". Way below them, to the southwest, the real thing shimmered in the June sunlight. The small crowd that had gathered around the still-veiled plaque were restive but good-humoured: some of them, Jean guessed, had never before set foot in the Spinney and were remarking on the fabulous views it offered of the city.

'It's really breath-taking, isn't it?' She could hear the note of wonder in Bee's voice. 'Dad took me up here once when I was little. I could tell how much he loved it up here.'

'Yes,' she said. 'Daniel loved this place.'

Her friendship with Bee was a wonder to her, not just a living reminder of Daniel but also something precious in its own right. The e-mails that flew almost daily between Cambridge and Malula were an unexpected gift that continued to astonish her. It had been Bee's own idea to spend a few days with her during her short stay in the old house in Paternoster.

'Looks like the dignitaries are here at last.' Bee gestured towards the black, stretched-Mercedes that was pulling into the reserved parking space.

As Leonard Crotty and the Mayor climbed out of the car, the

officer in charge of the guard of honour barked an order in Irish and the double-line of soldiers snapped to attention. The Mayor, small and bald, gathered his blue-and-red robe about him, fingered his chain of office as if to make sure it was around his neck, and waved good-humouredly. Len, she noticed, neither waved nor smiled. He had done himself proud, she thought, gathering in the Mayor and the military for his day out. The mayor and Leonard marched behind the officer as he led them past the soldiers, his sword sparkling in the sun, carried stiffly before him. The soldiers in turn, held their rifles in the honour position, hands white-gloved, faces impassive.

The crowd drew closer around Leonard and the Mayor as they took up their positions, one on either side of the maroon curtain, draped over the unseen plaque. The Mayor's speech was brief, a well-practiced compendium of jokes and platitudes together with a few necessary references to the matter in hand. Leonard's was longer, more serious. Feet shifted on the newly laid tarmac path. Bee caught Jean's eye and raised an eyebrow; they smiled conspiratorially at each other. Finally he finished. The drummer drummed a rolling flourish; the Mayor gathered the folds of the maroon drape in his hands and swept it expertly from the plaque.

'I now declare the John Crotty Memorial Park officially open!' he announced.

There was a smattering of polite applause. Photographers from the two local papers positioned Leonard and the Mayor and their cameras flashed in the sunlight. Within minutes the crowd began to disperse: this was, after all, no more than a minor moment in the life of the town.

She wondered what Daniel would have made of it. Whether he would have attended this official dedication of the Spinney to the memory of Leonard's father was another matter; yet she had decided, after much thought, to accept Len's invitation and to take Bee along with her. Long before the end, Daniel had known the fate of the Spinney. Tapping away at the computer in the cool of an African evening he'd suddenly yelled out in disbelief, and called her to his side. They'd read it together, there on the

Connacht Tribune's website, the news that Leonard's father would be immortalised in the renamed, revamped Spinney. And then he'd started laughing: "To think that I helped preserve that old buzzard's name!". His hand had found hers and they'd laughed together in the African night.

The two women made their way along the top terrace of the Spinney towards the small car park. Ahead of her Jean saw Leonard shaking hands with an older man; his great head nodded a couple of times before the other man waved a final goodbye and moved stiffly away. He caught her eye then and she drew Bee closer to her.

'Hello, Jean. Welcome home.' He came forward and kissed her cheek, formally, before taking her hand in his.

'This is Beatrice Best, Len,' she said. 'Daniel's daughter. Bee this is Len Crotty.'

'Mr Crotty, how d'you do?' Bee smiled, holding out her hand. 'You knew my father well, I gather?'

'Everybody knew your father, Miss Best.' He hesitated for a moment before releasing his hold on her and shaking Bee's hand. Was it, Jean wondered, the girl's beauty or her unconscious opening of old wounds that made Len seem so uncomfortable.

'Are you here on holiday?' he asked, changing tack.

'Just for a few days, then back to college.'

'What are you studying?'

'Environmental town planning. I'm finishing off a doctorate.'

'And after that?'

'Who knows?' Bee shrugged; the long, dark hair shook lustrously over her shoulders. 'Just getting away from the library will be wonderful.'

'After that,' Jean hastened to add. 'Bee is going to change the world.'

'Like father, like daughter!' There was no admiration in his tone. The bright day was darkened for a moment by his discomfiture, but as Jean watched he seemed to shake it off and haul himself back into his public mode. 'I have to go, I'm afraid. There's a lunch at the Great Southern and my wife is waiting for me.' He gestured towards the car. 'It's good to see you again, Jean.' Once more he shook her hand and nodded to Bee. 'Bye, ladies.'

Jean and Bee watched as the car purred away towards Taylor's Hill.

'He's sad,' Bee said quietly. 'He puts on a front but you can tell the sadness.'

'He'll get over it,' Jean couldn't quite keep the impatience out of her voice. 'He always does.'

'Am I stepping on toes here?'

'No, just "old stuff" that happened a long time ago.' Jean slipped her arm through Bee's. 'Not the kind of stuff we should be talking about on a beautiful day like this.'

Perhaps after all, she thought, it had not been such a good idea to come here: it brought back all that bad "old stuff", like Leonard pulling the plug on Kelly Carpenter the day he found out that she had miscarried. She was no longer his problem, he'd told her, and he'd kept his side of the bargain. Not until Daniel had finished the chemotherapy had she felt able to tell him. He'd just smiled and said it didn't matter any more, that he had a few bob and he'd help Kelly out until she got on her feet. That night had been long and wonderful, cradling his tired body in her arms, the hope rising in her heart that life would allow them some time together.

Arm-in-arm she and Bee sauntered on towards the laneway, where she'd had to leave the hired car. They were almost there when she heard her name being called.

'Doctor Martin!' The cry was hesitant, almost fearful.

When Jean turned she thought she recognised the caller, a thin, almost weedy fellow with just a greying tonsure of hair on his head.

'I'm sorry to shout at you like that, Dr Martin.' She could see the sweat glistening on his forehead. 'Maybe you remember me?' His tone made it clear that he didn't expect she would. 'I'm Stephen Conroy.'

'Stephen! Of course I remember you!' She had met him once, hovering outside the door of Daniel's room in the hospital; that night, too, there had been sweat on his forehead and nothing could persuade him to step into the ward – he had pressed the flowers and the get-well card upon her and scurried away along the corridor.

Once more she introduced Bee as Daniel's daughter. Jean saw his eyes light up and then he turned away, blushing, as though intimidated by her beauty. Yet she liked this nervous little man; having read Daniel's account of those days she knew how he had suffered.

'Tell me how your wife is, Stephen, and your girls . . . three of them, isn't it?'

'The oldest two are working in Dublin and my youngest is at University.' From under his brow he cast a glance at her with a trace of pride. 'She's studying medicine.'

'I'm delighted . . . and your wife, how is she doing?'

'She passed away last November.'

'I'm so sorry.'

'It was a relief to the poor woman.' He looked away towards the city below them. 'It's not so bad. I managed to leave Crotty's and got back into the office in the bus station, writing dockets like I did when I first came to Galway and met herself.' A smile lit up his face. 'It's all computers now but it's still the same job and I like it and . . . and my girls are okay.'

'Stephen,' she said. 'I'm so glad for you.'

'Anyway . . .' He had gone all fidgety again, poking at the ground with his shoe. 'I didn't want to talk about myself.' He turned to Bee, blushing as he looked up into her face. 'I knew who you were, Miss Best, ever before I spoke to you. I saw you once in the town with your father and Dr Martin. I just wanted to tell you that it's after him this place should be named and not after that . . . that other fellow. Your father was a decent man, Miss Best, a great man.'

'Thank you,' Bee said. There was a lump thickening in Jean's throat and she knew that tears were pushing upwards in her eyes. 'But, please, just call me Bee. Everyone does.'

He blushed deeper. 'He was a wonderful man, Bee,' he said in

273

a whisper, then seemed suddenly astonished by his daring and stepped back from them. 'I just wanted to tell you that.' He gave a little wave and withdrew another nervous pace. 'Good-bye now, Dr Martin, good-bye, Miss Best.'

They called goodbye after him but he didn't turn back. In silence they watched him get into an old estate car that rattled and groaned as he pulled away from the kerb and drove away down the laneway.

'I think,' Bee said, still staring down the empty lane. 'That my Dad bailed him out at some point.'

'He bailed out more than Stephen in his time,' Jean said. 'You must realise that.'

'He didn't bail Mum and me out.' In the younger woman's voice she could hear Daniel's own; honest and unafraid to look a sad truth in the face.

'He had to learn how,' Jean said. 'You realise that, don't you?'

'I didn't mean to be broody.' Bee was smiling again. 'I'm glad you and Dad got together and had some time together . . . and I'm glad I managed to see you both out there and both of you so happy.'

'Yes,' Jean said. 'We were happy.'

They'd spent the years of his remission back in her old hospital in Malula: Jean's African colleagues had hardly raised an eyebrow when she'd arrived back with a man in tow. A few months later her Order had finally recognised that its day had gone and left the hospital in local hands. Daniel had made himself indispensable, upgrading and running the hospital's computer system and taking charge of all records. Often she used to think that he had at last found for himself a role that had the measure of his many gifts. He never seemed to miss the writing: not even Gabriel's presence, for a long and hard-drinking week, could persuade him to pen a weekly "Letter from Nigeria" for *NewsTruth*. "The only thing I'll ever write here", she remembered him telling Gabriel on one boozy night, "Is admissions dockets and begging letters".

'Will you stay on out there?' Bee had asked earlier.

'Where else would I go? My life is out there. You know how they need me.'

'Yes, how could I forget?'

Three times Bee had visited them and each time Jean was certain she had come away surer than ever that her father had found a worthwhile place in life. On the last occasion, she had known that she would not see Daniel again. He was very ill but it was only afterwards that Jean told Bee that they had decided, together, against further chemotherapy, when his secondaries were diagnosed: "it would only have added to the pain, I had to spare him that", she had comforted her.

They were seated in the little car when Bee at last asked the question she had been expecting.

'So what was all that about, Jean? All that "stuff" that Stephen Conroy said, about naming this place after my Dad?'

'I suppose it's time you knew.' Jean started the engine. 'Daniel wrote the whole story down for you.'

'Did he? He told me he would.'

'When?'

'The same night he told me he had cancer. I was very upset at the time and afterwards, never pressed him about it. I thought he must have forgotten. What kind of story is it?'

'It's a long story,' Jean said. 'I'll let you read it for yourself. It is waiting for you, safe in the house.'

She'd been holding the manuscript back; now it was time to take the pile of typed pages out of the drawer in the bedroom in Paternoster and give them to Bee: they had, after all, been written for her.

'I hope there's a love story in it.' Bee winked at her, before turning her face towards the city below them and the unknown life that stretched ahead of her. 'Sometimes, I like a good love story,' she said quietly.

'It is a love story,' Jean said.

'About you and him?'

'Yes, but in a strange way it's more a love story about this town.'

'Why did he not publish it when he was alive?' Bee wondered.

'He made a promise . . . and stuck to it.' Jean smiled at her. 'It's yours now, to do what you will with it, Bee.'

Daniel Best's daughter touched her hand briefly, then Jean eased the little car onto the roadway and they moved off towards the old house at Number 1, Paternoster Lane.